CLOSE CALL

CLOSE CALL

John Nieman

For Scott

Chapter One

To this day, I tell myself I should have never listened to that damn telephone conversation.

On the other hand, I wasn't exactly eavesdropping. Like millions of multitasking Manhattanites, I was simply using the journey from point A to point B to soak in the sights and sound of the New York human zoo. The subway, of course, is the perfect place to do this. At any given moment, it's a compressed cross-section of overt New Yorkers. Here, even the most casual observer is bombarded with microplaylets of commuter's inner drives and outlandish behaviors. It's considered rude for a stranger to actually participate in these tableaus or even acknowledge their existence. No, everyone simply stares ahead blankly or pretends to bury himself or herself in some reading matter.

My cover was the bifolded edition of the *New York Times*. For the past several years, it had become a ritual of mine to look for Alba Gonzales's byline and see if my good friend from college had a juicy scoop. No such luck this afternoon. Unlike her occasional front-page crime stories, today she was relegated to follow-up piece on the governor's recent tryst. All the steamy, sensational, private details had been hashed over for days, and her story on page 4 addressed the secret psyche of a call girl. The lead, of course, was the governor's escort, who looked like an Ivory soap model—99 and 44/100 percent pure. According to Alba's report, no one suspected that the prostitute was anything but a struggling actress, presumably with a rich family to support her artistic quest to stardom. In this particular case, it felt like old news although the thought of any New

Yorker having a truly private life was a vanishing prospect it seemed to me. Perhaps call girls were the last remaining secret identities. Everyone else, everything else was "out there," for everyone else to see and hear in intimate detail. As I peeked above the fold of my newspaper and surveyed the crowded subway car, my theory was confirmed.

My Number 1 train was ambling along in the upper reaches of Manhattan. Earlier in the morning, I had been scouting apartments for a client's son near City College. While this was not my regular beat, I always liked this route because the train actually climbs above ground for a short spell. You feel completely inundated by New York City inside and out. Of course, there was more than enough to grab my curious attention inside the subway car. Like every line, it was filled with the daily swarm of workers, students, and shoppers. There was a group of young teenagers standing in front of me, busily flirting with each other.

"Wanna go to Ray's and get a pie?" the young teenage girl with the suggestive outfit offered.

"Too crowded," answered the Latino stud with the slicked-back ponytail.

"I don't want to eat it there, standing up. I don't like to do anything standing up," the other boy volunteered, apparently oblivious to the fact that he was doing exactly that—standing up—in the middle of the car for the past three stops.

The Asian girl suggested an alternative. "We could go to my house and eat it. My parents aren't home till eight."

"Yeah, then what could we do . . . after we eat it?" the Latino asked.

"Whatever," the Asian girl suggested with a raised eyebrow and a giggle.

"I'm down for that," the Latino nodded and winked at his buddy.

"Yeah! Whatever," the quiet friend joined in as he was orchestrating the seduction.

The business geek standing next to them seemed totally unaware to this by-play and everything else in the subway car. He was dressed in a gray pin-striped suit, blue shirt, and cordovan capped-toe oxfords—that faux British costume so popular among young bankers. He had folded his *Wall Street Journal* to the stock page and seemed to be circling stock picks with his pen as he listened to his IPOD. Given his Brooks Brothers look, it was probably the Eagles, Genesis, or some other once-hot band.

Next to him stood two obvious gays who were reading *Entertainment Weekly* and applauding the fact that Lance Bass of N'Sync had come out of the closet.

"It's about time," the more flamboyant, artistic type declared. "When we saw their concert, I had a hunch he was making eye contact with me."

"You wish!" his boyfriend teased him.

"Too bad I'm already spoken for." The man with the stubble and beret batted his eyelashes and stroked the purple tie on his friend. "I like that color on you," he cooed and nonchalantly turned his head in my direction. Just as nonchalantly, I reopened my *Times* and turned to the real estate section, acting as if I was reading each listing.

Over the past few years, I had become accustomed to how explicit most people were in public places. The once-upon-a-time taboo on holding hands, kissing on the lips, squeezing a friend's ass, and openly talking about "fucking this . . . fucking that . . . fucking A" was now *de rigueur* on today's subways

This is not a homophobic reaction on my part. I am equally amazed at how heteros talk about "getting laid tonight." Or how women talk about the size of their boyfriend's penis. Or how business cohorts talk about shafting "that asshole, Byrne at Merrill, who is clearly on the take with insider trading." All this within clear earshot of everyone on the subway car.

Maybe it's the Paris/Britney/Kate Gosselin society we live in. No one seems at all shy about revealing the most intimate details of his or her life. More importantly (unless you are already famous), no one seems to really care. I guess we are all too busy. As the kids say, whatever.

By the time we got to the stop on 125th, a morbidly obese black woman squeezed next to me on the seat. Given the extra eighty pounds of girth, she looked exhausted from the grind of the city. She was carrying three bags from Bed, Bath, and Beyond. They contained pillows, a poof, and a bunch of other ugly, squishy things. Do people really pay good money for those puke-green throw pillows? Evidently, yes.

She didn't say, "Excuse me," when she moved her oversized frame into the twelve-inch open space next to me. She just plopped down with half her butt cheek landing on my left thigh. I, on the other hand, did say excuse me when I extricated my smashed appendage from the heavy pressure and moved a few inches closer to the man next to me.

He was a nondescript man in almost every respect. Just a middle-aged guy in a peacoat and a stocking cap trying to get from point A to point B.

At least, that's what I thought. Until I heard that damn tantalizing phone conversation.

"Where the fuck is it," *the* man next to me complained to himself as he heard the muffled phone call. No fancy ring tones here. No boopee-dee-doop lilt or "You had a bad day" melody. Just a muffled *Drrring. Drrring.*

After checking the outside pockets in his jacket, my fellow commuter finally found the source of the sound in his right front Levi's pocket. "Yeah," the man answered gruffly.

As a courtesy, I turned my head toward the black woman next to me, just to give the man some psychological space. The fat woman was sitting quietly with her eyes closed and her head drooping down in prayer or in sleep. With the jostle of the subway car, she let out a grunt and tilted her head up for a second before letting it fall back on her ample bosom again with a slight satisfied groan. Obviously, a quick catnap.

The man next to me answered his cell phone and listened for a few seconds before responding. "Aw, c'mon, man. Not tonight. Too rushed. I don't think I can fuckin' do that tonight," my neighbor in the peacoat protested. "OK, what's the prick's name?" he finally asked as he reached for a pen or pencil in his pocket. I thought of offering him mine but knew the rules of subway, nonengagement etiquette. You're not supposed to overtly acknowledge a passenger's private moment. Certainly, you're not supposed to actively participate in any conversation.

"Yeah, I got it," the man continued as he scribbled some notes with the ball point he had found in pile of papers in his jacket pocket.

"Zeigler. Is that *ie* or *ei*? Forget it. Doesn't matter," the man quickly corrected himself. "Yeah, Martin Zeigler."

Wow, what a strange coincidence, I thought. In a city of eight million strangers, I actually knew a Martin Zeigler. No, let me correct that. I knew *of* a Martin Zeigler. The Zeigler I really knew was his wife, Melanie Zeigler. We worked together for three years in the Twenty-eighth Street real estate office of Stribling. We sold quite a few million-dollar condos together before inaugurating the plush bedroom of a vacated "classic seven" one quiet afternoon. It was the best, naughtiest sex I had ever had. The affair continued for a few months until Melanie felt too much exposure both from inside the office and at her home. Not that that her home life was any bed of roses. As she often told me after a clandestine breathtaking romp, her husband was a total asshole.

"He's a total asshole, I hear," the man next to me said into the phone, as if my thoughts had an echo. For a brief moment, I actually wondered if I had been mumbling out loud, but I never did so. No, that rumbling mumbling was coming from the large black woman leaning on my left shoulder.

"I know, I know, I know," the man on the phone continued. "Yeah, I already got the deposit from Melanie. I realize that. But does it mean I have to complete the assignment tonight?"

For the first time, he seemed to employ code language as a security precaution. *Assignment* was not the kind of language that flowed easily out of his mouth. In fact, he paused before saying the word, as if it were a euphemism for something else. Just to give the man enough privacy to continue, I turned my shoulder farther away from him and buried my forehead in my hands, as if I was trying to shut out the rest of the world. I wasn't. I was hanging on his every word and visualizing dear voluptuous Melanie.

"OK, where's he gonna be after his fuckfest tonight?"

Good Lord, I thought. Here, Melanie was always concerned about being caught in the act. And now it looked as if her asshole husband was going to be caught red-handed after a tryst. For a second, I wondered if he was actually going to photograph *in flagrante delicto.*

As my fellow commuter listened for instructions, I sat next to him somewhat amused and titillated by the irony. Melanie had often recounted her husband's overbearing, suspicious nature. "If he finds out about us," she told me once after a boff in a Murray Hill townhouse, "I'm really fucked. After all, he's Mr. Right and Wrong, and if you're wrong in his verdict, there is no mercy."

Apparently, Melanie had decided to turn to tables, perhaps spurred by her affection for me. All she needed to do was capture proof that Ziegler was not where he had promised he would be. With photographic evidence, Melanie could confront the double-dealing husband, gain a quickie lucrative divorce, and resume our afternoon pleasures.

"Yeah, yeah, yeah," the man next to me continued. "Let me write down the number. Barrow Street and what? Yeah, like the river," the man continued to write, evidently referring to the cross street called Hudson. "I would just rather complete the assignment next week."

There was a pause.

"OK."

Another pause.

"All right, but I want the final payment after the job is done. Tonight. By midnight. And yeah, OK, I'll delete this call. Look, the train is going underground so I'm gonna lose connection, and I'm getting close to my stop. Gotta go."

The man hit a few buttons on his cell phone, then clicked it shut, and began to rustle with some papers on his lap. The prerecorded voice on the subway system called out. "This stop . . . 116th Street, Columbia University." I slightly opened my fingers over my forehead like a venetian blind to see if others in the car had just overheard this same conversation. The teenagers were still teasing each other with innuendos. The geek was still looking at his stock listings. The gays were busy discussing what kind of gourmet meal they were going to jointly prepare tonight. And the large black momma to my left was faintly snoring by now.

"Shit, this is my stop," the man to my side mumbled as the subway train screeched to a halt. "Excuse me, excuse me," he said abruptly as he worked his way through the sex-obsessed teenagers toward the open door.

Inevitably, some new commuters would be impatiently waiting to hop on this number 1 train. Others would quickly reposition themselves closer to the straps. A red-haired businesswoman in her early thirties was headed for the now-empty seat to my right, as if she were playing the game of "musical chairs." She put her attaché on the seat to claim it as her own as the man in the pea coast squeezed his way through the closing doors of the subway car.

"This your phone?" she immediately asked as she took the empty seat.

I looked at it and immediately recognized that it was the same one used by man on assignment who had been next to me. I immediately looked at the doors to see if the man had made his exit. On the platform, he was reaching in his pockets just to make sure that he had remembered to pocket his cell. From the expression on his face, you could instantly tell that he had forgotten to gather all his belongings before exiting, as the PA announcer warns.

He squared around to view the seat now occupied by the redheaded businesswoman.

I got a good look at him. He was an Anglo guy about five feet ten. Probably Italian or Spanish in descent. Regular build. Nothing special. The kind of guy you might bump into at a Home Depot or in a Sears's tool department.

I don't think he got a good look at me. Just for good measure, I moved my head behind the closely pressed bodies of teenagers who were bumping into each other casually and intentionally as the train pulled out of the stop.

When we cleared the platform, I looked down at the familiar phone that the redhead was holding toward me.

I don't quite know why I answered as I did. Curiosity, I suppose.

"Yes, it is my phone," I replied in my most grateful voice. "Must have slipped out of my pocket."

"You've got to be careful," she gently admonished me. "These things are expensive to replace."

"Very true," I agreed. "Thanks."

I put the phone in my pocket and took one last look at the vanishing platform as the pea-coated man stood there alone and watched us disappear into the darkness.

Chapter Two

At my 14th Street exit, I had a vague notion to deliver the missing item to the MTA police or at least check on the procedure for lost goods.

When I headed toward the officer, an older woman who looked a little like Edith Bunker had beaten me to the question of lost and found. "I found this cake box on the train," she said and offered it to the man in blue. "I think the guy who was sitting next to me in a brown suit must have left it behind."

The officer opened the box and discovered a nine-inch New York cheesecake—the kind with that soft fragrant consistency made famous by Junior's Bakery. The MTA cop shrugged and then smiled at the woman. "I think he must have wanted you to have it."

"No, I think he must have mistakenly left it behind."

"Well, we don't have a lost and found here. It's at Grand Central Station. But, lady, I wouldn't bother. Ninety percent of all the stuff left on these trains is never claimed."

"But maybe it's for a special occasion or something."

"Lady, just enjoy it."

She sadly closed the box and reluctantly walked away.

The officer then looked at me as the next person with some weird senseless request.

"Can I help you, sir?"

I put my hands in my pocket and felt the newly acquired cell phone. I then looked toward the herd of people climbing the stairs toward Union Square.

"Yeah, when I exit this station, which way to Fifth Avenue?" I asked.

"Go up the stairs and bear to your right," he told me.

"There are signs that will point the way."

"Oh, there are signs. That's so good to know," I remarked incredulously, like a first-time subway rider from the wheat fields of Kansas.

"Just follow the signs," the cop wearily repeated and walked away toward the token booth.

I joined the crowd up the stairs and walked to my apartment on Fifteenth Street.

It had been my home for the past six years and was one of the inevitable perks of being a real estate agent in the Manhattan market. I got a great deal on it. For thirty years, it had been a rent-controlled apartment building until the new buyer came to Stribling with the desire to convert it to a luxury doorman condo unit. At the time, it was my job to canvass the current residents to determine which units would be purchased and which ones would be vacated and available for sale. I got lucky when I spoke with Maria Onuska, who had lived in 14B for the past sixteen years with her three cats.

Maria was like hundreds of thousands of middle-class New Yorkers who were caught in the squeeze of downtown gentrifications. She had been paying below market value for her place and barely had enough money to meet that monthly payment. The chance to own the apartment was an alien concept to Maria. It was also a financial impossibility, even with an attractive "insider's price."

Her place had been decorated in the manner of a sixty-year-old spinster. The Ethan Allen traditional furniture, realistic seascape pictures, and beige walls gave it a bland and busy first impression. However, as one learns in the real estate biz, the "bones" of the place were promising. Eleven-foot ceilings. A living room wall of big floor-to-ceiling windows and two legitimate bedrooms. From my notes, I already knew that the place was twelve thousand square feet with an insider price of $487,000, which was actually about 70 percent below the comparable retail prices in the neighborhood.

When Maria scoffed at the very idea of a $100,000 down payment and told me she was planning to move to Fort Myers anyway, I simply suggested an easy scenario for her to live in comfort with a bounty she never anticipated. I offered to buy her rights to the unit for a half-million dollars. I knew the neighborhood. I knew the market. Most importantly, I knew some Stribling lenders who could help me with a 4 percent down payment and favorable interest rates.

Admittedly, it was a slightly shady, opportunistic transaction, but not an uncommon practice among Manhattan real estate brokers. Since I paid above the insider's price, I was legally clean. Maria Onuska got enough living money to enjoy the sunshine of Florida's West Coast. She found a place to accommodate her three cats. I had the makings of a spectacular habitat.

When I entered the building, the evening doorman greeted me with his usual professional cheer. "Welcome back, Mr. Witt. No packages today. No visitors."

"Thank you, Javier. How was your day?" "Uneventful."

"Sometimes, that's good," I answered as small talk, not intentionally trying to link it to my subway event. I grabbed the mail from my box, waved a good-bye to Javier, and headed for 14B.

Over my first few years of occupancy, I had transformed it into a very chic crash pad. From my experience as a realtor, I had learned that clutter kills a place. A few choice pieces and open flooring make an apartment look twice its real size. From my earlier years as an actor, I also knew the value of some selective theatrical pieces. The anchoring visual of the living room was a large four-by-six-foot poster of Bertolt Brecht's *Three Penny Opera* in which I had played a supporting role about twelve years ago.

In the hallways, there was a gallery of twelve-by-fifteen-inch enlarged play bills of productions in which I had participated—Sam Shephards's *True West*, Ionesco's *Six Characters in Search of an Author*, Israel Horowitz's *The Line*, and a handful of others. Granted, this would ordinarily count for clutter, but the uniform framing and track spot lighting gave it a more focused unity.

I had painted the walls terracotta, sage, and dove and invested in dimmer-controlled Italian lighting to give the place drama.

The theatrical decor was all that remained from my days on stage. A decade ago, I had envisioned my name in lights above Forty-second Street. I had dreamed of marquees, which screamed *Death of a Salesman*, starring Dustin Hoffman and Jackson Witt, *Da* with Bernard Hughes and Jackson Witt, and *The Producers* starring Nathan Lane and Jackson

Witt. Instead, I landed a small role in *Three Penny Opera* and various off-Broadway, limited-run productions, which were quickly forgotten by the public but enshrined in my play bill gallery.

I did get a fair amount of commercial work. Usually as "the best friend" in my early twenties, then later as "the dumb husband." I was the guy who bought the wrong brand of toilet tissue, the wrong calling plan for his kids, or the wrong gift for his wife on Valentine's Day.

I suppose my looks typecast me as "everyday Joe." People say I vaguely remind them of Kiefer Sutherland on a bad day or a younger Jeff Daniels on a good day. Not completely unattractive. On any street corner of New York, I figure I can hold my own. But in an acting cattle call that brings out clones of Rob Lowe, Brad Pitt, and Matthew McConaughey, I end up as "the best friend or, worse still, background."

Like a lot of struggling actors, making ends meet was always a financial struggle. My single-parent mom had passed a year after college, so there was no longer a parental dole. I supported my calling by waiting tables and making those annoying phone solicitations for home improvements, medical insurance, and cable providers. Between those jobs, I auditioned.

One particular series of tryouts made me think twice about the acting profession. I was called back for a role in a vignette commercial as one of two buddies on a road trip. I was the driver of the car. My "buddy" was in the front seat, surrounded by about ten used wrappers of Hershey's Crunch bar. I had one line: "Quit hoggin' 'em." One screen, it would last about three seconds.

"Can you do it a little whinier?" the casting director suggested. I did and was called back again a week later.

This time, the casting director wanted a more humorous approach. I did my best imitation of a dejected Buster Keaton and actually cracked up the ad agency biggies. They called me back for a third audition.

Now they wanted an angrier interpretation. I became Travis Bickle in *Taxi Driver* and actually got a standing ovation. A week later, they cast the agency copywriter in the role. It was my last audition in showbiz. The next week, I enrolled in a night course to get my real estate license.

I always enjoyed looking at other people's apartments. It's a fascinating peep into people's tastes, behaviors, and dreams. Not unlike acting, it's easy to fantasize about the real lives of those who inhabit that environment.

It was a small class, and I rather enjoyed the study. It's not difficult. Yeah, you have to learn some technical things like balloon mortgages, prime rates, and housing starts, but most of it is common sense and contacts.

It's steady. It's respectable. Financially, it has a very nice upside, especially if you hustle. It also offered a surprising benefit, which I only later learned was a mixed blessing: it led me Melanie Zeigler.

Chapter Three

Melanie and I had not spoken with each other for the past eight months. It saddened me. I had never been so immediately attractive to a woman since my college days with Alba Gonzales. But this was completely different.

For one thing, she was older than me. For another thing, our dance was downright naughty.

In retrospect, it's fair to say that she seduced me. However, I admit to being a willing partaker. From the moment I walked into the Stribling office as a twenty-seven-year-old rookie, there was an instantaneous physical, intellectual, and psychological simpatico on both our parts. I was introduced to everyone in the office as "our newest associate." I shook hands with all my new compatriots and competitors. Most had that veneer of outgoing friendliness that characterizes New York realtors. But as I soon learned, pit one possible commission against another and it's as cutthroat as any business on earth.

Melanie was not like the other agents. For starters, she gave me more than a handshake. She gave that kind of body-to-body hug usually reserved for family members or former college roommates. I still remember her first words: "Welcome to the real world, Mr. Actor Boy." And then she whispered in my ear, "I've got a hunch you're going to be very satisfied here."

She had the looks and gamesmanship to get away with a test bomb like that. In her bare feet, she was only five feet six, but in her heels, she could look like an elegant runway model. Not an ounce of body fat. A confident carriage. Almost pale, but actually a healthy complexion, since she eschewed tanning beds so popular with other women on the Upper East Side. I guessed her to be about thirty-eight—right at the peak of her sexual maturity.

She wore a wedding ring. However, as I soon learned, her marriage was an unusual one. She was the second spouse of a big-time federal judge, who was twenty years her senior. Under normal circumstances, the term *trophy wife* would apply. However, Martin Zeigler didn't seem to squire her around town very much. He would trot her out for political purposes at election time and provide her with an outstanding Rolodex of prospective customers, but other than that, it was a lopsided one-way relationship—with Melanie providing all the support, spark, and sunshine.

I provided some spontaneity. It was a usual role for me since I have always tended to be the more cautious, observational type person. It's not that I'm timid. I've just always been perfectly content to view the ever-evolving kaleidoscope of human nature. You could say I like to watch. Thanks to Melanie, I also learned to participate.

At first, it was just words. A little tease here. A volley back. An off-color joke that was normally just told in girl cliques or in guy circles. One day, we had an effortless discussion of the Paris Hilton technique in her sex tape. Then dirty text messages. Then a comparison of our favorite nine hundred numbers. Then decidedly lewd cell phone messages on both our parts.

This went on for a very good six months since we both promised to be careful with gossipy office politics. At the time, it was important to Melanie to ostensibly honor her marriage vows. For her, it meant never having to admit to Martin V. Zeigler that she had actually had a true physical affair.

That changed when we started previewing empty apartments together. The first romp in a Sutton Place bedroom was a tour-de-force tryst. Unlike all the months of verbal foreplay, this was silent seduction. We both just looked at each other and started stripping. It was a two-hour bang in every orifice and every Kama Sutra position. When we dressed and walked out the door, Melanie summed up the morning succinctly.

"That was fun," she understated.

The next week, we boffed in a one-bedroom previewed apartment in Murray Hill. It was every bit as good as the first time.

The following week, we discovered the wonders of a Tribeca loft. According to our subsequent sales sheet, the master bedroom had a spectacular view of the Manhattan skyline. However, we scarcely viewed the panorama. Too busy with our lusty tryst in the owner's platform bed.

It was a fairly easy thing to arrange these assignations. As the primary listing agent, Melanie would contact the seller in advance and set up a time for photo shoot and descriptive analysis of the property. She would insist that the owner would vacate the property for a scheduled two-hour window. It would take us approximately fifteen minutes to measure all the rooms' dimensions and take some wide-angle photos that would make every apartment look like a minimansion. That would leave more than an hour for wild sex in the owner's bedroom. In the remaining minutes, we would make sure the "surveyed" property was completely returned to normal. We had it down to clockwork science, but it was more than math. It was magic.

Over the next two years, we sampled the beds in every neighborhood of Manhattan. We christened multimillion-dollar townhouses and small studio apartment. We utilized futons, foldout couches, and four-poster kings.

Of course, it was dangerous. While Melanie had the exclusive listings, there was always some risk that another broker might ring the bell and want to take an unannounced peek. We always feared that the owner might return early, but it never happened. We brought our own blanket to mask any telltale signs of our intercourse and normally had plenty of time to smooth the sheets, shower together, remake the beds to their perfect pristine appearance, and view our naked entwined bodies in the dressing mirrors before donning our real estate duds.

We rarely wondered where all this would lead. As Melanie often reminded me, "We should just enjoy our time together and thank our lucky stars that we both are getting something we really want and need from it." Even so, it was impossible not to project. Did I really envision that she would leave her highly regarded judicial spouse? Probably not, but I did know that she seemed happier in her trysts with me than at any other time during her day.

More to the point, did I want her full-time? The honest answer to this is a little trickier. In my grown-up days, I had enjoyed some long-term relationships, including one with Alba Gonzales that had lasted for a several college years. For the most part, it was wonderful. I liked waking up to a kindred spirit next to me in the morning. I loved knowing her thoughts, questions, and insecurities and sharing some of mine. It even felt good doing nothing together. But the mutual breakup was painful—more than I thought at the time.

Typical of me, I put on a brave front and vowed to spare myself from a similar heartbreak. Just too agonizing. Over the next five or six months, I learned to live by myself. Maybe it was a defense mechanism, but I didn't find it too, too difficult. I had lots of acting auditions to keep my busy and the attendant friends that come from that merry-go-round of rejection. I had this gypsy dream to chase. I rather enjoyed seeing movies alone. I liked Chinese takeout. And as for sexual release . . . well, Melanie was damn good at that.

However, it would be inaccurate to deny the fact that a more complete relationship hadn't crossed my mind. After all, I was no longer a starving artist. I now had a full-time job, with certain secret benefits. I was making money. Maybe it was my time to become a real grown-up. And maybe Melanie, away from the prison of an overbearing husband, could provide that, along with lots of satisfied smiles.

I know this: I at least wanted what we had to continue. Consequently, I didn't push for a greater commitment from Melanie. Perhaps she was right. Perhaps we should just enjoy our time together. Invariably, I did. Every time I viewed our bodies in those various bedroom mirrors, I believed our magical afternoons were definitely worth preserving.

I always remarked, "Damn, we look good together." A few times, I wanted to take pictures of our mirror-perfect poses, but Melanie always rejected the notion. Her *joie de vivre* would instantly drain.

"No! No pictures. We can never have any evidence of what goes on between us. "Martin would never understand."

"Why would he give a shit? He's always out with his lawyer friends or his buddies or judicial lectures," I typically countered.

Quite obviously, I couldn't begin to understand her home dilemma.

* * *

According to the cynical saying, "If it's too good to be true, it probably is."

I suppose that might apply to these rendezvous. As much as Melanie and I relished these moments together, we always had a sense that they were precarious. After all, we live in jealous, puritanical, right-of-center world.

Melanie often reminded me of the imminent risks. She would always inspect the ceilings for hidden cameras and wear shades in the hallways. She always feared that her suspicious husband would discover her transgressions. Despite these concerns, it didn't seem to inhibit her wild sexuality once she felt safe in the bedroom.

Melanie was a truly adventurous lover. She loved different positions and multiple orgasms. However, she was not a screamer nor a bondage queen. No, just straight-ahead lust. In some ways, it was a teacher-learner situation. I studied how to bring her to ecstasy and discovered more than few ways that a woman can bring surprising sexual pleasure to a man. It was damn fun.

I could only assume that her sexual appetite was not well served at home. However, we did not spend much time talking about her husband. The few times our conversation would veer in that direction, she would steer it back to the subject at hand, above her, or below her. "Let's don't go there," she would caution me. "Too complicated." Instead, she would then throw herself even more vigorously into our lovemaking.

However, the specter of Martin Ziegler always presented a dark cloud. As a conservative law-and-order judge, he was evidently very concerned with decorum. I remember one time she did tell me, "It isn't easy being married to a judge. It can turn one into a Stepford wife if you're not careful." Yes, we approached our hidden trysts with careless abandon. On the other hand, once outside the bedroom, we were careful.

When we would exit an apartment, we both tried our best to exude a businesslike, professional relationship. Of course, we didn't always succeed in this pretense. Too much inherent heat. Occasionally, we would carry our passion outside. But for the most part, we were able to compartmentalize our ardor inside the seller's master bedroom. Or so we thought.

In time, water cooler gossip in the Stribling office created a problem. No one ever said anything directly to me or to Melanie. But in the last few months of our physical affair, Diane Farin, the manager of our office, began to suggest that Carol Welton or Hannah Banks or any of the other female brokers start accompanying Melanie on her scouting trips. The manager began to load me with last-minute appointments or "very important" chores that would conflict with our liaisons.

Melanie assumed that people suspected. I would later learn that her instincts on this matter were flawless. We never knew if anyone in the office suggested anything to Martin Ziegler, but Melanie began to fear that loose lips could translate to major upheaval at home.

After a few painful weeks of sturm and drang, she asked to be transferred to the Eighty-sixth Street office so she could be "closer to home and her husband." I incorrectly assumed that this would mean we could resume our bed hopping with more anonymity. Instead, she sadly announced to me that it was over.

"If anything ever changes in my relationship with Martin, we'll be back together in a flash," she told me. "But until then, I don't think we should even talk. I just can't risk it."

It was the first time I had ever seen her cry.

Chapter Four

After an uneventful afternoon in the real estate office, I picked up some Chinese takeout for an early dinner. Since my college days, it had become my regular nosh.

Today, it was stir-fried chicken and broccoli. Granted, it was not a very exotic dish, but tasty all the same. I put down my chopsticks and approached my favorite ritual of the meal: the fortune cookie. One, I like the taste and crunch of these little triangular bites. Two, I always get a kick out of the little sayings inside.

Don't get me wrong; I don't really consider myself a superstitious person. I never read horoscopes. My key fob is not a lucky rabbit's foot. I rarely believe that I am destined to win the megamillion lottery (although that would be very nice). But I always look forward to these cryptic predictions. I view them mostly as an entertaining curtain call after a meal. But sometimes, the messages do seem to capture how I'm feeling, or perhaps it's the other way around.

When I cracked open the cookie and read the contents, I couldn't help but feel that this fortune was prescient. It said, "Without curiosity, you discover nothing." It couldn't be a more apt description of my mood.

I wanted to call Melanie Ziegler.

I had thought of doing so many other times but always fought that urge. On our last night together, I had reluctantly agreed to honor her tearful request: no further contact unless her relationship with Martin somehow changed. With that overheard conversation on the subway, I couldn't help but think that it had.

What a curious irony life is! Melanie had shied away from any intimate photography, but the man on that number 1 train would evidently capture her husband in the act or at least at the scene of the infidelity. While she had ultimately decided to play by society's rules, her uptight judicial husband had evidently decided to be the scofflaw.

I looked back at my fortune cookie, then at the cell phone lying on my granite kitchen island. It was a Verizon LG model and looked well used, with a few wear-and-tear scratches across the front of it. I opened up the device to see if it had any ownership information. The screen photo was a generic picture of hills, trees, and clouds—the type that comes from the Verizon factory, nothing customized about it. I flipped it shut and put the cell back on the island, pushing it a few inches away as if it were a living, dangerous creature.

No sooner than I placed it down, the phone lit up and began that familiar *drring* monotone I had heard in the subway. For a second, I thought it must be Melanie telepathically trying to reach me. Then it dawned on me. She wouldn't be calling me on someone else's cell phone.

Drring. It went again, and I picked up the contraptions. The little window on the front revealed that it was a call from 212-438-6261. It also said Home. Of course, it was no home I knew, no number I recognized, and undoubtedly no person I had ever met . . . unless it was the guy who had left it on the train. Of course. He wanted to track it down and get it back.

Drring. It droned again, this time almost impatiently.

I just wasn't in the mood to deal with this interruption right now. It was the wrong person. I picked up the cell and carefully hit the End button, immediately silencing the incoming rings. In a few seconds, the lights faded on the telephone screen. I flipped it shut again and again slid it a few more inches away from me.

In stone-cold silence now, I viewed the mysterious cell phone and wondered what had happened to her relationship with Martin. I also wondered what I would say to Melanie. I admit to feeling some butterflies, almost like a middle school kid trying to make his first nonchalant "What's up?" call to his secret heartthrob.

"Hey, I was just thinking of you." Too overt.

"Hey, long time no hear." Too casual.

"Hey, how are you?" Probably open-ended enough to unleash some honesty, especially if she was alone and free to talk. I reminded myself, she would indeed be alone. I had already overheard that her husband, Martin, was going to engage in a West Village fuckfest this evening.

Instead of using the purloined interrupting cell on my kitchen island, I reached for the landline just paces away. I knew the number by heart. It rang twice, and then I heard the familiar female voice. "Hi, you reached the Zeigler household. We're not in right now, but if you leave a message, Marty or Melanie will be glad to return your call. Listen for the beep."

It beeped. And I hung up. At first, I wasn't quite sure why. Maybe I just wasn't prepared for broadcasted message in the Zeigler household. No, more likely I didn't want the risk of a tongue-tied message being played to Martin Zeigler, if he were the first person home to hear it.

The chances of that were slim. And the more I thought about it, the more it would be easy to cover my ass in that eventuality.

I redialed the number. Again, I was greeted by the recording machine. After the beep, I said, "Hi, this is for Melanie Zeigler. This is Jackson . . . uh, Jackson Witt, and I am a broker in the Twenty-eighth Street office of Stribling. Today, I met a prospect that evidently has done some business with you, and I wanted to be his broker . . . but I didn't want to step on any toes or possible commission. Give me a call tomorrow, if you can, and we'll figure out a fair way to proceed. Good-bye . . . for now."

I hung up the phone.

"Good-bye . . . for now?" What was I thinking? I stormed around the kitchen shaking my head but ultimately decided it was harmless enough. No big deal. Just a late-night business call from an associate who was trying to play by the rules. Hell, it was even an hour when a broker might conceivably be discussing a property. Almost 9:00 p.m.

I looked again at the magic cell phone on the island and considered opening the private diary to discover the hidden world. I even toyed with idea of visiting Barrow Street and Hudson to witness the surprise on Martin Zeigler's face, but I really had no idea when that encounter would take place. Besides, it was enough excitement for one night.

I looked in the *Post* and discovered there was a 9:30 screening of *Avatar* just two blocks away. I had been meaning to see it and just wanted to lose myself in the faceless crowd of dimly lit moviegoers.

As I left the building, I said good-bye to Javier and entered the anonymous night.

Chapter Five

I didn't anticipate that *Avatar* would still be such a runaway hit three weeks after its widely ballyhooed initial release. Seeing the ticket-holder line stretched around the block, I promptly went to the window, only to discover that the 9:30 screening was already sold out. The next screening, at midnight, was not exactly enticing, especially since I did have this thing called a day job, where I was expected to be somewhat awake and aware.

The overflow crowd had filled the nearby video store. I knew what that meant. Only two-year-old movies would be available, and I had already seen just about everything I wanted to see.

I suppose I was in the mood to see something I had never seen before. Almost unconsciously, I headed in the Union Square subway entrance, swiped my prepaid Metro card, and took the E train to West Fourth. I didn't need an MTA officer to tell me where Hudson Street was. I was familiar with the stop. One of my best friends from college days lived in that neighborhood, and I often visited with him.

I climbed the nearly deserted stairs and braced for the brisk October air. It was one of those perfectly clear New York nights that make for great tourist photography. Maybe it's the neon in the shop windows or the old-fashioned streetlights, but the city always appears more exciting and romantic when the sun goes down. On this kind of night—sweater weather—it's particularly fetching.

This area, mind you, is not as electric as Times Square. It's a residential enclave with a few restaurants and delis and tons of townhouses and apartment buildings. The residents are mostly independent literati with a few professional creative types thrown in for good measure. It has a profile similar to the Upper West Side with one notable difference: given the fact that it is very West Village, it has a sizeable, significant gay population. In large measure, this factor alone helps explain the superb upkeep of the buildings and the dramatic decor clearly visible in the windows, even from street level.

It's a quiet neighborhood. There were few pedestrians on the streets. Mostly couples (both gay and straight) headed for a late-night dinner and an occasional single walking his daschund or Labradoodle, replete with a white plastic baggie, ready to scoop up any sidewalk "accident."

I always liked the neighborhood. However, it is not an easy sell, as we like to say in the real estate world. Given the demographic profile of the residents, it is not a particularly good district for schools or playgrounds, and that seems to be top of mind for many co-op prospects, especially the young couples who are looking for a good safe place to raise their little darlings. Not exactly "kid friendly," as they say.

On the other hand, it is "thirty-something cool," and there are plenty of prospects that easily fit in that type. As I approached Barrows Street, I couldn't help but wonder what type exactly Mr. Zeigler would be fancying tonight. Perhaps she would be an art director from one of the big ad agencies. Nah, no chance he would ever meet her unless he faked his Match.com profile. Perhaps a legal aid or social worker, one of those do-gooders that frequent the courthouses. Or perhaps an NYU professor. Maybe she was researching the judicial system, and they met . . . and then fucked.

As I approached the intersection of Hudson and Barrows, I told myself there was no point in continuing this blind conjecture. I would find out soon enough. Or more likely, I would never find out. After all, I had no earthly idea when the "assignment" would transpire. It could be in the next five minutes or five hours from now. My man in the peacoat had neglected to announce the exact time into his cell phone.

Also, whoever said that the photo would take place in a street? For all I knew, it was a behind closed doors, *en flagrante* shot that would capture the venerable judge spread eagle with an "omigod, who sent the paparazzi?" expression.

As I surveyed the empty street, I began to question the sanity of this stakeout. On the one hand, I felt like a sad voyeur. On the other hand, perhaps as a result of too many Stanislavski acting classes, I reminded myself that this was an "in the moment/follow your instincts" reaction. As my stage directors would encourage me, "It's no different than the response when a doctor strikes your knee with a little rubber hammer. It's a knee jerk. Don't question it. Don't overthink it. Be natural. Go with it!"

Come to think of it, I had not exactly "chosen" this path. I was just pulled into it. More accurately, sucked into it. I was just following my innate feelings and responding in kind.

It's all good advice when you are trying to realistically perform onstage. But when you're standing in the middle of a street at Hudson and Barrows without an audience, it's a little weird. After another few minutes in the solitary darkness, I became self-conscious and decided to busy myself by ordering a cup of coffee.

I could see the *Open All Night* neon of the A&R deli up the block.

"I'll have a cup of coffee—cream, no sugar," I told the Pakistani man behind the counter when I entered the store.

Like a zombie, he took a Styrofoam cup and filled it with java, put it in a bag, and included two of those little creamer thingies.

Without saying so much as a thank you, he took my buck fifty and went back to stocking the shelves. With the coffee warming my hands, I headed back to the intersection and vowed to eyewitness the event, provided it took place before I finished my cup of Joe.

With a coffee cup as my prop, I now felt less conspicuous standing by the parked cars on the street. Within a few minutes, a man walking his little Yorkie puppy passed by and nodded as if I totally belonged in the neighborhood. He probably figured I was just a visitor finishing my coffee after an outdoor smoke. Nothing unusual about that these days, especially in the smoke-free New York environment.

In fact, there was a man about forty yards across the street doing just that—finishing his butt and stomping it out with his foot. Rather than connect uncomfortable mutual stares, I slid behind the parked van and took another sip. The man apparently wanted to get his fill of outdoor smokes. I could see him reach in his pocket and take out another cigarette. When he fired up his lighter and illuminated his face, my instant response was to duck and hide even farther behind the van.

I knew that face. I knew that peacoat. I knew that stocking cap.

I admit that my first reaction was fear. If the familiar man from the crowded subway car recognized me, what then? Surely, he would wonder why I was there. Perhaps he'd even suspect that I took his cell phone. That could even lead to some tussle. *Wait a minute! Relax,* I told myself. There was no reason to believe the man in the peacoat even noticed me in the same car. He was too busy looking for a pen and yammering into his cell phone.

Just as an added precaution, I made sure that my perch was behind the van's tinted glass. Since I was under no streetlight, there was little chance I would be silhouetted through the car window.

The man in the peacoat took another drag and then reached in his pocket and took out some photos. He was looking at them intently, and I wondered if he had taken them earlier of Judge Zeigler and whether these new shots would simply be more icing on the cake. After studying the photos for almost a minute, the man put them back again in his pocket and looked up and down the deserted street.

I had never met Martin Zeigler, but I certainly knew what he looked like. Melanie had shared with me some candid photos of the man and sarcastically commented that he was way too old for her current interests. In addition, I had seen him on the news with some high-profile cases and, more recently, when he had won his latest election. He was distinguished enough looking fellow, with character actor features—the kind of guy who could easily play the father of the bride in any Broadway musical.

There he was! From my vantage point behind the Chrysler Pacifica, I could see Martin Zeigler now exiting a townhouse across the street. And who was with him? No one, at least not yet. He was coming out alone. When he reached the bottom of the stoop, he looked right and left in vain for a cab coming in either direction. There were none.

Rather than hang back and take a surreptitious photo, the man in the peacoat approached Zeigler quite casually, almost as if he were to ask the man if he had a match. When Zeigler motioned no, the man in the peacoat reached his gloved hand in his right pocket and pulled out a knife. Before Zeigler could utter a word, he was stabbed in the abdomen—again, again, and again. With each thrust, the judge was visibly lifted off the ground. After the third stab, Zeigler slithered down like a lifeless marionette. The man in the peacoat bent down over the fallen figure and seemed to reach in the judge's pocket. Then with absolute nonchalance, the murderer stood up and casually walked away from the scene as if nothing had happened.

I thought I was going to faint. Throughout the entire gruesome ritual, I spilled my coffee. I also thought I was going to scream. However, it all seemed to take place at such warp speed. I could barely get a breath. People sometimes claim that tragedies seem to occur in slow motion, but that's only if one is a participating victim. If you're a bystander, it's amazing how rapidly everything unfolds. It's just stab, stab, stab, and down he goes!

I felt some impulse to race to the fallen judge. I even stumbled between the two cars to gain a clearer view of the lifeless heap of a man. But I resisted the urge to move closer. What if the knife-wielding killer was still on the block looking for witnesses that needed to similarly silenced? Would I be his next victim?

I did see a gay couple walking down that side of the street, hand in hand, walking their twin fox terriers. When the taller man got closer to scene and could recognize that the pile was not some bag of trash but rather a slain human, he screamed. The other man took out his cell phone and immediately started punching numbers. A few lights from the apartment buildings began to go on.

I watched behind the van, absolutely immobile for a few seconds, and then decided that I certainly did not wish to be part of this chilling discovery. It's not really a cognitive decision. If you are ever unlucky enough to be in a similar situation, the natural impulse is just to flee. You just want to turn your head and run away.

Something inside told me that would not look good. Rather than race away from the scene, I walked away in a dazed state, catatonically retracing my steps to the Fourth Street subway station. By the time I had gone one block, I could hear the police sirens racing to the scene. I took one last look back and, in the distance, could see a small crowd gathering by the lifeless lump as the first police car zoomed past me on his way to the late Martin Zeigler.

Chapter Six

I could still feel my heart pounding as I stood in front of the Fourth Street entrance. To my ear, the pa-poom, pa-poom, pa-poom was amplified, almost as if it were being broadcast across a football field. At the same time, I could scarcely grab a full breath. I remember closing my eyes and imagining that the gruesome scene of a few minutes ago was just a bad nightmare. However, I instinctively knew I had actually witnessed a brutal murder. And when I opened my eyes again, I saw an ambulance screeching through the intersection.

It surprised me just how quickly the brain becomes scrambled. It simply reruns the same horrific moment over and over again. As I stood there gripping the railing, I tried to unsuccessfully clear my mind, but it was hopeless. It was stuck on instant replay.

How could I break this paralysis? For a brief second, I actually thought of circling around the scene of the crime and visiting my good friend Leandor who lived just a few blocks away. He would surely welcome me, but then I would just as surely relive the incident with him in minute detail. No, not now. My mental memory chip was already doing enough of that.

In this discombobulated state, I evidently entered the subway station and headed uptown on the E train. I almost missed my Union Square exit. Fortunately, I was able to squeeze through the closing doors and stumble my way out of the subway car. It was only 10:45 p.m. However, given the rush of activities that night, it already felt like 3:00 a.m.

As I somehow negotiated my way through the streets of my neighborhood, I couldn't help but focus on the victim's last moments. I had never seen a real human being die before. I had "suffered death" dozens of times in plays, and I now had to admit to myself that all my portrayals were sadly unconvincing. I always tended to stagger, shiver, and kick a bit for the benefit of the back row. In real life, it was very different. There are very few histrionics. You just slump and die.

The more vexing thing was the role that Melanie might have played in this sick event. Was it actually intended as a photo shoot that went berserk?

Of course not, I told myself. Was she capable of such a hideous setup? Were there dark unspoken problems between Martin and Melanie that no one knew? Did she love me so much that she wanted her husband forever out of the picture?

"Back early, Mr. Witt!" Javier greeted me as I staggered into the lobby of my apartment building.

"Oh, hi," I answered, happy that I had unconsciously arrived at the safety of my home. I then responded to his question. "Yeah, I didn't like the movie much. Left early. Bad plot. Complicated."

What the hell was I doing? I was always such a bad liar. Rather than just nod and move forward, I tend to overexplain my fibs, as if more details will make the prevarication more believable.

"Well, it's been a slow night, Mr. Witt. Not much going on," Javier shrugged.

"Really? Yeah," I answered.

"Good night, Mr. Witt." He tipped his hat as I entered the elevator. "Sleep well."

I knew I wouldn't. Too many unanswered questions. Who was the man in the peacoat? How had he ever met Melanie Zeigler or vice versa? Did she actually participate in this horrid scheme? Hard to believe, knowing her. Melanie had always had such a quiet fear of the upright judge but was clearly unwilling to leave him. Otherwise, why would she transfer out of the downtown office and work closer to her home? Had things become ugly between the two of them?

I poured myself straight vodka and tried to answer the puzzle, but my mind kept reliving the play-by-play of the stabbing. I wondered if anyone other than me had witnessed it. I wondered if Martin Ziegler had been pronounced dead.

Perhaps it was already on the evening news. I reached past the mysterious cell phone and grabbed my television remote. Nothing on the local news, nothing on CNN or Fox or MSNBC. Of course not. It had only happened fifty-five minutes ago. Chances are, the police had not even identified the body yet.

Just then the killer's cell phone began to ring. I jumped out of my stool and raced toward it. I immediately recognized the number as Melanie Zeigler's private line.

Holy shit, I told myself. Dear Melanie was in fact somehow involved. She was probably checking to see if the deed had been done.

Drring. Drring. Drring. The phone continued to beckon.

I was tempted to pick it up and hear her voice but was not prepared for the answers yet.

Five minutes later, the phone rang again. Again, Melanie.

I fixed myself another straight shot of vodka and turned off the TV. Then I turned off the phone, opened my cabinet, and placed it in an empty coffee cup. As I carefully closed the cupboard door, I realized that this little message machine was a dangerous device. If it were ever to get in the wrong hands, it would implicate dear Melanie. Despite the fog in my head, I convinced myself that would be a very bad idea, especially if she had done all this for me.

I sat in the dark silent kitchen, swigged my vodka, and began to consider my options.

Chapter Seven

After a toss-and-turn night, I finally decided to give up the pretense of sleep and see what the news rags had to say about the Martin Zeigler murder. I threw on a pair of jeans and a T-shirt and headed for a 24-7 deli around the corner. At five forty-five in the morning, this city has an eerie calm. Mind you, it's not totally quiet. It never is. There are a few Wall Street early birds hailing cabs, some bakers making their early-morning deliveries of baguettes and fresh bagels, and the usual insomniacs. With the streets dewy wet and the sun streaming over the skyscraping water towers, the effect is of an overcranked movie set. All that will change within forty-five minutes, when daily commuters start checking their wrist watches, racing for the subways stops and arguing for empty taxies. But for now, the pace was slower and more human-scaled. It had all the earmarks of just another morning, which, of course, it wouldn't be for Martin Zeigler. Or Melanie Zeigler, for that matter.

I entered the Malabar Deli, nodded nonchalantly to the morning man behind the counter, and poured a cup of self-serve coffee. Just to the right of the counter were the piles of morning newspapers. The headlines of the *New York Times* covered the latest surge in Afghanistan. The *Daily News* blasted Bloomberg on the bridge toll hikes. There was nothing whatsoever about Judge Zeigler's death, at least not on the cover. The police report must have missed the headline deadline, I suspected. I added both newspapers to my coffee cup on the counter. I paid up and scurried home, seemingly the only anxious person in the prerush hour calm.

In the privacy of my apartment, I tore through the newspapers. *Daily News* first.

Nothing on page 2. Or 3. Or 4. Nothing throughout the entire edition.

Now the *New York Times*. Again, nothing on page 2. And page 3? Wait, wait, wait! There it was right below the fold. A two-column story titled Judge Mysteriously Slain in West Village. In it, they identified the victim as "the Honorable Martin V. Zeigler, who had served on the circuit court of New York for eighteen years." The cause of death was called a homicide, and according to the article, "there were no known suspects at this time." Other than that, all the information was sketchy and biographical—where Zeigler was born, his ascent to power in the judiciary, and his survivors, including Melanie, who was listed as a "real estate executive in Manhattan." It was all so cursory and brief. There was no explanation for this lack of sensationalism other than a crushing deadline that resulted in this blurb of bare essentials.

The morning news shows were hardly more illuminating. Channel 4 had a thirty-second report on the "illustrious judge's violent demise," with a promise that "as more details unfold, we will bring them to you." Channel 7 announced that "the police pledge a full investigation to apprehend the perpetrator, or perpetrators." Channel 2 spent most of its coverage cataloguing Judge Zeigler's high regard as a tough law-and-order justice.

I was just slightly hung over, actually more fatigued from my lack of sleep, but I knew I had to move forward, get dressed, and head toward the office, like every other innocent Stribling employee.

I anticipated there would be a buzz of concern in the office. Inevitably, there would be shock from some people who do not start their day with broadcast news. I had not prepared myself for the line of police cars and battery of New York detectives inside the Stribling office.

When I walked through the door, I was met by Hannah Banks, a woman who had worked at Stribling for about five years and one of the many that had replaced me on my condo reconnaissance trysts with Melanie. Hannah was a nice-enough woman in her midthirties who worked her leads doggedly, but without much personality. From the moment I saw her, I could see she was shaken. Her normally pristine mascara had run a bit down the right side of her face, and she was carrying a box of tissues.

"Did you hear?" she asked.

"What?" I thought it best to be in the dark about this whole thing. Not much advantage is blurting out that I had witnessed the brutal murder and said nothing.

"Melanie's husband was killed last night."

"No!"

"Dead."

"An accident?"

"Hardly." She took a tissue and wiped her eye. "He was stabbed to death down in the West Village. Pretty gruesome."

"Wow. Was Melanie with him?"

"Fortunately, no. She was meeting with some developer and his staff at the time."

"Well, that's some small consolation. Thank God for that. Did you talk to her?" I asked innocently.

"No, but Diane Farin did. Evidently, Melanie seemed pretty shook up. Hey, who wouldn't be?" Hannah took another tissue. "You should give her a call. She and you were pretty close, weren't you?"

"Well, in a professional way, yes. I admired the way she could consummate a real estate deal and size the market for a prospect's needs." Realizing that this dodge sounded far too formal for the circumstances, I added, "And she was always nice to me." However, I did not love the illusion to "how close" we were. No need to underscore that nature of our relationship, especially in view of last night's events. Like Melanie, I began to wonder if everyone in the office suspected. Eventually, I added, "Sure, I'll give her a call. I imagine everyone in the office will."

"We should," Hannah agreed. "The girl needs a support system now."

I looked around the office at all the Stribling staff. No one was seated at his or her desk. Everyone was having their morning cups of coffee, huddled in small groups, whispering to one another, as if it were a funeral. A few were talking to the police officers.

"What's with all the cops? What are they looking for?" I asked as I surveyed the room.

"Anything. Anyone who knows anything about the judge, his relationships, or the circumstances. I think they're just looking for any leads. They just want to talk to each of us and see if we can help."

"Pretty standard, I guess."

"I guess." She nodded. "I just feel so sad for Melanie. It's awful."

"It is," I agreed.

Out of the corner of my eye, I could see Carol Welton exit the temporary interrogation room, which, until yesterday, was the Stribling manager's office. It had apparently been commandeered by the NYPD for these employee interviews. Like many of the women in the office, I noticed that Welton had been crying and was carrying one of those small Kleenex boxes.

As soon as she walked toward her desk, a middle-aged NYPD officer appeared in the doorway of that interrogation room. He was looking down at his clipboard and then turned a page.

"Mr. Witt," the officer called out in the fashion of a schoolteacher taking roll call.

I held up my hand like a kid in class and motioned that I would be right with him. I poured myself a cup of coffee from the community urn and headed into the back office.

The officer greeted me in a friendly manner when I walked through the door.

"Jackson Witt?"

"That's me."

"Have a seat. My name is Detective Tommy Donovan, and I am attached to this case." He took out a card and pushed it across the desk. The detective looked like a man of about forty. I imagined that he was a lifer in the NYPD and may have come from a police family. He was a dark-haired man, probably second- or third-generation Irish-American, with a New York accident. In all respects, he seemed a nice-enough guy—the kind of fellow you might meet at a Mets baseball game. "We're just trying to gain some background information from all the people who knew Melanie Zeigler and perhaps her late husband, Martin Zeigler."

"Sure," I responded. "Anything I can do to help."

"You heard what happened?"

"I just did."

Donovan called out through the open door. "Officer Washington, can you join me here?"

While we waited, Donovan shrugged. "Police procedure these days. Always got to have two for any interrogation. No wonder everyone's taxes keep going up."

"Right," I smiled at his little joke.

Tanya Washington came into the room. She was a youngish black officer, probably about twenty-eight. *A little chunkette,* I thought and wondered how she was able to pass the police physical. I figured you only had to run the mile once to get in the force, and then you could load up on the donuts. She closed the door and took a chair next to Detective Donovan.

"This is just preliminary," Donovan began. "We're just trying to get a sense of the situation from people who may have known the Zeiglers. Mr. Witt, how long had you worked with Melanie Ziegler in this office?

"About three years until she transferred uptown."

"Ever met Martin Zeigler?"

"Never did," I answered truthfully. "Whenever we had a holiday party or a Stribling get-together, he was a no-show. I did see him on the tube and when he ran for reelections. But I think he was pretty busy with all that legal, judicial stuff."

"Ever hear Melanie talk about his enemies?" Donavon asked.

"No, not that I can ever remember."

"Uh-huh. Were you ever aware that she might have received some harassing phone calls? Either here or at her home?"

"No, did she?"

Officer Washington, who was taking notes, looked up at me. "Well, that's what we're trying to ascertain, Mr. Witt. That's why we're asking questions." The woman had a definite attitude. I figured that the best course of action was not to argue with her about who should be doing the interrogating.

"No, I don't know of any harassing phone calls," I stated.

Detective Donavon was looking through his notes, saying "uh-huh" several times as he ticked off check marks. I figured I was getting close to the bottom of the sheet. "Let's see here," the detective sighed. "Ever see any unusual characters come in the office here or meet with Ms. Zeigler?"

"You mean other than the unusual characters who come in here every day looking to buy an apartment?"

"Yes, other than that," the detective smiled.

I knew the value of timing from my days in theater. I just looked at the sky for a few seconds and shook my head no. "I never saw her with anyone who would raise any suspicions whatsoever," I answered soberly.

The detective nodded and looked again at his notes. "That's good, Mr. Witt."

I should have learned my lesson about asking questions, but I just felt the urge to learn one little thing, especially given the insinuation of the last few inquiries. "May I ask you one question?"

Officer Washington lifted her glasses and looked at me. Detective Donovan closed his notebook and said, "Sure."

I looked at both of them and asked it as sincerely as possible. "Is Melanie Zeigler a suspect?"

Officer Washington harrumphed. "Mr. Witt, at this point everyone is a suspect."

"Everyone?" I interrupted.

Detective Donovan finished the thought, "Everyone! Until we can get to the bottom of this thing. And I can guaran-damn-tee you the powers that be definitely want us to get to the bottom of this case."

"Wow," I said involuntarily.

The detective looked at the young black officer. "You got anything else, Officer Washington?"

"Well, yeah . . . I got one other inquiry. I'm not trying to pry, Mr. Witt, but as I've talked with a few of the employees here, I get the feeling that you and Mrs. Zeigler had a . . . 'friendship.' Uh, some might even say . . . a 'special' relationship."

"Who said that?" I shot back.

"No one in particular," the officer immediately responded. "We're just talking to everyone and trying to figure out who knew Melanie best. And your name has come up a few times."

I was looking directly at Officer Washington, but I could see that Detective Donovan opened up his notebook at this new line of questioning. I didn't like that this new area warranted a fresh page of notes.

Tanya Washington was more than capable of returning my stare. She slightly raised one eyebrow and continued, "Well, how then would you describe your relationship with Mrs. Ziegler?"

"I would not use the term *special*!"

"Well, what term would you use?"

"*Businesslike. Professional,*" I answered. "Look, we were assigned to do the research on new real estate listings together. Just like you two are assigned to do your jobs together. Would you call your relationship special? Officer Washington, Mr. Donovan, would you call your relationship special?"

Tanya Washington looked at Donovan and, for the first time, showed a slight smile. "I would not call our relationship . . . special."

The detective almost chuckled. He looked at Tanya, then at me, then back at the officer. "It's nice though."

"Exactly!" I jumped in. "A nice relationship. That's the relationship I had with Mrs. Zeigler. A nice businesslike, professional relationship."

"Good, good. Have you spoken with her by any chance, Mr. Witt?" Donovan asked and then amplified, "You know . . . like in the last few days or the last week?"

"I have not," I stated. Admittedly, it was a Clintonesque response. Technically, I had not actually spoken *with* her. True, I had tried to reach her and even left messages, but I had not actually had a conversation with Melanie.

"One more question, Mr. Witt." The detective leaned back in his chair. "Can you account for your whereabouts last evening . . . say from nine to midnight?"

I sighed. I didn't want it to look like I was getting agitated. Hopefully, it just came off as fatigue. "I went to a movie."

"With anybody?"

"By myself. I do that quite frequently."

There was a silence. I've often believed that people who have never watched a film solo find it difficult to understand those who do. From the looks on their faces, I could see this mode of behavior was foreign to them.

"Lots of people see movies alone," I explained. "Especially if they live alone."

"Right," Ms. Washington finally said. "What did you see?"

"*Avatar.*"

Another pause.

Just to break the ice, I added, "It wasn't that good."

"Well, I'll keep that in mind next time I see a movie alone," Detective Donovan said with a smile. "You know, we got a lot more interviews to go through here," he said, looking at Washington to suggest a wrap-up. She looked back and gave a slight nod.

"If we have any other questions, we'll get back to you," he detective said as he finally closed his notebook. "And if anything else occurs to you—anything at all—you have my card. Call anytime."

I picked up the card and put it in my pocket. "Yes. Of course." As the two authorities of the NYPD stood, I did too, shook their hands, and exited the small room. I couldn't wait to get out of there.

Well, that barely went OK, I told myself. I looked around at all my co-workers in small groups and wondered which one had suggested that Melanie and I had a "special" relationship. Just then, Hannah Banks walked up to me and handed me a fresh cup of coffee.

"How'd it go?" she asked.

"Fine. They just wanted to know if I had seen anything strange," I answered.

"Yeah, same with me. But I never saw anything strange or anyone strange.

Did you?"

I took a sip of my coffee.

"No. Nothing," I quietly answered.

Chapter Eight

By the time I arrived in my apartment after a day of shock in the Stribling office, the story of Martin Zeigler had broken wide open.

My first clue was the blinking red light on my telephone answering machine.

Once I heard all the solicitations for dish TV and credit cards, I listened to the message from my college friend, Alba Gonzalez. "Jackson Witt? Alba. I've been assigned to cover the Zeigler murder for the *Times*, and I know you knew them. I need some background fast. Meet me at the Riviera Café on Broadway at six. Please. If you can't make it, give me a call. Need to fill in a lot of blanks. It'll be a big help. You're a sweetie. Please meet me."

I always loved hearing from Alba even though these days our communiqués came too rarely. Her clipped staccato diction was as recognizable a feature as her dark brown eyes. I used to kid her that her "I'm in a hurry" delivery was a proud, even braggadocios, display of her language mastery beyond her native Columbian roots.

"I can speak just as fast in Spanish," she would crow, "but I'm afraid you wouldn't understand a word of it since you only took two snoozing semesters of a foreign language. God forbid, Jackson Witt, if you ever have to play Don Quixote! Of course, I could always help you get the exact accent."

I also got a kick out of the fact that she had this habit of calling me by my first and last names. "You should get used to it," she'd advise me. "That's what the master of ceremonies will call out someday at the Academy Awards."

We had met as sophomores at Temple University. While I was in the theater department and she was in journalism, we found ourselves seated next to each other in a few communications courses. Late homework led to late lattes, which led to a full-fledged two-year romance. In fact, most of my friends considered us an off-beat, undeniable item, but competing schedules drove us in different directions. I was always rehearsing till midnight, and she was always chasing stories in the morning. We could both feel the drift of our conflicting ambitions. Before graduation, she cared enough about me to suggest the breakup. "You've got to chase the American dream and devote yourself to becoming a star. Do it. Focus, Jackson Witt. I believe in you. You can be really good, but you've got to give it 100 percent. At least for now."

I hated hearing her advice at the time, but as usual, I did appreciate her blunt honesty. Just to soften the blow, she admitted that she too would have to work around the clock for several years to create true journalistic credentials.

It sounded harsh. In real time, it wasn't. To this day, I think she really meant it as sympathetic, realistic jump start for both of our professional apprenticeships. From a practical standpoint, I reluctantly agreed. However, the heart is another story. I remember feeling dazed and discombobulated for days. I never asked if she felt the same way but assumed those same emotions may have descended on her before our talk. Even so, I always had this instinct in my solar plexus that timing conspired against us, and still did.

After four years with the *Philadelphia Enquirer*, she landed at New York's great gray lady a few years back. At the time, I was transitioning out of the theater and in the early months of my love nests with Melanie, so once again, our timing was bad. Even so, we'd meet every few months, partly because I loved her nose for news and her amazing, unforgettable smile.

I would gladly get together with her. For one thing, if anyone knew anything about the inside story of Zeigler, it would most likely be Alba.

While changing into Levi's, I turned on the tube. The New York City mayor, Carl Woodson, had held a press conference surrounded by the chief of police and several detectives including Tommy Donovan. In it, the mayor pledged "the full resources of New York City to solve this heinous crime."

He also extolled the judicial career of Martin Zeigler. As the mayor put it, "While this by-the-book judge may have been one of the more conservative justices on the bench, he was an honorable man who meted out justice as he believed it was due, and we are all saddened and sickened by this senseless act. Rest assured, we will catch the perpetrators."

All the TV channels covered the sensational story. The questions of why Zeigler was in the West Village, who his supposed enemies were, and his tough rulings on gay adoptions, pornography, and prostitution would clearly be more than enough to fill hours of airtime. A few stations covered the lovely Melanie, who was described as a "high-powered New York City real estate executive." According to most reports, the widow was "in seclusion and grief-stricken."

I arrived at the Riviera Café a few minutes before six, remembering that Alba always hated waiting alone at a bar. When she entered, she looked breathtaking, as usual. Dressed in a fitted black business suit, which matched the jet sheen of her hair, we looked like an odd poorly art-directed couple, but always did. I rose when I saw her coming and gave her a kiss on the cheek.

"Thanks for coming, Jackson. Can we get a quiet table in the corner?"

"Sure. God, you look great," I said.

"Thanks. C'mon." Alba was never one for small talk. I always admired that about her. No games. No guile. And those amazing looks, but let me not get ahead of myself. She motioned for me to follow her and walked across the room to an open table away from the bar crowd.

As soon as we sat down, she took out her pad and expelled a huge breath and shook her head quickly, as if to clear her mind from all the previous interviews and to launch into this new one. "Wow, this is a wild story, Jackson Witt. Glad you could make it."

"Me too."

"I'm really up against a deadline, and I know you could help."

"Tell me how."

"Well, for starters, the widow Melanie Zeigler. Tell me about her 'cause I know you know her."

"I do?"

"Jackson, c'mon. You mentioned her when I first came to town and told me she was one of the people who made your entry into the real estate world easier. And as I've been chasing this story, it's pretty clear you knew her more than professionally."

Rather than protest the accusation to a friend, I simple answered, "She's a nice woman."

"Could she have murdered her husband?"

"No way."

"Could she have orchestrated the murder?"

"Geez, I don't think so."

I really didn't. Despite the fact that her calls were on the cell phone, it was inconceivable to me that she could actually give an order to slash the judge. "Is she suspected?" I was afraid to hear the honest answer but knew I would get it from Alba.

"Of course, she is!" my college flame almost laughed at the question. "In every death of a spouse, the other spouse is always the first person of interest, and evidently, theirs was not a perfect marriage."

"I know that," I admitted.

"But the woman seems to have a rock-solid alibi. She was locked in a meeting with this big developer and his staff for several hours. Six witnesses say she was there.

Alba pressed on. "Do you know Robert Lévesque?"

"The real estate developer?"

"Right. Is there a sexual relationship between Melanie Zeigler and Robert Lévesque?"

"God, not that I know of. Why? Does the police think he may have done it?"

"Right now, the police are looking at anyone with motive, including you . . . but I'll get to that soon enough."

"Wait. Wait. Wait," I interrupted her. "Go back to that last sentence."

"Don't worry. There are a lot of people in the suspect line in front of you."

"Such as?"

"Did you ever meet the judge?"

"I never did."

Right about now, the rat-a-tat of her questions was beginning to fatigue me. Fortunately, the waitress was hovering at our table, giving me a welcomed respite.

"What can I get for your folks?" the waitress asked.

"I'll have a latte," Alba responded while looking at her notes. Then she looked at me and added, "For old time's sake."

"I'll have a Diet Coke. Again, for old time's sake," I requested.

Immediately, our waitress left, and Alba looked at me with a slight smile.

After a beat, I waded back in. "Tell me about this long line of suspects."

"This is a very weird case," she said.

"How so?"

"The judge was a real hard ass when he was on the bench."

"So I hear."

"But he was rather inviting soft ass when it came to his private life."

"What are you saying?" I'm not stupid. Inherently, I understood what she was implying, but I wanted to hear the dirt.

"This judge, Judge Zeigler, was widely considered the most right-wing, hang-'em-high antigay justice in New York."

"Uh-huh."

"But he had a secret sex life with a gay prostitution ring."

"Really?" I asked incredulously. I flashed on Officer Washington's questions about the judge's private life. So that was where she was fishing. "Martin Zeigler was gay," I asked.

"Big time."

"One latte and one Diet Coke," the waitress said as she brought our drinks.

"Thanks," Alba said and actually waved the waitress to move on. *Wow,* I thought. *No point in being polite when you're on a deadline.*

"How big time?" I asked.

"The police are just finding out. Evidently, he had a regular account with a few gay prostitution syndicates, like Adam's Apple and Gayfair. Ever hear Melanie mention these firms?"

"Never."

Alba actually paused for a breath and took a sip of her latte. "What this means is that Judge Zeigler may have been killed by the very people he sent to prison."

"Wow," I said. "So that's a long list of suspects."

She nodded. I took a sip of my soda, letting this all sink in. "They are sure he was gay?"

"Very." She motioned to me to move closer as if she wanted to share a secret that could not possibly be overheard. "In the autopsy, they found a welt of a heart on his left butt cheek. And he had a cock ring in his jacket pocket."

I'm sure I had a look on my face akin to opening a dirty sock drawer. However, part of it was that I simply didn't understand the term. "What's a cock ring?" I innocently asked.

"A little ornament they put at the base to provide stimulation for both parties."

"Yeesh, and that was in his pocket? His outside pocket?" I asked, clearly remembering the peacoated killer slipping something in Zeigler's jacket after the stabbing.

Alba looked at me with a curious expression. "What difference does it make? Quite honestly, I didn't ask whether it was the right, left, inside, or outside pocket. I just know he had a cock ring on his person and heart welt on his ass."

"Right," I shook my head, comprehending with some astonishment.

"So did your friend Melanie ever mention anything about this? Any gay activist visitors to your office? Did she ever mention any gay threats? Jackson, think back. This could actually help her."

"Alba, all this is news to me. I'm telling you, I never heard a peep about any of this."

"Well, maybe you two were too busy discussing sweet nothings," Alba countered, for the first time showing some potential jealousy. Or at least I could fantasize as such. I rather enjoyed hearing this hint of a barb. It suggested some latent interest. Besides, her earlier reference to Melanie and me definitely caught my attention.

"You mentioned my name earlier, Alba." I felt it the time was right to change the subject, especially given her hints that I was in the circle of some suspicion. "Are the police really interested in my so-called relationship with Melanie?"

"They definitely know about your so-called relationship," Alba countered with air quotes and the kind of sarcasm I loved from her when we were together. "However, they also know it was seven or eight months ago. And that there were probably other paramours of Melanie after you."

"Really?" I asked.

"Sorry to break it to you, buddy, but you are not the first . . . or, evidently, the last."

I took a sip of my soft drink and leaned back in my chair. As I did so, I took a good look at Alba. My god, she was attractive. She was drawing lines through a series of words, thoughts, and questions on her notepad. When she looked up, she caught me staring.

"You really don't know anything about any of this?"

"I don't. And I didn't hear anything about it on the news."

"Well, you wouldn't. Not yet." She closed her notebook. "Nobody thinks we have any code of ethics in journalism. But it does exist, at least on the legit papers. We're not interested in bringing the judge out of the closet or exposing his gay sex life unless we know it somehow has a bearing on his death. At least, that's the way the big papers work. Of course, there are other so-called news-slash-gossip sources these days. God knows what will be out there in the next twenty-four hours."

I just nodded. "I wish I knew more," I told her.

"I do too,'" she answered, finishing the last sip of her latte. "Jackson Witt, do yourself a favor. If the police start asking question—and they are asking questions of anyone who had any relationship with the Zieglers— answer them as straightforwardly and honestly as you can."

"Of course," I answered, as if by rote.

"I'm serious. They are not kidding around with this case. They want to pin the tail on some donkey. And if anyone starts giving them bullshit, they are going to pin the tail on that particularly donkey."

"I'm not capable of bullshit," I answered, as if it were true.

"I have never thought so," she said. She stood up and gave me kiss on the cheek. "Jackson, I have to file a story by nine, and I have a few more interviews to do. Can you cover this?" "My pleasure," I told her and winked good-bye and good luck. As she walked away, I followed her slinky silhouette past the crowded bar. I took another sip of my Diet Coke and felt the hit of the news I had just learned.

Chapter Nine

I have never been fond of wakes, but I was looking forward to the memorial of Martin Zeigler more than any I had ever attended. Everyone from the Stribling office would be there. Many city officials would be there. More importantly, Melanie Zeigler would be there. I had tried repeatedly to reach her via telephone. Not surprisingly, she was evidently too tied up with details to get back to me.

I took the subway up to the funeral parlor on Madison Avenue. Ever since the incident in the West Village, I had become anxious on these underground journeys. I always imagined I would bump into the man in the peacoat, or worse yet, he would bump into me with a knife in his gloved hand. On this particular trip, I tended to look like a guppy in a fish tank—jerking my head right, left, right, left, behind me, forward— keeping a lookout for anyone who resembled the Zeigler murderer. He was nowhere to be seen. As usual, the subway was filled with commuters, students, and shoppers, all yammering away about the intimate details of their daily lives.

Unlike my usual carefully calibrated antennae for gossip, I was only able to decipher snippets on this journey.

"I think my boss is on the take."

"My kid is having a drug problem."

"Ellie is gaining a ton of weight. Especially on her thighs."

"I am sick and tired of Ben's inability to get it up."

I just couldn't key into the full content of these conversations. Perhaps it was right/left shifts of my concentration. More likely, it was my forward focus on the Zeigler wake. I wondered if Mr. Peacoat would make an appearance. Probably not, I hoped. But given all the publicity, I did figure that the place would be packed.

The Frank E. Campbell Funeral Chapel was accustomed to big crowds. Over the years, it became known as the last resting place for celebrities and had served the likes of Rudolph Valentino, Judy Garland, Jackie Onassis, John Lennon, Leona Helmsley, Luther Vandross . . . and now, Martin Zeigler.

When I approached the funeral home coming out of the subway stop, I could see the overflow crowd gathered outside.

Mixed among them were a few co-workers from the Stribling office—Diane Farin, Kathy Lacey, and Hannah Banks. Hannah was grabbing a smoke, and the other two were there just to keep her company.

"Big turnout," Hannah said as I walked toward her.

"Like an opening night," I quipped, flashing on my Broadway days. "What's it like inside?"

"Crowded. Even the mayor is in there, and all the big government muckety-mucks. And of course, Melanie . . . who seems to be bearing up pretty well under the circumstances."

"That's good." We both stood there speechless for a few minutes while Hannah took another drag or two.

"Want one?" She took out another Marlboro Light and lit it from the end of her previous butt.

"Nah, I should go in and pay my respects."

The parlor itself is a model of understated decorum. All beige and gray-greens and soft lighting. The stairway to the upper rooms is unusually wide, but in no way flashy or pretentious. Just a few touches of dull metal and mahogany and faint-print carpeting. One of the things that makes the place feel so surreal (other than the fact that there are dead bodies in caskets) is that there are no pictures on the walls. Just wide expanses of paint. Also, the pervasive aroma of flowers. From the moment you walk inside, you feel like you are in the midst of a tropical paradise.

A man who evokes the image of a somber concierge greets you as you enter the palace. Instinctively, you know he is there to give directions. I looked right at him and said, "Zeigler." In that hushed sympathetic tone, he slowly pointed to the left and said, "Parlor A."

Obviously, it would be parlor A. It was the one with a jam-packed attendance. Evidently, there was another wake upstairs in parlor C. Very few people were walking in or out of that room. *Sad,* I thought, *to play second fiddle your last night on earth.* Right then and there, I decided I would never plan to be waked in a place that could attract more people in an alternative room than my own. Too depressing. Not that one would exactly be aware, but it would be so depressing for those who attended. They'd begin to feel like they were there for a loser.

Well, Martin Zeigler was definitely not a loser, at least from the crowd he attracted. When I entered the room, I could see Melanie close to the casket, greeting a long line of well-wishers. Of course, she was dressed in black as she accepted sympathetic handshakes from one visitor after another. Even in this hour of horror, she looked sexually hot. Rather than stand in the long line, I surveyed the different enclaves in the parlor.

There was Mayor Woodson and his entourage. About ten feet to their left stood a group of people who had all the earmarks of lawyers and judges. The judges were the sober-looking types, and the lawyers wore cufflinks. All of them mingled easily and quietly and evidently knew one another from more heated courtroom battles.

To my right was another group. It would be difficult to not immediately typecast them as gays. It's not as if there is a definite gay costume although the bulk of these men were more fit than the lawyer/ judge enclave, and they tended to wear more European suits. However, the dead giveaway was not the attire. There were no women in this group. These men seemed inherently comfortable being around one another and did not appear to be uncomfortable in a funeral home, perhaps because they had been there many times before for dear departed AIDS victims.

I looked around the parlor to see if others noticed the distinct discreet gatherings in the room. No one seemed to. Everyone was too busy chatting away in hushed tones.

I signed the guest register and joined the line to see Melanie. Along the way, I passed a succession of standing floral displays. "Dear Judge," "Dear Co-Worker," "Dear Brother," "Dear Husband," and several "Dear Friend" bouquets. While waiting, I checked a few of these "Dear Friend" presentations to see who sent them. One was marked from "your friends," and the others were sent anonymously. *Curious,* I thought. I suppose if the antigay judge had friends in the gay community, they didn't want to identify themselves.

By now, I was just a few people in line from Melanie. I could tell she had noticed me a few paces back when she looked up and sent back a faint smile and a quick wink. Almost immediately, she went back to her widow duties, accepting the outreached hands of those in front of me and nodding an understanding agreement to each person's recollections of Martin Zeigler.

"Melanie, please accept my condolences," I said rather formally when I approached her with a kiss on the cheek. "It's awful."

"Terrible."

"Horrifying."

"A nightmare."

"Devastating."

After a beat, Melanie broke the rhythm with a slight smile. "Well, I don't know that I would go that far," she said and looked around the crowded parlor. "But he obviously had a lot of friends. I'm just trying to get through this ordeal."

"I called you a few times."

"I know, but I just couldn't respond at the time."

"A lot to do."

"More than you know, Jackson. There are all these details to handle at the funeral parlor. And given the nature of his death, there's the police to deal with. The investigation. The news media."

"Just tell them all to stuff it until you're done dealing with your grief," I offered, as if she really did have a traditional relationship with her husband and a mourning consequence.

"It's not that easy," she answered, rolling her eyes.

"I know. I've been watching the news coverage. It's nonstop."

"You don't know the half of it."

"I've got an idea," I told her. Actually, I had more than just some idea, but this was not the time to discuss cell phones and eyewitness murders. "If there's anything I can do . . ."

"I'd love to talk to you," Melanie finished my sentence and reached out again to hold my hand. *Finally,* I thought. The woman does want to get in touch with me; she just wants this to blow over and then . . .

Just then, a tall man joined the two of us by the closed casket. He was about forty and didn't easily fit in the category of any of the three visiting enclaves. Not a lawyer. Not a judge. Not a gay. He had all the air of a successful businessman with his dark suit, mauve tie, and tanned visage.

"Melanie, if you wish, you can take a break from all this. Get off your feet. Have a cup of coffee in the back room. Everyone would understand." As he spoke, he reached out to her and gently held her elbow.

"No, Robert. I'm fine."

The man just stood next to her and planted himself as if he belonged. After a moment of awkward silence, I reached out to shake his hand. "Hi, I'm Jackson Witt, and you are . . . a friend of the family?"

He smiled. "I'm Robert Lévesque, the developer. Friend of Melanie here. Actually, a business associate of Melanie."

Melanie jumped in the fill of the dead air. "You've probably heard of Mr. Lévesque, Jackson. He develops all those high rises on the east side. I was actually in a meeting with him when . . . when . . ."

"When the event happened," Lévesque said, tilting his head to the casket. "Sad," he added, unconvincingly.

"I'll say." After another uncomfortable pause, I decided to conclude this visit. "Well, you've got a long line of people to speak with. Melanie dear . . . if there is some way I can be of help . . ."

"I will definitely call you," she said.

"On my landline," I stupidly added, as if she would continue to keep ringing the cell phone of Mr. Peacoat.

She looked at me quizzically. "What do you mean?"

"My cell phone is on the blink," I added with a shrug.

"OK. I will call you . . . on your landline," she said.

"Very nice to meet you," Mr. Lévesque said as he patted me on the shoulder and moved me through the line so Melanie could great the next visitor.

As I walked away from the casket, I couldn't help but look back at the tableau. There was Melanie, gracefully acknowledging the next visitor with understanding nods and handshakes, and the tall tanned Mr. Lévesque standing next to her like a bodyguard.

"Do you know Lévesque?" a vaguely familiar voice asked.

I turned to my right and discovered Detective Thomas Donavon standing next to me. "Oh, hi. Wow, I didn't recognize you without your notepad."

"Yeah, I clean up nice for these events."

I looked back at the casket area. "In answer to your question, I don't really know Mr. Lévesque. I've heard of him. Everyone in the real estate business has, but uh . . . no."

"I guess he's sort of stepped into the role of chief consoler," Donavon said with some purpose. I couldn't tell whether he was saying this to goad me or make me jealous.

Hell, I didn't even know how much he definitely knew about Melanie and me. I looked back at Donovan, who was staring noncommittally at Melanie.

"She seems to be holding up rather well," the detective remarked.

"Maybe so, but it can't be easy," I answered sympathetically. When I looked back at her, I noticed that Robert Lévesque had exited the scene. He had taken a solitary seat off to the right. In his sartorial splendor, he seemed uninterested in mingling with any of the three groups. Instead, he appeared to be focused only on her.

Perhaps he had decided that standing by her side for an extended time didn't look good. However, he was clearly exuding an interest in the woman. I wondered if Donovan had noticed the chemistry.

"We may need to ask you a few more questions, Mr. Witt," he added without turning his head toward me.

"Sure."

"You going to the funeral tomorrow?"

I looked back at Melanie, who continued to greet those in line. I decided it was best to underplay the closeness of my relationship with the widow. "Wasn't planning on it," I said in an offhanded manner. "You know, I'm not that close to Mr. Zeigler. As I told you before, I never really met him."

"I remember," Donovan answered. "Is it OK to call on you in the afternoon at your apartment?"

"Sure, whatever is easier. I'm off tomorrow. You know where I live?" "Oh yeah. I got it from your office."

"Good," I answered with fake enthusiasm.

Of course, I knew it wasn't good. But the advice of Alba Gonzales rang in my ears. "Don't play around with the authorities. Answer their questions as honestly and directly as possible." I vowed to do so, within definite limits.

Chapter Ten

By the next morning, the news stories on Martin Zeigler had begun to spin toward the prurient. Village Justice, screamed one headline. It began to chronicle the judge's history of antigay rulings and then hinted at allegations that he had an equal fascination with the gay lifestyle. The *New York Post* headline, Sicko Judge, was more direct and brutal. It essentially called Judge Zeigler a two-faced public servant. It came right out and claimed that the judge had a secret life that included gay porn sites and gay brothels. None of these articles, however, alleged that the actual murder was perpetrated by a gay activist.

Alba's article in the *New York Times* was more sober. It focused on the hunt for the killer. According to Alba, police were combing the West Village for leads but had not yet identified any suspects. The article also intimated that Mrs. Zeigler herself was being questioned, as well as many business associates and friends of the family that might have motive for such an act. It only hinted at the gay connections by suggesting that a full investigation was underway to better determine the full extent of Mr. Zeigler's personal lifestyle and any links that may have to the slaying.

As I read her article, I couldn't help but feel that the top brass had heavily edited it. Leave it to the *New York Times* to makes sure that any steamy claims were fully vetted and substantiated. Even so, Alba did conclude the article with the following text, "Given the high profile of the victim, increasing speculations about his private life and city-wide fear that a brutal killer is on the loose, police authorities have doubled the detail to solve this mystery as soon as possible."

I took the mysterious cell phone out of coffee cup in my cupboard and carefully placed it on the island. I believed it held answers, and it was time to unlock them. I turned on the device and discovered that there were four messages in the inbox and eight voice mails.

The texts had all come from a familiar number—Melanie Ziegler's cell phone.

With some trepidation, I began to scroll and review them for any incriminating evidence.

The first one was from three weeks ago. It simply stated, "Glad to have been introduced 2 U. Sounds positive. Good luck." Hmm, I couldn't help but wonder who had made the introduction.

The second one, sent a week later, was more cryptic. "Did U get pix?" On some level, this supported my theory that Melanie's sole intention was to get embarrassing photos of the philandering judge.

The third message was sent on the morning of the judge's murder: "Locale 2 come."

Perhaps wisely, Melanie had not left any message after her late-night calls on the evening of the slaying. There were no other typed messages whatsoever. They had either been deleted or the callers had opted to not leave a trail. True, Melanie's messages did indicate that she had contact with the man in the peacoat. However, that was not news to me. On the other hand, there was no mention of Martin Zeigler, no hint of a hit, no signal that any physical harm should come to the judge.

And yet, fatal harm had indeed come to the judge, and someone had set those wheels in motion on the number 1 train by 125th Street. I thought back to the time of my overheard phone conversation. To my recollection, it was somewhere between 11:45 and noon on that fateful Tuesday.

I switched the cell menu to missed calls. There were several from the same 212 number that I presumed to be from the killer. There were the two late-night calls from Melanie. And there were two calls from unrecognizable numbers. I wrote them down on a sheet of paper for further investigation.

Unfortunately, there was no record of a missed call during the time frame of my overheard train conversation. I presumed that the killer had followed the caller's request and succeeded in deleting the message before the train headed underground. Damn.

Perhaps there was an answer in the voice messages. Unfortunately, I could not access these calls. Without the password code, it was impossible to open this mailbox. I tried 1234, 1111, 2222, and several other combinations but quickly realized that this search was futile—as pointless as trying to predict the NY lottery numbers in advance. I had the urge to call the number of those repeatedly missed calls and learn the identity of the mystery murderer but wasn't quite sure what to say when one answered. Better to rehearse that call and know exactly what information and answers I wanted. As I mused over different scenarios, the phone rang with that familiar *Drrring. Drring.* I looked on the screen and saw that it was the New York number as those missed calls. In the right corner of the screen, it also displayed a sign that indicated Low Battery. And then the phone went dead.

Good, I thought. It would give me more time to prepare for my reconnaissance return call, provided I could juice up the cell phone again.

I tried my current Verizon charger, only to discover that it didn't fit. The magic cell phone was an older model. I checked in my photo gear for any other undiscarded chargers. There were three. God only knows why I save this shit. The first one was marked Sony, probably for a disc player. No good. The other two looked like old phone chargers. The first didn't fit. But with the second, voila! I plugged in into the magic cell and decided to replenish its energy source.

When I heard the buzzer from the doorman, I physically reacted with a jolt. A little jumpy, I had to admit. I hit the buzzer button and heard Javier's voice. "Mr. Witt, you have a visitor. Mr. Leandor."

"Leandor? Send him up right up," I cheerfully instructed.

Leandor Montgomery was a good friend from my college days at Temple. He was a great costume designer and had worked on a few of my plays. Like me, he had enrolled in the acting school, but by freshman year, he realized that his calling lied behind the scenes. Part of his decision came from certain affectations in his diction style.

Shortly after leaving his high school home and enrolling in college, Leandor came "out of the closet" and declared his homosexuality to the world.

Having repressed it so long, he threw himself into a more flamboyant carriage and sibilant voice. I used to kid him about it, as only a good friend can.

"Leandor, what's with the queen voice cadence?" I would ask.

"I just don't want anyone to make any mistake about what side of the fence I now sit on," he would answer.

At the time, Leandor had all the bearing of an African-American leading man but was tired of the diets, abdominal crunches, and the charade. A year after he had come out, he gained about thirty pounds but still carried himself with elegance and pride, perhaps more so today since his true personality was no longer sublimated.

When the doorbell rang, I opened it and immediately received a big bear hug from Leandor.

"Hello, darling," he said and swept into my apartment. "I was just in the neighborhood and knew you would be oh so hurt if I had not stopped in and said bonjour. How's life for the real estate maven of Manhattan?"

"Crazy! Berserk! The world's gone haywire."

"Tell me about it. You been following the news? Did you hear about the murder just a few blocks from my apartment? Cops everywhere," Leandor said and walked into the kitchen. He put his copy of the *Advocate* newspaper on my island and opened up the fridge. "That pretty little gay-bashing judge got what he deserved. All my friends in the village are up in arms! Some of them even knew the guy since he liked to sneak his way into the forbidden clubs wearing sunglasses, which fooled absolutely no one. Hah!"

"Can I help you find something, Leandor?"

"No, I'll just help myself," he answered as he rummaged through the lower refrigerator sections. "He put a bunch of my neighbors away for pornography and then liked to partake on his own time. What an asshole! A very nice tight asshole from what I hear, but that's a completely different story. Got any brie? Smoked salmon? Want to go out for brunch?"

"I don't think I can do that right now," I answered. "But I would like to speak to you, maybe dinner sometime."

"Oh, that would be kismet. Love it." He then continued his scavenger hunt through my fridge and found something to his liking. "Yes! Ahh, wonderful. Some havarti. Have you got a knife?"

"In the drawer. How's the theater treating you these days?"

"Oh, you know. I work a show, I'm off a show, and then I work a show. Life of a gypsy!" As he said this, he extended his hands in the air dramatically, like Auntie Mame. "Just did the sound for 'Million Dollar Quartet.' See it?"

"No. But I hear it's good."

"It's wonderful. I created this sound montage of Elvis, Carl Perkins, Johnny Cash, and Jerry Lee Lewis. It's pretty chilling. Got any crackers?" He had already opened up my cupboard door and discovered some Carr's wafers. "Here!"

I always enjoyed Leandor's visits. He would stop by every month or so, usually unannounced and always full of emotional confetti. I loved the way he felt completely at home. Normally, I would visit with him for hours, partly to keep plugged into to my ever-vanishing theater world but mostly just to enjoy his spontaneous company. However, this exact moment didn't feel so perfect. "Leandor, I would love to have dinner sometime soon. Especially as relates to that double-dealing judge, but now is not such a good time to talk."

"I'm really miffed about that asshole Zeigler. I'm sure Zeigler read the *Advocate* for vicarious ideas," he said, pointing to the newspaper. "That's why I got the paper. I'm going to write a letter to the editor and tell them 'Gays only need apply.' I want them to quit running ads encouraging curiosity. This is sick, my friend. It pulls in the voyeurs like Zeigler. And look what happens!"

Just then, the doorman buzzer rang again.

I moved over to the device and hit the button.

"You have more visitors, Mr. Witt. A Mr. Donovan and a Ms. Washington.

Should I send them up?"

"Send them up," I said.

"Leandor, this is really not a good time," I said without trying to hurt his feelings.

"I'll just finish this havarti and get on my way," he said as he cut off another several slices and reached into the box of crackers.

Chapter Eleven

"Come in, Detective Donovan. Ms. Washington."

"Glad we could catch you at home," she said with a smile.

The gregarious Leandor walked around the island and bounded to the door, chomping on his havarti and crackers. He held up his fingers dramatically to emphasize his manners (no talking with your mouth full). As soon as he finished his self-made canapé, he extended his hand to my two new visitors. "Leandor Montgomery. Nice to meet you. Welcome to our humble abode."

A humorless Thomas Donovan looked directly at me and then Leandor.

Ms. Washington asked, "Roommates?"

"Oh, Jackson only wishes! But not so fast, buddy," Leandor said in his mock overly gay persona, which he liked to assume for the shock of strangers. "You're going to have to wait till after tonight's dinner. Call me dessert."

I would have liked to have been a camera in the corner so I could see a replay of my face. I tried to smile and imply that it was a big ha-ha joke, but I'm sure I looked like a panicked Richard Nixon in a David Frost interview. "Is this an OK time, Mr. Witt? Are we interrupting something?" Ms. Washington asked with some sensitivity.

"It's perfect," I said. "No problem. I want to help any way I can."

"I can help with havarti and crackers," Leandor said and opened up the fridge to pull out the cheese tray.

"I don't think they are here for snacks," I corrected my friend.

"It's scrumptious," Leandor said. Looking at Officer Washington, he smiled and teased her, "You look like you'd like a little slice or two. Whadya say, honey?"

"Not hungry," she cut him off abruptly.

"Hey, OK. No need to get huffy about it," Leandor reacted like a cat.

"Leandor, really," I admonished him. "Not a good time. I will talk to you later."

"OK, I can take a hint. Between the lines, I can see that it's toodles for me." He reached onto the coat rack to grab his muffler. "Jackson, darling, you keep that copy of the *Advocate*. Take a good look, and you'll see what I mean. There are plenty of ads in there that say, 'Hey, curious? Come on over. Walk on down!' You'll see. OK? Gotta scoot." He then raised his hand and did a little bent hand finger wave. Just for good measure, he blew a kiss to all of us sitting in the apartment.

When he closed the door, there must have been a good four or five seconds of silence. It felt like four or five minutes, but I'm sure that was just my mind racing.

I stood with my back to my two police visitors and finally turned around with a forced smile. I motioned for them to have a seat in the two living room armchairs. I then sat on the couch and kept my silence. From my old acting days, I tried to transport myself into the next theatrical scene. I closed my eyes and, after a few seconds, opened them with a question posed as calmly as possible: "How can I help you?"

"We just have a few follow-up questions," Officer Washington said as he opened up her steno pad.

"How was the funeral?" I asked in the direction of Detective Donovan, trying to change the subject.

"A lot less crowded," he said soberly.

I wondered if Robert Lévesque attended the final interment but decided not to ask. Too easy for the detective to interpret it as schoolyard envy. In my bones, I knew it was important to show no emotions or interest in Melanie Zeigler's personal life.

"A few things don't tally up," Detective Donovan stated.

I shifted my stance on the sofa to look at her and asked innocently, "Such as?"

"In the Stribling office, you stated that your relationship with Melanie Zeigler was a nice, professional, businesslike relationship. We have it on good authority that your relationship extended beyond just business."

"I would still characterize it as businesslike."

Donovan leaned forward and looked at me skeptically. "Would you characterize midday sexual liaisons as a normal part of business?"

I could feel myself pulling back into the sofa. I took a deep breath as I stalled for an adequate riposte. "Detective Donovan, I would call that a jealous reaction from some parties in the Stribling office that must have wished for such a liaison in their own private daydreams. There is absolutely no proof or evidence that such a relationship ever existed."

The self-director in me had to quietly applaud. It sounded so damn definitive.

Officer Washington then followed up, "Mr. Witt, you say you went to the movies the night of the murder. Do you, by any chance, have a receipt from that cinema?"

"No. Now that I no longer claim livelihood as an actor, I don't have any need to save film receipts for tax purposes."

"And what time did you attend that movie?" she asked.

Before I could answer, the magic cell phone rang. It rang again and again.

Almost like an alarm bell, all three of us sat there frozen.

"Go ahead, you can answer it, Mr. Witt," the detective said.

"Nah, that's OK," I answered.

Again, the phone rang. And again.

"Excuse me," I finally said and walked over to the cell phone and hit the Clear button. I walked back to my place on the sofa as if nothing had happened and said, "Where were we?"

"What time did you attend the movie, Mr. Witt?" Tanya repeated

I rubbed my temples, trying to indicate sincere thought. "So much has happened since then. But I think it was a 9:30 start, at the Quad Cinemas on Fourteenth Street."

"Makes sense," the officer said, but with a puzzled look. "See, Mr. Witt, this is one of those things that don't quite tally up. According to your doorman, Javier Sanchez, you returned that night sometime between 10:45 and 11:00. According to the running time of the movie, it didn't end until 12:35, which would put you back at your apartment around 12:40 . . . 12:45 if you stayed to watch the final credits roll."

I was silent.

"So you got back before the movie was even half over."

I took a beat and looked at both interrogators and then remembered my words to Javier upon entering the co-op. "I left the movie early. Didn't like it. No point in wasting my time. I think I already told you folks that."

"Do you remember who took your ticket that night?

"Ah, Jesus. No idea." In a crowded New York City movie theater, who could ever remember?

The detective leaned back and checked his notes. "Any chance you might have gone somewhere else that night instead of going to the movie and leaving early?"

Before I could answer, the damn cell phone rang again.

Drring. Drring.

"Why don't you get that?" Officer Washington said.

"This is more important," I answered.

Drring. Drring.

"Excuse me," I said and walked over to the island. This time, I hit the End button to power down the phone. I opened up the cupboard and put it back in its proper resting place—in the empty coffee cup. As soon as I did so, I turned back to the police duo and announced, "No more interruptions."

Detective Donovan heaved a long sigh and then hit me with the brutal truth. "Do you understand, Mr. Witt, we have a job to do here. We need to chase every possible lead that has any motive in this incident. Given the rumors about you and Ms. Zeigler, there is reason to believe you might have an incentive for Ms. Zeigler to be single. If so, we need to fully investigate your story." He took a long pause for emphasis. "I advise you to tell us the absolute truth because I can guaran-damn-tee you . . . we will get the truth from every suspect in this case."

I appreciated the honesty, but not the message. "Are you telling me that I am a suspect?"

"Not at this point. But your situation interests us. We need to get answers, and we're chasing every avenue that feels unanswered."

"Including Mr. Zeigler's gay connections," I suggested, as if I was offering an easy solution to their case.

"Yes, including that," Officer Washington answered.

Donovan jumped on that bait. "You have an issue of the *Advocate* on your kitchen island. Do you often read that publication?"

"Aw, come on," I answered. "You know damn well that my friend Leandor left that for me, by accident."

"I don't believe in accidents," Donovan responded.

"Well, I'm beginning to," I answered, flashing back on the accidental overhear of the "assignment," the accidental acquisition of the magic cell phone, and the accidental viewing of the eviscerating murder.

Detective Donovan stood up, satisfied that the basic interview was over. "Do you have a passport, Mr. Witt?"

"I do."

"Under the circumstances, I think it best that we see it," he said.

"You've got to be kidding! I don't feel comfortable with that," I answered quite instinctively.

"Well, I'm sorry you're not comfortable with police procedures," Detective Donovan scolded me. "But we are taking every precaution on this case. If you feel your rights have been violated, you should feel free to retain an attorney."

The words stung. "Are you advising me to get an attorney at this time?"

"No, we are not at that point . . . necessarily," Donovan answered.

"However, that is every client's individual, personal call."

"Should I have a lawyer?" I asked in plainer English.

"It probably wouldn't hurt to make a few legal inquiries," Tanya Washington helpfully answered.

I left the room, retrieved my passport from my file cabinet, and presented it to Detective Donovan. He wrote down all the pertinent information—the date of issue, the city of issue, and the passport number.

"Don't leave town," the detective advised me.

"I don't plan to," I told him and showed them the door.

After an uncomfortable pause, Tanya Washington softened the blow. "Mr. Witt, I just want to reiterate the invitation we made to you in our first interview. If you can think of anything that might help shed light on this case, please call us. It could have been an event that may have seemed insignificant at the time or just a little strange. Maybe something that just seemed a bit suspicious that you may have observed. Think about it. It might help us get to the bottom of this case. And it might help you."

I looked over at Donovan, who didn't seem too pleased that his subordinate had requested me to come up with alternative theories or even a better alibi. "I will think about it," I answered. "Especially in view of this latest interview."

Then I showed them the door.

Chapter Twelve

Given the tightening dragnet around me, I felt the need for a second opinion. The biggest burning question was what was to do with that damn cell phone. Of course, it would help to know who owned the phone and who had made the call on the train. More to the point, it would also help to know how to preserve my own innocence without completely throwing Melanie under the bus.

I believed that Alba Gonzales could provide that insight. For one thing, from our years together, she understood me better than most people on this planet. She would instinctively know that I was incapable of this imbroglio. Most importantly, she was a truth seeker. Perhaps that's what made her such a successful reporter and such an attractive personality. Besides, she might be able to shed some light on any progress from the police in finding the real perpetrator.

I had chosen to meet her at the Tocqueville Restaurant bar in Union Square. Since the cocktail lounge was primarily a gathering place for predinner guests, I was fairly certain that it would be a secure place for a sensitive conversation, especially at 9:00 p.m., when most diners had been seated. When I arrived at 8:45, there was only one other couple finishing their aperitif. In five minutes, they too went to their table, leaving the place perfectly empty for privacy.

When Alba arrived, she greeted me with a warm hug. "Long day," she said with an eye roll.

I agreed and ordered her a glass of wine. Despite her breakneck schedule, she always had a knack for looking fresh. Her pin-striped skirt and mauve sweater almost gave her a preppy look, which she definitely was not. I always loved her eyes. Even with obvious fatigue, they danced and lit the cocktail lounge. I knew better than to attribute it to long hours of sleep. She was a hard worker but loved it. I believed that's what gave her such an incandescent aura.

Once she had settled in, I laid out one parameter. "Alba, what I'm about to tell you is off the record. I don't want to see it in print. I just need some advice about a certain predicament."

Alba took a swig of her wine and said, "Go on."

"No, you've got to really promise that this is not a work interview."

She reached over and touched my hand. "Hey, right now, I'm here as a friend, Jackson Witt. Not as a reporter." I then launched into my entire chain of events—my overheard one-way conversation, my discovery of the cell phone, my witness of the murder, all the way to the surrender of my passport information to the NYPD authorities. She took it all in for about fifteen minutes without interruption or a notebook, which I appreciated.

"Dear heart, you are knee-deep pile of someone else's shit," she summed it up.

"I feel that."

"You should turn over the phone to the cops and let the chips fall where they may."

I winced. On a commonsense level, I knew it made sense. But the consequences of delivering this piece of evidence would potentially bury Melanie. I knew what she was capable of and what was unimaginable. Quite frankly, it seemed unfair to put a noose around her neck, especially since there was nothing definitely incriminating in her text messages. "I can't do that," I quietly stated. "I was thinking I should tell Mrs. Ziegler that I have that cell phone."

Alba immediately interrupted me, "That's the absolute worst idea ever. Jackson Witt, do not—and I repeat, do not—tell her you have her text messages ordering a hit."

I let this wisdom sink in and took another swig. "See, that's the thing. I don't believe she actually ordered a hit."

"Then who did?"

"Well, I'm not sure anybody actually said, 'Kill Martin Zeigler.' But there's only one man who could answer that—the man who did kill him. Incidentally, he's the same guy who keeps calling on that damn cell phone. I guess he wants it back." This truth got me thinking. I then presented another possible scenario. "I could call the killer and tell him that I, a very good Samaritan, found his phone and want to return it to him . . . if he would only give me his address."

Alba put her drink down and stared at me. "You're not really thinking straight now, my friend."

I began to like my little plan in the hatching and began to build momentum.

"And then I could call the police anonymously and give them a tip that the killer lives at . . . at the address he provided me. The police nab him. He tries to pin it on Melanie, but without the cell phone, there's no evidence she did anything. And everybody lives happily ever after."

"Jackson Witt, you've been reading too many fairy tales, my dear boy."

"I think it could work."

"Nothing in this world works that smoothly."

Rather than try to convince Alba, I decided to downplay my conclusion. "It's just a thought." I motioned for the waiter to refill our wine glasses.

"Jackson, here's my advice. You give the cell phone to the police and call it a day. If you're not ready to do that, then I would hold on to that phone for dear life. Don't give it to Melanie Ziegler. Don't give it to the killer. If shit starts to fall around you, that phone is your lifeline."

"I believe that." If push came to shove, the phone could always exonerate me.

"One more thing, Mr. Amateur Detective," Alba gestured for me to come closer. "If I were the man who lost that phone, I would just buy a new one and cancel all the messages. Including the ones on your phone. Ever think of that?"

I smiled back at her, rather proud of the investigative groundwork I had already covered. "He can't," I said smugly. "I called Verizon to check on that. The messages stay intact until you press the buttons on that phone to delete them. Can't do it from another phone."

"Well, OK . . . there's at least that," she avowed.

I wanted to know if the cops had made any headway and figured Alba might have a clue. "I just wish the police would get off their ass and find the real guy rather than wasting their time interrogating me."

"I need to warn you of this, Jackson dear. The department is not fucking around on this case. They need it resolved, and quickly. But all they have right now is you and your friend Melanie. Yeah, there are some rumblings about the judge's private sex life . . . but no witnesses or evidence. You've got the answers they need."

I nodded, fully aware of the powerful evidence in my pocket.

"Jackson Witt, listen to me. I would not let this spin too far out of control. You're not a suspect yet or a person of interest, but there is intense pressure on the police to name one. If they decide you are their easiest target, it will be bad for you."

I agreed and knew that the some action must soon be taken.

"You're a good guy. But you're a little blinded right now. I get the sense you're trying to protect someone you think may not be completely guilty. That's may be admirable, but also may be stupid, especially if the blame ends up falling in your lap."

"I appreciate the advice, I really do."

"I'm saying this because I give a shit about you and don't want to see you to get hurt."

I must admit, I loved the fact that she still gave a shit about me. I trusted the fact that there was no ulterior motive other than my own best self-interest. She was always good that way. At the time of our breakup, I still remember her parting words—"Right place, wrong time." Right now, it felt so good to have her in the right place—sitting across from me and in my corner. But once again, time was our enemy.

She took the last sip of her wine and explained that she still had some work ahead into the deep dark night. She then added, "If you're not going to turn the phone into the cops, I would not give it to anyone."

"I hear you."

When we exited the restaurant, Alba took my muffler and tightened it around my neck like a real friend would. She then gave a warm embrace. "Take care. Don't be a stranger. Be careful. Be smart. Don't do anything stupid, Jackson Witt."

"I won't," I stupidly promised and waved good-bye.

I took a deep breath of the crisp October night and tightened my muffler a little more. As I did so, I looked across to Union Square Park and viewed all the people milling around, going about their business as if nothing had ever happened.

This particular park used is a haven for drug transactions until the neighborhood became gentrified and the police increased their foot patrols. Like most of New York, it had become safer with increased police presence. In fact, there was still a good dose of NYPD around the fringes, just to keep things clean.

One officer was standing at the edge of the iron fence. With his militaristic stance, he looked familiar. I squinted across the traffic at him and could see the resemblance to Detective Thomas Donovan. He seemed to have an eye out for me. As soon as the man saw my gaze, he moved his face slightly away so I couldn't be completely swear to it.

My god, I thought, *my mind is beginning to play suspicious games with me.* I considered going across to the park for a closer look but figured I had enough excitement for one day. I turned down the sidewalk, threw the long end of my muffler over my shoulder, and strolled back to my apartment.

Chapter Thirteen

With the benefit of twenty-twenty hindsight, I would now suggest that it's a very bad idea to meet face-to-face with a cold-blooded killer. However, at the time, it seemed like a pretty amazing way to gain a positive ID of the perpetrator and get to the bottom of how this crime was committed or even commissioned. I also figured it could provide the ultimate "free pass" if the cops ever decided to incorrectly point fingers at me.

I had listened to Alba's advice: don't give up the damn phone. I had chosen to ignore the other part of his sentence: "Unless you turn it over to the police, which is the right thing to do." I just couldn't. Too many doubts about Melanie's real role.

I put the fully charged cell phone on my island and waited for the killer's call as I smeared a bagel with chive cream cheese and enjoyed a morning cup of coffee. Thirty minutes later, the phone was still silent. I checked the missed messages and discovered that, lo and behold, there was another from that oft-repeated 212 number. It was tempting to just return the call and speak with the mystery man. But I envisioned a grander, more elaborate plan. First, I needed to check one feature of the phone. Did it have photo capability? Would I, in fact, be able to snap a picture of the killer and provide the perfect alibi? I scrolled several features on the LG device and discovered the answer. Yes! Perfect!

Like an actor in the wings, I walked away from the phone and prepared myself for a performance. I rotated my neck to loosen the tension and shook my hands several times for a relaxed presentation. One more long cleansing breath. And then I dialed that number.

After two rings, the voice answered.

"Hello. Who is this?"

In my most cheerful, helpful voice, I answered. "Hey, did you lose a cell phone? Because I think I may have found it and wanted to return it . . . if it's yours."

There was a pause. "Who is this?"

I looked at my play bill posters on the wall and improvised a name from the *Cherry Orchard* production. "I am Henrik Ibsen," I answered.

"Well, Mr. Gibson . . . I did lose a phone and want it back."

I decided not to correct him on his mispronunciation of my instant pseudonym. Instead, I resumed my performance as Mr. Cheerful. "Gee, that's great! Then it's yours. By the way, what is your name, sir?"

"My name is not important. But I would like my phone back."

His reticence threw me a little, but I powered forward. "Well, I am glad it's your phone. Yeah, I found it in the street just last night."

There was a beat as this new information sunk in. "You found it on the street? What street?"

I hate it when I overlie. It leads me down a blind alley of more severe prevarications, and I decided to nip this fib in the bud. "Some downtown street. I don't really know since I'm basically a tourist in town. That's why I always get lost in Manhattan. Can't keep the streets straight." I began to nervously laugh and decided to take control of this conversation again before he could speak.

"If you give me your address, I'll be glad to drop it off at your apartment or your house . . . or wherever you live."

"No, that's not going to work. I'll come and get it from you. Tell me where you live."

Time for more lies. "Me? Where I live? Well, that's the funny thing. I'm actually homeless."

"I thought you said you were a tourist."

"Yeah, a homeless tourist." Another nervous laugh on my part.

There was pause on the other end. I decided to fill the gap. "Hey, here's an idea! I'll meet you at Grand Central Station. Right in the main terminal under the clock where they have the train schedules. You know the place?"

"I know the place. What time?"

"Let's say noon." I liked the idea of a busy terminal, just in case anything went wrong.

"Noon," he repeated.

"But how will I know who you are?" I asked as innocently as I could. Just for emphasis, I added, "I don't know what you look like . . . at all."

"I'll be wearing a peacoat."

"A peacoat?" I responded with faux puzzlement. "Oh yes. Like the navy boys wear. Oh yes. I haven't seen one of those in a while."

"Just bring the damn phone at noon."

"Perfect. That's why I'm calling. To return it to its rightful owner. Where it should be."

There was a click on the other end. I put the cell phone back on the island as if the device was toxic and slowly backed away from it. I took another deep cleansing breath and wondered how I could ever call myself an actor. I told myself it's ten times easier to do a stage portrayal than a real-life impersonation. Perhaps that's why I never became the Broadway star I envisioned for myself. Enough thinking about this.

I had an hour and forty-five minutes to prepare for this role and meet the mystery man. From past experience, I knew it would take me no more than an hour to get into costume.

*　*　*

Toulouse-Lautrec arrived at Grand Central with ten minutes to spare; I had chosen this outfit from a trunk of old costumes I had saved from college. I liked the fact that with spirit gum, the beard looked completely authentic. Given the requirements of the character, it meant I would be wearing a hat and small glasses. Wisely, I decided to dispense with the short bound legs and walk as a normal full-sized human being.

The costume seemed like a good precaution given the rather menacing tone of my earlier cell phone conversation. I didn't want the mystery man to recognize me. Of course, I reminded myself that, in all likelihood, he had never seen me. At least, I hoped not. However, better safe than sorry.

In my subway ride up the Grand Central, I was quite proud and satisfied that no passenger on the train even gave me a second look. They were all engaged in their private conversations, which they incautiously broadcast in full earshot of every fellow commuter. I was convinced that the costume seemed normal enough in not-so-normal New York.

I stood up by Michael Jordon's Steak House on the mezzanine and saw my peacoated subject standing by the clock kiosk in the center of the terminal. He was a man of about twenty-eight, well built, and impatient. He looked right and left and through the crowd for some homeless tourist who might have his cell phone.

For a brief moment, I wondered what kind of man this was. What sort of job is it to kill people or photograph people in a compromising moment? No one in high school consciously chooses this path or even suggests it to their high school guidance counselor. I figured some life in crime dictates this limited option. Maybe he was a victim of Martin Zeigler's by-the-book justice. Maybe he was a jilted lover. Nah! He definitely didn't look gay. Not that one can easily tell these days

As often happens in Grand Central Station, there are tourists taking photos for posterity. On the balcony above the main terminal, a young Japanese couple in wedding regalia was being photographed by their father. Other tourists, enamored with the spectacle, joined in snapping photos of this moment.

I decided it was a grand opportunity to gain a long-distance snapshot of the mystery man.

Toulouse-Lautrec took the cell phone camera out of his front pocket and seemingly focused it on the Asian lovebird. Instead, I moved it two inches to the right to zero in on the man by the clock tower. Snap. Replay. Yikes! Someone stepped in front. Another snap. Damn! He turned around. Another snap. Barely OK. It is probably a hundred yards to that clock kiosk. And all parties are miniscule in this primitive camera. Upon playback, I realized that the ID photo was not sufficient.

Hey, no big deal. Toulouse-Lautrec needed to move a little closer. I walked down the gracious staircase and gingerly moved toward the schedule kiosk. As I did so, I constantly looked in an opposite direction from the target so as to prevent any clear view. I looked at the train schedule up on the wall to the left. I scanned the throng of rushed commuters and lollygagging tourists. There were two elderly couples pointing to the ceiling and remarking about painted constellations in an indecipherable Eastern European language. There was a procession of parochial grade school kids, ambling hand in hand, evidently on their way toward some school outing. Then I turned my back to the kiosk to seemingly eye three preteen African-American girls walking through the terminal, as if this old man in costume was enticed. This created five more steps toward the target. With my back toward the kiosk, a Midwestern couple asked me to photograph them in Grand Central Station.

"It's a point-and-shoot camera," the man from somewhere like Omaha suggested. "Could you just get a picture of us in the Big Apple?"

I agreed and took a happy snap of the two of them in front of the terminal midpoint with the killer clearly in sight. I then handed back their Canon camera and was struck with an inspiration.

"Would you mind I got a picture of the two of you?"

"Us? Really?" the Midwestern man asked quizzically.

"Yeah, I'm a tourist here myself, and I'm trying to get a flavor of my visit here and a feel for the people in Manhattan."

The woman looked at her husband, shrugged, and said, "I suppose it's OK." She then took his arm and smiled at me.

I reached in my pocket and took out the LG cell phone and pretended to aim it at the couple. I moved it a few inches to the left and saw the man in the peacoat. He seemed to still be scanning the terminal, looking for the person he came to meet.

Click.

As soon as the picture was taken, the man looked directly at me. He cocked his head down a notch and focused on the cell phone. It all registered. He then stared directly at me and held out his hand for the phone.

For a few seconds, we were both locked in a frozen face-off. I assume he wondered what kind of bearded man in black clothing would have his valuable cell phone. I certainly wondered what kind of man in a peacoat would—indeed did—kill a judge so cleanly and dispassionately.

The man across from me then snapped his fingers and held out his hand again for phone. He then took a step toward me.

I whirled away and scurried through the main terminal. I could see my mystery man bump into the Midwestern couple and soon become entangled in the tourist group of grade school students, all of whom were still holding hands and now in a double line Perhaps from countless recesses of Red Rover, Red Rover, they had learned how to grasp each other tightly. However, their grip was no contest for the agitated man in the peacoat. In his rush to follow me, he clumsily broke through the line of darlings and actually knocked down two young girls. The teacher, a burly man in his midforties, screamed at him and physically restrained him.

Given our post 9/11world, there are armed military police everywhere in Grand Central Terminal. Two of them raced up our mystery man, and I could hear one officer admonish the man in the peacoat. "Hey, slow down, pal. You'll catch your train."

"What's the rush? Hold on there, fella," the other officer said to him.

I'm sure the man was facile enough to explain that he was just running late, but by then, I had reached the subway entry.

Thank God, I had a Metro card. I ran down the most unrushed turnstile and took the number 7 express train up to Bloomingdales. Once again, no one seemed to notice my superb camouflage.

In character, I walked to Central Park and, in the cover of autumn trees, reached into my pocket to see the image. Not the best quality in the world, but definitely usable. The man was staring in the general direction of the lens. It was probably one second before he recognized the cell phone. By now, I assumed he was out of Grand Central and into a damn tizzy at someone who looked amazingly like Toulouse-Lautrec.

Chapter Fourteen

In the comfort of my apartment, I took off my costume, gingerly removed the beard, showered, and poured myself vodka on the rocks as I considered my next moves.

Since I had successfully endured one confrontation, I felt emboldened to face another. I had this urge to quiz Melanie. Call it curiosity. Like a fly being attracted to the light that might zap it, I instinctively knew that this might pull me further into a vortex of danger. But given the police suspicions about me, I already felt in some danger. It would help to know Melanie's level of innocence or guilt

By the time, I finished my Smirnoff, I decided to call her and learn the answers to those vexing questions.

"Melanie?" I asked tentatively, when my landline phone rings were answered.

"Jackson Witt! Well, hello, hello. I tried to reach you this afternoon, but you must have been out and about. Your phone wouldn't accept my message. So it must have been telepathy that you called me back."

As I heard her words, I looked back at my answering machine light, which was blinking, indicating Messages Full. True enough. Maybe.

"What did you call about?" I asked innocently enough.

"Advice."

"God, I don't know that I am one to give it these days," I reflexively answered.

"Why do you say that?"

"No reason. Just an expression. Just false humility, I guess." I decided to quickly change the subject. "I wanted to see how you were holding up with all . . . you know, all that's swirling around these days."

There was a pause on the other end.

"It's a mess, Jackson. You have no idea."

"I can only imagine."

"And it's confusing."

"Really?"

"Very."

"I called to see if you wanted to have a lunch."

"I would love that. How about tomorrow?"

*   *   *

Michael's on Fifty-fifth is considered a power breakfast, lunch, and dinner spot.

The ingredient that contributes to this is a clientele that dearly wants privacy in their business conversations. It is a place of hushed whispers and widely spaced tables. Given its locale, the restaurant had fond memories for me. About nine months ago, Melanie and I had a wild romp in condo 23b a few doors to the right. We had also "inaugurated" a two-bedroom co-op across the street and a studio down the block. I wondered if she remembered it as indelibly as I did.

As I waited for her at the bar, the wondering eyes of several business moguls alerted me that Melanie had entered the restaurant. She had that effect on men. Even in these days of crisis, she could be on the cover of *Vogue*—dressed in a slinky navy blue designer dress with a mostly taupe scarf draped on her shoulders.

I arose to great her with a hug and a kiss on the cheek. "You look dazzling, as usual."

"Please, I can barely pull myself together these days," she answered modestly and squeezed my hand like a prom queen. "Jackson, I'm glad we could get together."

It didn't take her long to get into the nitty-gritty in our corner table near the back.

"The police are all over me, Jackson."

"That's to be expected." I shrugged. "A friend of mine told me that the spouse is always an automatic suspect."

"I suspect so," she sighed as she gracefully took the Pinot Grigio to her lips.

"But there is nothing to fear," I added with an even bigger shrug. "Unless, of course, you have something to fear."

She put the wine glass back on the table and looked around the restaurant to make sure she was out of earshot. "Well, that's the thing. It's complicated. And confusing. And I am not completely in the clear."

I was somewhat disarmed by the honesty of this confession. On the one hand, she was admitting some complicity. On the other hand, she was clearly flummoxed by the ultimate result.

"What happened?" I asked in an open-ended fashion. I had learned this technique in communication classes with my friend, Alba Gonzales. As Alba always reminded me, the best investigative question is nonaccusatory. It allows the accused to answer in an unburdened way that may ultimately reveal the truth.

Melanie took another sip of her wine and looked me straight in the eye. "I had no idea that any of the actions I took would result in the Martin's death. But it's not real clean."

I could tell she needed to unload, and I didn't want to impede her flow. "Talk to me," I encouraged her.

"Martin had pictures of us coming out of one condo after another. He even had hidden camera pictures of us in a condo down the street from here. By the way, we looked pretty good together."

Yep, she did remember. Rather than dwell on the juicy flashback, I gestured for her to continue.

"Martin wanted a no-contest, no-settlement divorce. Meaning, no money."

"Melanie, that would not be the end of the world. You're a star in the real estate business. For the past five years, you probably made more money than he did."

"Not really. There is big money in the Zeigler family tree. But there would definitely be no money for me if I would be portrayed as a slut . . . which he promised to do in the tabloids."

"Ugly," I winced. I took another swig of my Pinot and ventured forward. "I hope to God you have those photos under lock and key."

Melanie shook her head and answered matter-of-factly. "I don't know where they are."

I almost choked and did a spit take with my mouthful of wine. Quite frankly, the fact that compromising photos of Melanie and I were floating around somewhere gave me shivers. I could only imagine what kind of reaction Detective Thomas Donovan would have if he ever viewed them. No, let me correct that. I instinctively knew what conclusion the detective would reach. It would cinch the matter of motive. I could feel the noose tightening around my neck.

When I could grab a breath, I responded like a deer caught in the headlights, if not the crosshairs. "Melanie, you've got to find those pictures. Did you check his desk?"

"Nothing."

"A home safe?

"Not there."

"His safety deposit box?"

"Zero."

I leaned back in my chair and let this import of this missing evidence sink in. It truly was a disaster in the making. If the pictures were ever unearthed, the Melanie-Jackson link would be toxic in a no-holds-barred investigation.

"Let's hope they are never found," I uttered, more as a prayer than a statement.

From her nod, I could see she felt the same way. Time for a slightly different but related tack.

"When you talked with the police, did they ask about us?"

"Over and over and over again. I guess the gossip mill at the downtown Stribling office talked."

"And what did you say?"

"I have repeatedly described ours as a friendly but very professional relationship."

"How much emphasis on the professional?"

"Almost 100 percent, but the police seem convinced that we enjoyed each other's company."

I knew this to be true from my own police interrogation. "I have said the same," I assured her. Almost to convince myself, I added, "You know,

Melanie, there is no sin in actually enjoying a 100 percent businesslike, completely professional relationship."

"Right," she answered with that familiar sly smile, as if acknowledging that we both knew better.

The waiter brought our chicken Caesar salads, interrupting the flow. As he sprinkled fresh pepper on our meals, I took another swig of the pinot and let this new data sink in. Wow, it was clear that Melanie was feeling victimized in her marital relationship. Her responses to the police actually protected me. Just as telling, she seemed to be denying any intentional culpability in the death of her husband. At least so far.

When the waiter had moved on to his next station, I attempted to reassure her of this conclusion. "So you needn't worry anymore. All this is private matter. It's not criminal. Fun, amazing, promising . . . but not criminal. So far as I can tell, you did nothing to get in trouble with the police."

The ensuing pause was longer than I wished.

"There's a part B to this story," she whispered as she leaned closer to me. "I told my friend, Robert Lévesque, about all this."

"The real estate developer?"

"Right. He tells me he knows how to get me equal money in a divorce. And more than equal dirt on Martin, the gay caballero."

"How does he know how to do that?"

"A, he's a lawyer. And B, he's a real estate tycoon, meaning he's connected."

"And C, he's more than just a friend," I added. I tried to camouflage my jealous suspicions but instinctively knew it was a bad performance.

Melanie quickly reposted, "That's not the point here, Jackson. Stick with the plot."

"I'm listening."

"We go in this together. Robert hires this guy. His name is Joey Roach. He's supposed to get compromising pictures. I agree to pay. And the next thing I know, Martin is stabbed to death."

I put my fork down after my last bite of romaine lettuce. Almost as an out-of-body experience, I could see myself from afar, exhaling a huge sympathetic sigh.

"Well, I see what you mean, this complicates things for you."

"It gets worse," Melanie continued. "I never intended any of this as a 'hit,'" She whispered to me with air quotes and then prepared me for her knockout punch. "There's a record of my phone calls on a certain cell phone to Joey Roach."

I feigned indifference to this concern. "So what? He would never reveal that. It would implicate him."

"I know. But I can't reach him on his cell phone."

"Maybe he left town," I suggested, trying to bring a happy ending to this part of her story.

"No. He didn't. Someone else has that cell phone."

"Maybe he just misplaced it," I said.

Melanie shook her head, indicating that none of my suggestions were possible. She leaned toward me and announced the real purpose of her lunch with me. "I don't know how and I don't know where, but I know it's you. You've got the damn cell phone."

I tried my best to mask my shock. *How could she know? Had the killer identified me? Did the damn cell phone have GPS?* Fighting my instinct to reveal my jaw-dropping head jolt, I instead laughed out loud and put my hand in my pocket, feeling the cold LG cell phone in my right jacket pocket. I hoped to God I had turned it off. "You've got to be kidding," I said a little too loud for this quiet restaurant.

Melanie was undeterred in her delivery. "Jackson, I need that cell phone.

If you still feel anything for me, you'll hand it over."

"I don't know what you're talking about," I protested.

Melanie was undeterred in her pursuit. She took a breath and made a proposal. "OK, this brings me to the advice I called you about. What will it take to get the phone back?"

I simply looked at Melanie with my best quizzical face. "I'm telling you ... wow ... This is weird," I stumbled through a response as I stalled for a new line. "Why would you think I have this dangerous cell phone?"

Melanie quietly shook her head and looked down at her perfectly manicured vermillion-colored nails. She then regarded me smugly. It was a look I was not accustomed to seeing from her. "Jackson, do you remember last year's Halloween party at Stribling?"

I did. It was the culmination of a memorable bed-hopping, condo-scouting week with Melanie. "I remember it well," I admitted.

"Do you remember wearing that great Toulouse-Lautrec costume to the Halloween party?"

I endured a flood of instant flashbacks. Yes, she was right. "I don't recall that," I answered.

"Jackson, I was overlooking the whole scene yesterday at Grand Central just to make sure he got his damn cell phone back, and I could get on with my life. Joey Roach contacted us and assured us it would be returned at noon. I was up in the restaurant called Meze with clear view of all that happened."

"And what happened?"

"Joey Roach didn't get his phone back."

"No?"

"No, Toulouse-Lautrec ran away with it."

I took my last swig of wine and signaled for the bill. "Melanie, no. Whoever has that cell phone, it isn't me. Maybe it was the real Toulouse-Lautrec, or some Hassidic Jew, I don't know. I wasn't there." As I said these words, I gripped the phone in my right pocket, reminding myself of Alba's advice: do not part with my lifeline.

At this juncture, Melanie's warmth turned to ice. She put her fork down and stared right through me. I have to admit; I had never seen that look in her eyes. It was accusatory.

"Jackson, I know it was you," she repeated.

"You must have mistaken me for someone else," I responded.

For about the next five or six seconds, Melanie and I just looked at each other, waiting for each other's next move. I understood that she desperately wanted that cell phone. If I were she, I would want it too. By the same token, my gut instinct told me that I might need this evidence now more than ever. Neither one of us would budge. It was an uncomfortable confrontation for two people who had been through so much together. Perhaps she felt the same way.

Finally, I saw the upturn of a slight smile on her face. She then turned into the more familiar nice Melanie. "Jackson, maybe you are doing this to protect me. I don't know. But my best protection, my best safety, my best alibi is to have that damn cell phone. I really need it."

I was able to continue the face-off a few more seconds and then added, "Do you ever think of us late at night?"

"Often."

"And what about this other guy, Robert?"
"He's a dear friend."
"And what am I?"
"Jackson, you are a dear, dear friend."
It was a nice try, but I no longer believed it.

Chapter Fifteen

The lunch left me in a tizzy. Despite the fact that Melanie had dubbed me twice as dear as her new friend, Robert Lévesque, I decided to take some self-preservation precautions upon leaving the restaurant. It was now clear to me that the cell phone in my pocket was widely coveted, and the sooner I stashed it in a safe place, the better I would feel.

What was not clear was Melanie Zeigler's actual participation in her husband's demise. I tended to believe her ignorance about the ultimate consequence. And yet, her contacts on Roach's phone were the only identifiable numbers. I considered the role of Lévesque. Obviously, he was her new main squeeze. But was lust enough reason to orchestrate a high-profile murder? Doubtful. Unfortunately, his deleted messages provided no clue.

As I walked down Fifth Avenue, I thought about Officer Washington's invitation to contact the NYPD with any inkling that felt dubious. The whole Melanie-Lévesque-Roach connection definitely fell in that category. Unfortunately, with so many missing blanks, all suspicion would point to the widow. I reminded myself that the NYPD was still fishing and that the cell phone was actually enabling me to discover new information in ways that the police would most likely not be able to uncover. No, it was premature to surrender this tool. But something told me it was dangerous to carry it on my person.

Rather than endure another subway barrage of private conversations, I decided to walk down toward midtown, constantly protecting of the preciousness of Joey Roach's phone. Ultimately, I decided to stow it in a locker at Grand Central. After checking with several MTA officials, I discovered that all such lockers had been removed from the terminal as a safety precaution in the aftermath of 9/11.

I needed another place of safekeeping. There was only one other lockbox that came to mind.

I made a rare visit to the New York Health and Racquet Club near my apartment. I had joined as a New Year's resolution and used the facility a total of maybe ten times in the past year.

Fortunately, I remembered my combination lock and placed the cell phone underneath an extra pair of dirty gym shorts. I made sure the device was turned off, just to preserve the reserve power, and buried it away from any prying eyes. *Ahh, at least it is now safely stored,* I thought.

Exercise is not really my thing, but a huff-and-puff run on the treadmill, a sauna and steam does tend to wipe away the worries of a day. In the terry robe they provide, I nursed myself with orange juice and watched the local news with several other members, none of which knew me or vice versa.

"The curious case of Judge Martin Ziegler's gruesome murder remains a mystery," the chirpy female broadcaster reported. "However, chief of police Bratton, in a press conference today, did express some confidence that certain leads would soon yield positive results."

The chief looked exhausted but attempted to cooperate with a salvo of pressing questions from the press corps. His answers exuded a calm confidence and showed deft experience with dealing with a news-feeding frenzy.

"No, we do not have a suspect at this time, but we are zeroing in on several persons of interest."

"We are not yet convinced that it is sexually related crime of passion."

"No, the wife's alibi appears to be rock solid. Her whereabouts at the time of the judge's death is well documented. And we have no reason to question her involvement."

"I will not comment on the judge's personal life or behavior."

"Yes, it's true that the judge had enemies. Every judge does. That goes with being a public servant. I'm sure I have enemies as well. Perhaps we all do. But there is no reason for it to result in this type of action. And that's why the police are on the case."

"No, we do not believe there is any ongoing threat to the New York public at large. We believe this is an isolated case."

Without announcement, the TV above the juice bar flipped to ESPN. I casually turned around to see that a man in a similar terry robe was holding the remote control.

On the tube, Chris Berman was now opining about the upcoming football games.

The man next to me simply shrugged and seemed to accept the change. "Nonstop sports," he mumbled to me with an eye roll. I faintly smiled back, which only encouraged him.

"I hear that judge was a real prick. You know?"

By now, I knew better than to engage in this line of questioning. "I don't know anything about it. Never watch the news. Other than sports."

"Really?"

"Really," I answered like a dullard and soon headed home.

Chapter Sixteen

I should have suspected something when Javier greeted me at the door and gladly announced that my electrician had finished the job in the afternoon.

"What electrician?" I numbly and dumbly retorted and headed up the elevator, only to discover a completely ransacked apartment. The contents of every kitchen cupboard were emptied. My shoes were strewn across every room and the clothes in my closets dumped on the floor. The stuff in every drawer was piled on my bed.

My first reaction was one of extreme shock and personal violation. Someone had touched all my underwear, rifled through my video collection, and actually separated the dirty clothes in my hamper. Yech!

I immediately called 911 and gave the dispatcher my information. About ninety seconds later, my emotions changed to anger. Someone knew exactly where I lived. Someone knew I had something of value to him or her. And most important, someone didn't give a shit whether or not I was in my apartment at the time and could potentially be collateral damage.

As I waited for the police to appear, I tried to gather my wits. Only two people knew that I had the dangerous cell phone—and Alba certainty had no reason to do anything like this. Just as obviously, it wasn't Melanie herself since she was sitting across from me during our curious lunch. But God only knows whom she told.

The blinking light on my kitchen phone would provide the answer. I hit the Play button and heard a chilling message:

"Hello. Hey, Jackson Witt, you fucking asswipe. This is Joey Roach. I don't know how you got it. But one way or another, I'm going to get . . . that . . . fucking . . . phone. You hear me? You ain't gonna know from where or when, but I'm coming after it. A little birdie let slip who you are. And now I know where you live. If you get in the way, I'm coming after you. So play ball now. Don't be a dumbshit."

Wow. What an impulsive, dangerous guy, I thought. I listened to the message a second time and then a third time. It was damn sloppy of Melanie to guess who I was in front of Roach. I presumed that she had her plan to retrieve the cell at our lunch, but the impatient Roach decided to take matters in his own hands. Damn. He was definitely an uncontrollable, unpredictable guy. At least, I had stowed the damn thing in a safe place, I told myself. Unfortunately, that didn't make me feel any safer.

As I was beginning to feel this fear rise within me, there was a knock on the door. "Police," a voice announced. "You made a 911 call?"

"Yes!" I answered from the kitchen with some relief. I wish I had five more minutes to gather my thoughts. Instead, I called out "Be right with you" toward the direction of the door. In the next fifteen seconds, I unplugged my landline phone. I definitely did not want an interrupting call from my burglar in the midst of my police report.

I opened the door. Before me stood two young NYPD officers who looked as if they been on more than a few similar calls this very week.

They routinely showed their badges, and I invited them in.

"A burglary," the thirtyish male cop offered with a keen sense of the obvious as he tiptoed and zigzagged his way over piles of dirty clothes strewn in the living room.

"What's missing?" the younger female cop asked.

"Nothing that I know of," I answered honestly.

"Nothing?" the male cop asked suspiciously.

"Nothing that I know of. But I haven't checked everything. I think it just happened."

"TV?" the female cop asked.

"Still here."

"Cameras?"

"Still here."

"Stereo?"

"Still here."

"Curious," the male officer interrupted the cadence.

After a few seconds pause, I filled the gap, "Right. And that's why I called you."

"Curious," the young female cop repeated, as if echoing her superior would eventually gain her high marks and a possible promotion.

The more senior cop slightly expanded on this repetitive vocabulary. "It's very unusual, Mr .... Mr .... Mr ...." He looked down at his notes. "Mr. Witt? Yes. It's very unusual when a burglary occurs and nothing is actually taken."

"Very unusual," the female subordinate eagerly agreed.

"Mr. Witt. A very direct question. And we can verify your answer, so please respond truthfully. Do you have any police record of drug incidents?"

I took a deep frustrating breath and buried my head beneath my knees. No wonder the police solved no mysteries. They always resorted to the simple idiotic conclusions. After a dramatic pause, I lifted my head and alternatively looked at both officers as if I had a major confession. "I have absolutely no history of drugs. I have never used drugs. I will never use drugs. Feel free to check my record in this or any other state of the union. Drugs are not implicated in any way in this burglary."

"Well, there is no need to become so defensive," the older cop admonished me.

"Look, I'm just trying to be a good citizen and report this crime," I answered.

"I do not expect suspicion of being somehow guilty for calling 911."

"Hey, hey, hey, hey . . . We're glad you called," the woman tried to calm me.

"Mind if we look around?" the older cop essentially ordered my way.

"Help yourself," I answered. Immediately, the officers ran automatic and pointless dusting exercises for fingerprints despite the fact that this leads to arrests in less than 1 percent of the cases in NYC. However, it looks good.

After an infuriating sixty minutes of dusting, every available glass, shaving bowl, and candleholder, the two police officers approached me in their eager beaver best attitude.

"Mr. Witt, I hate to break this to you, but sometimes burglaries are inside jobs."

I tried to respond to this widely known fact as if it were news.

"Wow. Is that so?"

"How well do you know your doorman, Mr. Javier Colonel?"

"Nine years," I answered. As the last consonant exited my lips, I hit the intercom and asked Javier to join us in my apartment. Upon my request, he immediately agreed.

"We would rather interview him in private." The younger officer smiled.

"I would rather you not," I answered as the doorbell rang. Before any officer could respond, I invited Javier into my apartment, which was his first entry in nine years.

"Oh. Mr. Jackson, I am so, so sad about this incident. I did not know. I did not know."

I looked at the older male cop, who appeared to know the difference between the truth and the cover. Clearly, this nervous Latino was telling the truth.

"Do you have surveillance camera in the lobby?" the officer asked.

"Not now. Next year," Javier answered.

"Well, maybe we should request this crime to be committed next year!" the young female cop shot back, as if this would somehow embarrass Javier. Perhaps it was also intended to impress me, the injured party. However, I interpreted it as a dig. No wonder minorities have a distrust of police authority.

"Short of any reliable photographic surveillance (just to rub it in, Javier), could you describe the man who described himself as Mr. Witt's 'electrician'?"

"He was maybe thirty or forty, average height," Javier answered honestly but nervously. "Maybe Hispanic or part black or maybe Mediterranean. He had a signed voucher for electrical work."

Javier then shuffled through his papers nervously. "Here it is," he gleefully announced. "Mr. Henry Gibson." It was a makeshift voucher available at any Staple's office store. No masthead. Handwritten on the top of the page was the fictitious business called Gibson Electric. No phone number. No address.

"Describe him," the female officer requested.

"He was wearing a stocking cap and a navy-colored peacoat and sunglasses. Green lenses. Maybe brown."

"Long hair? Short hair? Did he have any tattoos or scars?" the female officer asked.

"None that I could see. And he was wearing a stocking cap," Javier explained and then looked at me. "I feel really bad about this, Mr. Witt. I assumed from his paperwork—"

The male officer interrupted him and turned to me, "You know someone who fits that description, Mr. Witt?"

I just shook my head in frustration. "It could be any of a million people in Manhattan."

"*Suficiente,*" the officer responded, knowing this would lead to nowhere.

"I am so, so sorry, Mr. Jackson." Javier bowed as he walked out the door.

The two cops somehow knew the power of the dramatic pause. After Javier left the room, the older cop actually took five paces across my living room floor before delivering his closing argument. "Mr. Witt," he intoned. "There is very little probability we will solve this, given the sketchy leads. But we will keep this case open for the next six months. Sometimes, events unfold. Sometimes, the truth is told. Sometimes, even when the case is cold, we find the culprit."

From a poetic standpoint, I was disappointed in the interruption of a triad rhyme but recognized the futility of this search and thanked the officers for their routine investigation. I invited them to keep me informed of any new developments, fully aware that none would come.

After a few seconds, I called Leandor and asked for an evening to reassess my new, even uglier, situation. And a safe haven from the gathering storm.

Chapter Seventeen

Leandor had said an early adios to his afternoon paramour, an Asian flight attendant named Ash, in order to hear me out. I needed to unload my ongoing accelerating agita.

"My life is totally berserk," I admitted. "And unless I can redirect events toward the truth, I will end up getting butt-fucked in the federal pen for thirty years."

Leandor leaned back in his favorite possession, a genuine Eames chair, and smiled. "Really! And what would it take to earn this pleasure?"

"Continued police incompetence. They seem clueless in their search for a perpetrator, other than me."

I then explained everything to Leandor—from my overheard conversation on the train to the break-in in my apartment. Throughout this account, I could see Leandor biting his tongue and resisting the urge to stop me at least a half dozen times. When I finished my saga, I heaved a huge sigh and then looked at my friend for a reaction.

"Well, what a fine mess you've gotten into, Ollie," Leandor summed up my situation with a comic-relief reference to Laurel and Hardy. *What a good friend,* I thought. Perhaps as a result of a life overcoming certain prejudices, he always tended to be a glass-half-full sort of guy. Just the tonic I needed in the midst of storm clouds.

"Look at this way, my dear super sleuth," Leandor said cheerfully. "At least you've got a picture of the real culprit, just in case."

"At least that."

"You know, your friend Alba is right about the phone. At this point, you should turn it into the cops and throw your double-crossing former friend Melanie under the bus."

"I probably should," I admitted for the first time.

"But you probably won't because you don't really think she masterminded the whole thing," Leandor answered. He did know me. I had to smile.

"I've got the phone safely stowed away," I finally responded. "And you should know where it is."

"I'm not sure I want to know."

Ignoring his counsel, I proceeded, "It's in my locker at my New York Health and Racquet Club. Just in case."

"Just in case what, darling?"

"Just in case I can't easily get to it. Just in case . . ." I didn't need to complete the sentence. With an angry, desperate, ransacking murderer who now knew my identity and home address, we both understood the inherent danger.

Leandor had ordered Chinese delivery. For the next hour, we shared pot stickers, tangerine beef, pork-fried rice, and contraseasonal Rose wine. In this oasis of Asian smells and spices, we reminisced about easier days—when our most pressing problems were college workloads and underrehearsed university productions. Leandor always reminded me that I had a gift for stage presence, which I doubted given my current real-life performances. At the time, he had argued quite persuasively against splitting my attention with real estate. He initially interpreted it as a rejection of artistic idealism. In the ensuing months, when the career turn actualized, he eased up. "Are you happy with your choices?" he would ask as if he were a Temple drama teacher, questioning an actor's interpretation.

"Very," was my repeated answer, and in time, he would raise both arms in the air and encourage me to "go with it."

He was one who had lived through my Alba Gonzales liaison, which vicariously thrilled him. "Not my persuasion, mind you," I recall him telling me. "But she is one hot tamale, and nobody's fool. And Jackson, here's my favorite things about her: she doesn't fall for your usual bullshit."

He had never met Melanie. Had no desire to do so. Part of this was bundled up in my eventual exit from the theater world, which he finally forgave. A bigger part of it, of course, was the surreptitious nature of our relationship, which invited no spectators, other than those nasty missing Martin Zeigler photographs.

"I never completely trusted Melanie," Leandor admitted as we reached for our meal-ending fortune cookies.

"Yeah, well, she's got a complicated life," I countered.

"Bullshit. We all do. All I know is it's really complicating your life, and that's not fair. No matter how you slice and dice it, she blabbed to someone and put your life in danger. There's no other explanation. Think about that, my friend."

I silently nodded.

Evidently satisfied that he had made his point, Leandor lightened the moment.

"What's your fortune cookie say? If you're destined to meet a tall dark stranger, then you must have gotten my cookie by mistake."

I looked at my fortune and frowned. "The fall will be your spring," I reported. "What the fuck does that mean?"

Leandor just laughed. "It means the fortune writer ran out of understandable things to say. I don't know."

"And yours?"

Leandor read his, "There are two sides to every story."

"See! We just need to find that other side."

Leandor smiled and continued to look at his small slip of paper. "I say you follow this fortune."

"Right, whatever that means."

"Listen to me: There's is a good idea in this, Jackson. You feed to the police the other side to the story. You got a decent picture of the killer?"

"It's fairly clear."

"This is good. I say you send it anonymously to the cops. Get them focused on this lead. If nothing else, it will compel them to chase another suspect, other than Jackson Witt."

I silently let this new piece of advice sink in.

"What's the risk?" Leandor pressed.

I held up my hand. For a minute, I considered any negative ramifications.

"They may not choose to chase the lead," I admitted. It was the only downhill consequence I could imagine, especially given the NYPD workload and the rush to find a suspect.

While pulling out his the mattress of his sleeper sofa, Leandor offered the perfect rebuttal, "Then send it to the press as well. Create pressure from the media." He went to his closet and threw two poofy pillows on the bed.

"It can't hurt," my big gay friend encouraged.

He was right. I couldn't hurt. And I knew just the perfect press amiga to send it to. "You're a good friend, Leandor."

"I just hate to see wrong judgments made about good people, especially those who don't know any better than to try to be their own detective."

"Maybe so," I admitted.

"Send the pictures. Do it first thing in the morning."

"I will."

"And sleep tight. If you get lonely, I'll be in the other room, in a big comfy real bed . . . waiting."

It was the standard, customary faux tease that marked Leandor's banter with me. We both knew it meant nothing, but it never deterred him from fishing a new line.

"And if you get cold in there . . ."

"Good night, Leandor."

"Good night," he said and turned off the light.

"And thanks," I added in the darkness.

*   *   *

It was not a particularly good night for me.

I woke up about 6:00 a.m. after a toss-and-turn battle and finally decided it was futile to just lie in bed. There isn't much in TV that is worth watching at that time on a Sunday morning—just a few early evangelists, the shopping network, and paid programming for the Sham Wow, Ginsu knives, and the Clapper. After a few minutes of channel surfing, I finally gave up and flipped off the TV.

Fortunately, my host's Braun coffeemaker was prefilled, so I turned on the machine and looked forward to the ritual of java and the *Sunday*

Times. To my dismay, there was no big fat newspaper outside Leandor's apartment door. I went to his magazine bin and discovered my only reading matter would be a stash of gay *Advocate* newspapers, both current and several back issues. Oh well. Better than staring into space.

The headline on the current edition did catch my eye: Murder of Double-Timing Judge Exposes Dangers of the Closet. The article was more direct about Martin Zeigler's secret life than had been reported in any mainstream publication. Evidently, the judge had a rather well-documented history of secret liaisons and gay one-night stands. Dozens of his affairs were disclosed, albeit anonymously. According to one unnamed source, "the judge would hang out in gay bars wearing his sunglasses at midnight, as if it would somehow give him cover. He would gay-bash during his day on the bench and prowl the streets at night, looking for young men who would gladly accept his $300 cash gifts."

The article went on to delineate his scorching decrees against gays. *Wow, this guy was beyond right wing,* I began thinking. He had ruled against gay pornography distributors, gay prostitution rings, and gay advertisements in any newspaper. In one landmark case, he had decreed that a Craig's List gay personals ad, which promised evenings of joy was "a bridge too far."

"What this dramatizes," the news story concluded, "is the quasi-gay, antigay attitude of those who continue to live in the closet and refuse to confirm their own innate sexual orientation." Unaccustomed to such direct opinion, I looked at the top of the page just to see if this was listed as an editorial. Nope. Upon further reflection, a publication called *Advocate* would undoubtedly have a point of view in every article, especially given its audience.

I closed the paper, enjoyed a sip of my slowly cooling Columbian blend, and reflected on the difficulties and challenges of being a closet gay. It couldn't be easy for a right-winger like Martin V. Ziegler. As a Connecticut-born, Upper East Side-raised pillar of the community, he had obviously concealed his true inclinations all his adult life until those natural impulses finally contributed to his undoing.

I grabbed my cup of coffee and went toward Leandor's bedroom to see if he was stirring. The bear was still snoring and soundly asleep. From the doorway, I looked upon him and admired his courage. At the same time, I despised Ziegler's duplicity. The article was right. The closet is an awful place to live.

I refilled my mug with caffeine, cut it with half and half, and looked at my watch. Only 7:30. There would still be nothing of merit on TV. Only more articles of the *Advocate* to pass the time. Unfortunately, there was little else in the back issues that were germane to my situation.

After paging through several back issues, I was attracted to one article from a purely prurient and semiprofessional standpoint. The headline simple announced, Gay-Dedicated Co-ops Gain Steam. *What the hell is a gay-dedicated co-op?* I wondered.

There were ten listed in Manhattan. Four were in the West Village, four in Chelsea, one on the Upper West Side. Surprisingly, one was in Hell's Kitchen ("Purely a function of its unidimensional clientele," the article admitted).

As a real estate professional, I was somewhat aware of the phenomenon of gay-friendly co-ops, but a gay-dedicated co-op? Please explain.

The article did. These were co-ops that had amenities specifically geared to gays and lesbians.

The Number 1 top prize went to a sparkling new co-op at 355 W. 18th called the Orion House. In addition to oversized bedrooms (in comparison to the living room), it had some rather unusual amenities:

- A decorating bonus at closing. The new owners would receive a $15,000 credit toward interior decoration, courtesy of Lance Bainbridge, a well-known gay Manhattan decorator.
- Customized "his and his/her and her" bathroom suites. In contrast to the usual "his and hers" bathroom arrangement, this feature offered dual bidets or dual urinals. A rather ingenious amenity, I had to admit.
- Monthly mixers for all co-op owners with the freedom to invite two guests per month.
- A concierge service that would provide twenty-four-hour gourmet food service, including caviar, artichoke heart salad, Brie en Croute, and fig spread with whole wheat crackers, and a selection of Rose wines.
- A free lending library of LGBT videos (updated monthly). Free of charge.

As explained, the Orion House did not specify to prohibit heterosexual couples, but given the tailored amenities, none had applied. To date, it had a 100 percent declared gay and lesbian population.

According to the article, "The developer, Robert Lévesque, while not a declared gay, has a long history of antidiscrimination and business connections in the gay community. A notoriously private real estate developer, he declined comment on these rankings, instead stating through a press release, that 'all people deserve to follow their dreams in New York.'"

I reread the passage, just to make sure I was making the right connections. Robert Lévesque. Developer. Gay sympathetic. Usurper. Opportunist. Liberal groundbreaker. Machiavelli. Injured party. Bleeding heart. Poseur. Conspirator. Hitman enabler. OK, at least a few of those could not be true. But which few?

*   *   *

"I can't believe you don't get the *New York Times* on Sunday morning," I complained to Leandor when he stumbled out of bed at 8:30 wearing a way-too-furry bathrobe.

As he reached for bagels on the counter and a bread knife from the drawer, he stopped his breakfast prep to explain, "Unless I have dear guests, such as you, I like to meander about the neighborhood, find a paper, and open myself to new friends."

"I just made a new pot of coffee," I announced, having exhausted the 6:00 a.m. potion. As I poured his cup, I quizzed, "I get the sense from your newspapers that Judge Zeigler should have died."

Leandor accepted the cup of java and looked at his watch. "What is it, 8:35? It's a little early to get into a philosophical brouhaha. But I suppose you've been up for a while, and it's noon your time."

"Sort of," I ruefully replied.

Leandor took a sip and leveled with me. "None of my friends think this prick should have lived." He took the mug to his lips again. "Let me get another sip before you hit me with a harder question."

"Ever heard of Robert Lévesque?"

There was a legit pause and then a mental search. "Nope," he answered.

"Ever heard of the Orion House?"

"Never been there. But I hear it's grand. People rave. Wanna move in together?"

I simple chuckled and smiled at his resilient behavior. "You've seen the brochures," I asked. "But never heard of Robert Lévesque, who evidently developed it?"

Leandor raised his hands like Reb Tevye in *Fiddler on the Roof.* "Maybe he's the opposite of Donald Trump. Maybe he doesn't want his name on the front of every building." He then took a deep sip of his coffee. "Especially a homosexual building."

Just for added effect, he accentuated the word *homosexual* as if he were a foreigner pronouncing the words *shit, merde,* or *ca-ca.*

We finished our coffees with pleasantries. I promised to send the cell phone photos. We gave each other a big bear hug. Given the danger of returning to my apartment, he offered his apartment again for the night. There were other plans I was hatching, so I declined.

What a friend, I told myself as I walked toward my locker at the New York Health and Racquet Club.

Chapter Eighteen

Leandor's apartment was just two blocks from the scene of Martin V. Zeigler's murder. I had avoided the site since the night I witnessed the slaying. Too many shocking, painful memories. Too many police interviews after the fact. But for some reason, I felt compelled to revisit the scene of the crime today. Maybe the continuing specter of Joey Roach in my daily life induced me.

I walked the extra uptown block and approached the site from Barrows Street.

I passed the deli where I got coffee that night and walked on the same side of the street where I hid behind the van.

It was only six days since the event, but already street life seemed completely back to normal in this West Village neighborhood. There were no police barricades or taped crime scene cordons. Couples were walking their groomed fox terriers. Occasional joggers were returning from the morning exercise. No passersby were pointing to the stoop or even apparently aware that a brutal knifing had transpired on the steps of that brownstone.

I stood there again and squinted, trying to revisualize the horrific moment. It took no imagination. There was the man in the peacoat smoking a cigarette. There was Martin Zeigler coming out of the apartment. And there was Joey Roach approaching the judge. *Think*. Was there anyone else on that street at the time? Was there a suspicious car with its parking lights on? Was there any accomplice in one of the windows who was signaling that the mark was indeed on the street? Despite my attempts at subconscious memory triggers, absolutely nothing came to mind. I guess I was too preoccupied with the drama that was center stage.

I looked back at the precise scene of the murder; it had all happened so fast. There was a quick confrontation, as if asking for a match. And then stab, stab, stab, stab, stab, stab. Almost instinctively, I again turned my head from the imaginary reenactment.

It only served to reconvince me that this was no accident or photo stalk that somehow went haywire. No, this was a premeditated cold-blooded murder. There was a time and a target, and there was no ambiguity about Joey Roach's intentions.

Ironically, this made me more determined than ever to point the police toward this animal. No matter what Melanie or even Lévesque had thought might occur, Joey Roach took matters in his own hands and offed a human being. The killer deserved to be apprehended and ultimately confined behind bars. Of course, in the process of providing this lead to the NYPD, I would be removed from the suspicious list.

I immediately walked toward the New York Health and Racquet Club to retrieve the photo of Joey Roach and send this valuable tip to the police.

The cell phone was resting in the back of my locker. Before viewing the photo, I checked to see any new messages. There was only one new text from the Joey Roach number: "Return my damn cell phone. You are playing a dangerous game. Lucky I didn't catch you in GC. But I will."

Lucky I have it the damn phone in a safe place, I told myself.

I looked around the early-Sunday locker room. There were only a few guys putting on their running shoes, and one was busy talking on his phone. There would be little suspicion here of any member checking his phone messages or sending one.

I scrolled to the My Photos icon and took another look at Joey Roach. Not awful quality. Clear enough. I found the Forward button and reached in my wallet for Officer Donovan's number and typed it in with the following message: "This man killed Martin Zeigler. I saw him do it." I thought about signing it anonymous but thought that were too fancy. Better to just send it through, which I promptly did.

I immediately felt relieved. If the police were efficient enough to check the source of the phone, they would learn the identity of the killer. I assumed they had tons of whirring computers that could immediately spit out his name, address, IRS history, any police record, buying habits, and perhaps a GPS locator of the killer's every move.

At least, that's the way it's done in the movies. It would all come to fruition soon enough.

I knew Alba Gonzales's number and forwarded the same picture to her. The first two sentences of my message were identical to the one I sent to the police, with the following addendum: "I would like to speak to you about all this tonight. In fact, can I cadge a night in your apartment? No strings. But I have major complications in my apt. Call me back on my own cell.—Jackson Witt."

When finished, I turned off the cell phone and put it back inside my gym locker. After double-checking that my combination lock worked, I headed off to my Stribling office with a little bounce in my step.

Chapter Nineteen

For a real estate agent, open houses are a necessary evil.

On the one hand, it is a service one must offer as a listing agent. It convinces a client that you are working diligently on their behalf and are worth the commission. It also encourages the seller to get their condo in tip-top shape, dump the clutter, and make it presentably salable (very occasionally, when a client cleans up their apartment for a pristine showing, they fall in love again with the place).

On the other hand, the actual event is a pain in the ass. It takes the agent some research to prepare for the event—the nearby schools, subways, any financial complications with the condo, laundry facilities, bike rooms, etc., etc., etc. It usually means preparing some sort of glossy handout sheet of flowery sales points and floor plans, which had always been my happy scouting assignment with Melanie. It also entails getting sign-in sheets, clearances with the doormen, and occasional payola to the supers to make sure the lobby and hallways are impeccable.

However, the worst part is the stream of unqualified prospects that frequent these events. The vast majority is just window-shopping. At least 25 percent are habitual "free date" voyeurs who simple want to see how other people live. Occasionally, you will actually find "live" lookers, and even more occasionally, you will actually meet someone who is actively in the market to buy. Rarely does the open house result in a direct sale. That requires more repeated one-on-one private showings. Once in a blue moon, you will actually unite a seller and buyer, enjoying double commissions. In my case, this only happens a few times a year. However, given the million-dollar economics of Manhattan real estate, it only takes a few times a year to support you handsomely. Consequently, despite the downsides, it's worth it.

I had stopped at my local Stribling office and prepared for my 1:00-3:00 p.m. open house at 325 W. 18th. I did a quick review of client's notes on the property, grabbed my sales propaganda, sign-in booklet, keys, and headed for the condo.

I like to arrive about forty-five minutes before showtime. It gives me the opportunity to refresh my memory on the property's amenities and reconnoiter the neighborhood. I this case, I was particularly glad I had done so. The neighboring condo had made significant construction progress over the past few weeks. When I had last seen my listed property, this next-door development was only half-built. Today, the final eight floors now exhibited a skeleton of its structure, bringing the total height to seventeen floors. This would mean an obstructed view from the apartment. I looked back on the sales sheet to see how it was described. Partial view of the river. Well, at least it was factual.

Worse yet, the new building was only about twelve feet from my open house condo. It would have an outdoor elevator, now only half-built, that would eventually illuminate itself from the outdoor balcony of my highly prized property. Yikes!

I only hoped that my open house prospects would approach the open house from the east side so they wouldn't have to envision this atrocious neighboring structure.

I entered my open house property and gave the doorman my card and a forty-dollar gratuity "for his trouble today." I hoped it would also mean a welcoming smile to prospects. I headed for the elevator and prepared for the show.

*　*　*

The current owners had prepared the place to its best advantage. All the clutter had vanished, including some of the unnecessary furniture. The closets contained scant clothes, making them look generous in size. The refrigerator was cleaned, except for a few fresh red peppers, a few wedges of fresh cheese, and several bottles of white wine. There were fresh flowers in every room. As they had promised, there was coffee in the maker. I turned it on and placed my sign-in book on the kitchen island.

Perhaps the place could fetch 1.4 million, after all. With its L-shaped living/dining area, with its outdoor balcony ("ideal for late-night stargazing," according to my sales sheet), and with its two separated bedrooms, it might strike the right chord with the right prospect.

As I did one last run-through of the apartment, I couldn't help but pause in the master bedroom. It was irresistible to instantly fantasize. Only a few months earlier, on a reconnaissance mission of this property, Melanie and I would have "inaugurated" the king-size bed, posed naked in front of the full-sized strategically placed wall mirror, and commented that "we sure look damn good together." Given the events of this horrendous week, it seemed like years ago. With the encroaching police dragnet, I honestly wondered if it would ever happen again for me with anyone.

Just then, the doorman buzzed, announcing that my first viewers were on their way up.

Chapter Twenty

In the first hour, eight prospects visited the apartment. Most were couples.

As predicted, about four of them were completely noncommittal Sunday voyeurs. They had no questions and no issues with the neighboring condo, which crowded the otherwise open feel of the 1,150 square foot apartment. After cheerfully passing out my card to all and promising to answer any subsequent question they may have, I waited for hotter, more interested prospects.

There was a respite of about five minutes, which was fortunate timing for my cell phone to ring.

"Alba!" I answered, instantly identifying her number.

"Jackson Witt! Interesting goddamned message." She was never one to waste time with such pleasantries as "How you doing?" "Good to hear from you," or "What's up?"

"Yeah, I had a hunch you'd be intrigued by it," I answered.

"We need to talk," she said.

"That's why I sent you the message."

"And yes. Of course, you can stay here," she fast-forwarded to my next question.

"I appreciate that."

"Thought you might."

"But I'm hosting an open house for an apartment today. So I'll be awhile."

Just then, the doorman buzzed me and announced my next visitor.

"Call me when," Alba said.

"Yes. Thanks." I clicked off and prepared for the final hour of open house. It would be more promising than the one that preceded it. Yeah, there were a few maddening window-shoppers. But at least three or four prospects actually looked in the closets and tried to visualize their own furniture in the place. Encouraging.

But none were as promising as Mr. and Mrs. Robert Dolan and their young daughter, who showed up at 2:40.

"This looks nice," the attractive Mrs. Dolan immediately remarked as her husband signed the register. She was in her late twenties and looked a little like Rachel McAdams. She was about as bubbly too—full of wonder and optimistic imagination as she viewed the place.

Her husband, who, I would soon discover, was an advertising executive at McCann-Erickson, looked up from his autograph. With a Christian Slater aura, he viewed the space and raised an approving eyebrow. "Let's take a look," he agreed, and I showed them around.

"Nice," Mrs. Dolan said, seeing the kitchen cupboards.

"Nicer," she said upon seeing the bedroom.

"Hannah, can you see yourself here?" Ms. Dolan asked her one-year-old daughter, upon entering the second bedroom. Almost on cue, the nonspeaking infant giggled.

And then the buzzer rang. "Coming up," the doorman warned.

I showed Mr. and Mrs. Dolan and young Hannah the balcony, which I promised would always have an excellent partial view of the Hudson.

"I really like it," Mrs. Dolan gushed as she looked up to her taller spouse.

"Is the price flexible?" the ad-negotiating husband couldn't resist.

"Not a lot," I answered, sensing I wouldn't need to lowball this place to keep their enthusiastic fire alive.

Across the living room, the door slowly opened and an unfortunate interruption entered the room. At first I didn't recognize the new guest, given my preoccupation with the eager Dolan family. But with a double take, I definitely knew that navy peacoat.

It was the man I had come to know as Joey Roach.

Almost out of nervous habit, I asked him to sign the register. "I'll be with you in a minute," I acknowledged him.

Joey simply turned the kitchen chair around, straddled it, and lit a cigarette.

"Don't let me interrupt you," he announced with an evil smile.

*   *   *

I was determined to keep the enthusiasm and potential sale alive with the Dolans as long as I possibly could. But after about twenty minutes (and two more cigarettes from Joey Roach), the secondhand smoke had begun to invade every room and the luster of this apartment began to wane.

"I'm allergic," Mrs. Dolan told me when we revisited the master bedroom closet space and waved her hand toward the living room. Clearly, she wanted me to take up the issue with the intruder. From a purist standpoint, I totally agreed with her objections. But I shrugged. The quickly diminishing prospect of a sale was not worth a dangerous confrontation in my book.

"It's a free country," I said lamely and quickly tried to change the subject. "Isn't it a wonderful apartment? A beautiful space. Plenty of room for little Hannah. A gourmet kitchen. And a great balcony for nightcaps. This place just seems to be made for you."

I rarely sell this hard, but I wanted to entice the Dolans to spend more time in the place and revisit every room again.

When we walked back into the smoke-filled living room, Mrs. Dolan announced, "We should go. I know your open house is supposed to end at three, and we're supposed to see a few more places."

"Do you have a card?" Mr. Dolan asked.

I reached into my jacket pocket and handed him one.

"I'll have one of those cards too," said the murderer.

"Last one," I apologized to the intruder.

As the young family approached the front door, I tried one more ploy, "Let me escort you down to the lobby."

Joey Roach instantly reacted, "They're grown-up people. They can operate a damn elevator all by themselves. Can't you, folks?"

"Of course," Mr. Dolan answered and then shook my hand. "We'll be in touch."

I watched them silently walk to the elevator bay and eventually exit. Like a little kid in the driveway when Dad goes off to work, I waved at them and feebly said, "Bye."

I closed the front door and turned around to Joey Roach.

"May I help you?" I tentatively asked, playacting this encounter as if it were a legit real estate visit. Instinctively, I knew it wasn't.

"Where's your Halloween costume?" Joey Roach taunted sarcastically without moving from his chair.

Best to make this a case of mistaken identity, I figured. Of course, I knew it probably wouldn't work. After all, the man knew my name, my address, and my place of business. But there was no percentage in admitting my connection, especially in view of the fact that I didn't have his damn phone with me.

"I don't know what you're talking about," I answered.

"Yeah, you do," he smiled like a Cheshire cat and walked over to the front door. Maybe this is just a threatening taunt, I tried to convince myself. Maybe he'll just follow me as a constant reminder, and make my life miserable day after day. Probably not, I had to admit to myself, as Joey Roach carefully double-bolted the front door and turned back to me.

"I want my damn phone back," he said.

"I think you have the wrong person."

"No chance," he answered with an evil chuckle. "Your former girlfriend was there to make sure everything was returned to the proper owner. But instead, you try to get too clever. You dress up like a clown and try to get my picture."

I just shook my head like a simpleton. Like the lame denial in the Shaggy hit song, I said, "It wasn't me." I went over to the kitchen island and tried to gather my real estate belongings. "Now I really do have to go. I have another appointment."

"You're not going anywhere," Joey Roach corrected me and slammed his hand on the sign-in binder. "I don't know where you found my fuckin' phone. Maybe on a subway car. Maybe in the lost and found. I don't know. And I don't give a shit. I just want it back."

Time for a new tack. The mistaken-identity ruse didn't appear to be working.

"What's on this phone that supposedly I have?" I invited him to sit at the dining room table and discuss this like two adults.

"Nothing in the past twenty hours," the murderer smugly said. "After our little confrontation at Grand Central, I called Verizon to put a hold on all incoming and outgoing calls. He then reached in his pocket and plunked a brand new LG phone on the dining room table. It was still in its wrapper, apparently uncharged. "See, Mr. Smartass, I went and got myself a new fuckin' phone this morning. Want this one too?"

"No," I quietly answered.

"So my old phone that you have in your pocket will be obsolete and useless to you."

I hated this new information. My damn lifeline, as Leandor liked to call it, would soon be a nonfactor. Damn, it was the only leverage I had. But it raised a curiosity on my part. Why then would he give a shit about the old phone? If he could delete messages, why threaten me?

"So you got a new phone. I'm happy for you. Now can I leave?" I rose to walk to the front door.

"Not so fast, asshole." He beat me to the door and stood between my exit and me. "It's not so easy to erase the text messages . . . and other stuff." Meaning, a possible photo, I assumed. "I need that damn memory chip to delete everything, and I think we both know it's not in your apartment."

Ahh yes, at least part of the lifeline might actually survive, if only I could. I definitely had a sixth sense that this tête-à-tête could not endure much longer before Joey Roach would again erupt and demand his missing merchandise.

As long as we were on the subject of Melanie, I figured it was as good a time as any to clear up some missing blanks. "So this mysterious missing cell phone, which you think I have, might have text messages between you and Melanie . . . and she is the one who hired you to slash her husband?"

There. I took it to the bridge I wished not to cross. But I had been tortured with this thought. Was Melanie telling me the truth about her limited involvement in her husband's death? It would be nice to find the answer from the one guy in New York who knew the truth.

"I will only tell you this. She didn't hire me. The other guy did. And he's too smart to leave his any messages. He always demanded that I erase his calls, which I think I did. But the lady wasn't smart enough to think of that."

I was happy to hear this. It proved that my hunches weren't all wrong.

Roach was beginning to lose patience with this discussion. "So the damn cell phone is mostly dangerous for your friend, Melanie," he said. "It's also damn dangerous for me." At this point, Joey Roach stood up from across the table and looked me straight in the eye. "And, Mr. Jackson

Witt, I'm here to tell you that keeping the cell phone is very dangerous for you."

The logic of our sit-down reasonable conversation was over. As he stood, I stood.

In a gesture similar to the one he used at Grand Central Station, he extended his palm and flicked his finger. "Give me the fucking cell phone."

"I don't have it," I answered honestly.

"Give me the fucking cell phone!"

"I don't . . ."

"Quit lying to me!" he snarled and slowly walked toward me. As he circled to the left of the round dining room table, I rotated to the left. At a perfect diameter from this angry man, I knew that this impasse would not last forever.

Joey Roach grabbed the sides of the table and effortlessly tossed it in my direction. As he did so, the vase of flowers crashed toward me, shattering glass and broken flowers. "I don't think you understand who you are dealing with, dumbshit," he barked. "Give me the fuckin' phone. If you don't take it out of your pocket, I'll cut the damn thing out of your dead pocket." As he delivered this threat, he reached in his peacoat and pulled out a switchblade.

He flipped the button without looking and opened the weapon, as if it were a familiar action. I immediately recognized the blade from the Zeigler slaying. Up close, the knife looked much larger than from across the street at Barrow and Hudson.

I was a scared rabbit about to be skinned. And there was no place to hide.

I scurried behind the couch, but the killer, knife in hand, kept moving toward me. "Give me the fucking phone," he repeated.

I moved behind the large leather armchair, but Roach began lunging forward with his switchblade. "Give me the fucking phone" became his mantra.

There was no place to go but the balcony. I ran to it and looked to see if there was a landing I can leap to. Impossible. Only the nearby construction of the half-built neighboring condo.

When I turned my head back toward the living room, I caught the figure of Joey Roach racing toward me, with his knife in a right underhand motion, similar to that he used to eviscerate Martin Ziegler.

As a result of way too many stage-fighting class exercises, I reacted instinctively. I crouched, crunched into a ball, and felt his body crash into me, far too high for his intended target. Instantly, I charged my body to explode and unleash itself. I sprang open and forward like a frenetic, frightened cheerleader.

Suddenly, I felt the release of human weight. I turned around to see the floating body of Joey Roach flying over the balcony. It was like a slow-motion sequence from a Sam Peckinpah movie. Unlike the first death I had witnessed—the detached rat-a-tat demise of Martin Ziegler—this more personal journey over the four-foot railing was long and lingering.

I remember reaching over the balcony to try to grab the falling victim, but it was futile. He silently wafted down, down, down until he became smaller and smaller.

The momentum of my unbundled crouch had propelled Joey Roach a good several yards from the side of the building. In fact, his skydiving body was headed toward the unfinished construction of the nearby neighboring condo.

And then it disappeared into the half-finished open-to-the-sky elevator shaft.

I thought I heard a swish thump, but it may have been my imagination. In a state of shock, I closed my eyes to try to recollect any sound. I heard nothing.

From the vantage point of the balcony, I looked on the ground of the construction site to see any human debris. After all, perhaps I only imagined Joey Roach flying into an empty elevator shaft. Was there a broken body lying on the base concrete? Any sight of blood? Maybe the knife was released and lay there on a scaffold. Nothing.

I leaned over the balcony to try to see the disaster inside the elevator shaft.

From this angle, I could see nothing.

It did occur to me that someone from another balcony might have seen a peacoated man flying through the air holding a knife. Or worse yet, the real estate agent on that balcony who had accomplished the jujitsu moves to catapult the victim. There were about five other balconies on this side of the building. All were vacant, and most were shuttered for the upcoming winter. Thank God. No apparent witnesses.

Maybe there were people on the roof. I recollected that the apartment had a small rooftop terrace for tenants. Before cleaning up the apartment, I thought it might be a good idea me to see if there were any eyeballs who may have seen this tragedy from on high.

I took the elevator to the penthouse, roof level. When the elevator door opened, a young couple, each with wine glasses in hand, was waiting for the down elevator.

"Anything going on up here? A party?" I innocently asked.

"Nah, just the two of us, and we're leaving so you get the whole roof terrace to yourself," answered the chirpy girlfriend.

"How's the view today?"

"Same as always," said the boyfriend, who toasted me with his glass in a neighborly way. "Cheers," he added and the two of them got in the down elevator.

The roof garden was a pretty makeshift for an apartment building of this size. It had weathered redwood decking, a few patio chairs, and a picnic table. The entire area was about 20 × 25 and was surrounded by scraggly potted juniper bushes. For safety code purposes, there was a redwood guardrail around the perimeter. I walked the entire edge and looked in every direction to see what one could witness. To my relief, the deck was situated on the east side of the building, making it impossible to see any man from below falling through space.

No one saw anything, I reminded myself.

And what was there to see anyway from any vantage point? I climbed over the safety roof garden rail and snaked my way across the tarmac around the building mechanicals and extruding air vents toward the west side of the building, toward the unfinished half-constructed condo on the west side.

From a relatively safe ten feet from the edge of my building, I could see the open elevator shaft, but still no body. I took a few steps forward and was now about three feet from the unprotected edge of the building. Bravely, I peered downward. What I saw instantly sickened me.

The lifeless body of Joey Roach, impaled on two iron support rods, seemed to be staring me in the face. I instantly ducked down and almost fainted. I could feel my breath shorten, and my stomach begin to knot. I really did feel dizzy, which was not a good sensation just a matter of inches from the edge of the building.

After a few moments of confusing horror, I decided to take another look. Unlike my first glimpse, which was only a second or so, this time I decided to try my best to truly observe the mess. The first impaling rod had passed through his sternum. The other rod passed between his legs. From my distance, I couldn't quite tell if it had castrated him. It didn't matter. He wouldn't be using it anymore.

There was quite a bit of blood, certainly around Joey Roach's chest. There was also a rather sizeable pool of red around his head. His eyes were open and staring skyward. At first blush, it felt that they were aimed in my direction. Upon closer examination, probably not. It was just the way he fell and the angle of his head.

It looked as if death was instant, something that gave me some small consolation.

When all this data had registered, I still stared at the scene for another three or four seconds. Just letting it sink in, just feeling my own role in this event sinks me even further.

Eventually, I walked back to the deserted roof garden and sat in one of the patio chairs. Dazed and depressed, a flood of thoughts ricocheted in my head.

> *It was self-defense.*
> *No one saw it.*
> *I killed him.*
> *He wanted to kill me.*
> *What's still on the phone?*
> *Melanie didn't hire him.*
> *Thank God I got a picture.*
> *The police think it's me.*
> *Thank God I sent the pictures.*
> *Now the killer is dead.*
> *Tomorrow he will be buried in concrete.*
> *He can never confess.*
> *I'm fucked.*
> *I don't know whom I can trust.*
> *I killed a man.*
> *It was self-defense.*
> *No one saw it.*

After a half hour of such thoughts racing around in my brain and repeating themselves, I closed my eyes, hoping to shut down the mental noise. I took a deep, deep breath and slowly pushed myself out of the patio chair with the dexterity of an eighty-year-old man.

Still in a daze, I took the elevator down to the open house apartment. I cleaned up the shattered glass and wilting broken flowers and discarded them in the refuse down the hall. The dining room table appeared unmarked, having fallen on the plush carpet. I righted it and carefully placed the chairs around it, as if nothing had happened.

After one more flashback of the struggle inside this apartment, I closed my eyes once again to distance the image. I grabbed my real estate belongings, turned out the lights, solemnly took the elevator to the lobby, and stumbled into the life-as-usual buzz of the New York streets.

Chapter Twenty-One

It was too early to go to Alba Gonzales's apartment. My head was just too jumbled. More to the point, there was now no need to do so. Tonight, Joey Roach would not be invading my apartment, ransacking the place, or threatening me. Not after what just happened.

As I ambled through the New York streets, I found myself using such euphemisms—the event, what just happened, the incident. Even in the immediate mental blizzard bombarding my mind, I couldn't refer to it as the killing.

It was self-defense, I reminded myself.

It was lucky I was not run over by an automobile in this haze. Inundated with these thoughts, I can't recall stopping for any red lights or stop signs. I can't remember seeing any Walk or Don't Walk signals. In an almost catatonic state, I simply progressed one foot in front of the other toward my apartment.

About a block before reaching my place, I stopped in the deli to get myself a cup of coffee to warm my soul and wake up my senses. It worked a little. After a few sips, I did decide to visit my friend Alba tonight. It would be just too haunting to spend the evening in an apartment that had been manhandled by a man who was no longer alive.

A little more aware now, I approached the front door of my condo. When I reached the lobby, I was greeted by the two people I least wanted to see at this moment.

"Mr. Witt, welcome home," Detective Donavan said, rising from the lobby bench.

"We heard you had an incident," Tanya Washington quickly added.

I flinched and am quite certain I looked like a shocked, frightened lemur. She couldn't possibly have seen Joey Roach hurtling through the air from the balcony of the open house. *No one had seen anything,* I tried to tell myself.

"An incident?" I tentatively asked.

"Someone broke into your place," Ms. Washington answered.

"Oh, that incident," I responded with perhaps too much relief in my voice. "Yes. Yes. A break-in. No idea who could have done it. I filed a police report with two other officers."

"We saw the report," Detective Donovan said.

"You got it solved?"

"No, not yet," Officer Washington responded.

"Want to take a look around?" I suggested, trying to be cooperative. I walked toward the elevator and invited them to join me. The detective nodded soberly. "Yes, actually we do wish to take a look around. In a very specific way. We have a search warrant."

I found those words chilling. What would they be looking for in my apartment? The officers after the break-in had checked in every room and dusted many items for fingerprints. What else was there to find?

"A search warrant? What are you looking for?"

Once we had entered my apartment that was still in burgled disarray, Detective Donovan presented his document to me. Three items were listed: a red muffler, a Yankee baseball cap, and a knife, approximately a half-inch wide.

"What's this all about?" I asked, not so anxious to hear the answer.

"Mr. Witt, perhaps you should sit down," Tanya Washington advised. I did so.

Both officers joined me at my small dining room table.

Detective Donovan, as the senior officer, took the lead here. "Mr. Witt, we have reason to investigate you further in connection with the death of Martin Ziegler."

"Really?"

"There are inconsistencies in your story."

"Well, I am sure I can clarify any misunderstanding that may exist," I eagerly answered, feeling a growing pit in my stomach.

Detective Donovan launched in, "There's still this matter of your relationship with Mrs. Zeigler."

I was somewhat relieved to hear this opening salvo, especially since I could honestly now claim that there was now no ongoing relationship. Mr. Robert Lévesque had taken care of that.

"Have you asked Mrs. Zeigler about this?" I countered.

"Of course, we have. And she uses the same language you do—professional and businesslike. But that's not what any of the people in your office believe."

"I think we've been over this before," I said with some intentional weariness in my voice.

"Right," Donovan agreed. "But there is something more concrete that is far more troubling, Mr. Witt."

I was all ears and anxious to hear this shoe drop. So far, it didn't seem that the officers had anything new that should concern me.

"That movie you went to the night of the murder?" Tanya Washington reminded me.

"As I told you, I didn't stay for the whole thing."

"Right. That's what you said." She looked at me skeptically.

Donovan took over to deliver the body blow. "Here's the trouble, Mr. Witt. As part of our ongoing investigation, we checked the surveillance tapes at the Barrow Street subway stop—the closest stop to the scene of the crime. There weren't that many passengers at that time of night, slightly before the approximate 10:05 murder and shortly thereafter . . . but thanks to those surveillance videos, all the subway passengers are on camera."

I did not like this news. I could feel my body slump but did my best to correct it with an upright posture, as if I was interested in this, as an anecdote. *Good Lord, could I really be on tape right before and after the murder? Could I actually be placed at the scene of the crime?*

Donovan continued in measured tones, "There is one particular man on this tape—just before and after the time of the murder—who was wearing a red muffler scarf and a Yankee baseball cap."

"There have to be a million people in Manhattan that have Yankee hats," I tried to argue.

"Yeah, but the man on the surveillance tape looks remarkable like you, Mr. Witt," Detective Donavan finished his account and paused dramatically to let this information sink in.

Yikes! Is something like that admissible? Is the tape that clear? I'm not a lawyer but suddenly felt I needed one. I looked at both officers who continued to observe me for any reaction. I tried to show none.

Officer Tanya Washington broke the silence. "That's why we're here with a search warrant, Mr. Witt. We're looking for a red muffler scarf and a blue Yankee cap."

Donovan then decided to pile on. With his usual passive-aggressive tonality, he said, "And as long as we were in the neighborhood, we thought it might be a good idea to look through your knife collection."

"I don't have a knife collection."

"Well, we'll just have to take a look. Won't we?"

"Help yourself." I invited them to look through the piles of ransacked clothes on the ground. I didn't feel there was much of a choice, especially since they had a search warrant. And I knew what they would find.

As they began rummaging through my shirts, socks, and underwear, I moved to the refrigerator for a Diet Coke. Observing their search, I tried to imagine what all this would mean. Obviously, it was not good. I wondered if they had other viable suspects. I wondered if they had received the photo of Joey Roach I had sent earlier.

"Red scarf," Officer Washington yelled from my bedroom. She came into the kitchen with the item no in a plastic bag, and placed it on the island right in front of me.

It was almost like a taunt, I felt. She looked at me with a smile and went back to the bedroom. In a few minutes, she came back with favorite Yankee cap, similarly bagged.

"We need to go through your knife drawer," Detective Donovan said. "Care to point the way?"

I did so. They opened up my kitchen cupboard and saw my scant collection of utensils. I am not a big gourmet guy, but I do have a few kitchen tools. Wearing plastic gloves and a tong, Officer Washington showed a utensil to Donovan.

"It's a common steak knife," I suggested.

"Maybe," Donovan answered without even looking at me. "Let's bag it up and check it out."

He then handed the search warrant to Washington to go along with her pile of findings. As the female officer put exhibit A, B, and C in her satchel, Donovan stood cockily and officiously in the center of my messy living room. When he saw that all the items were properly tagged and bagged, he gestured to his junior partner that their business was finished here.

"Thank you for your cooperation, Mr. Witt."

"I have a few questions."

"Of course."

"What will happen with my things?"

"We'll be checking them out forensically and against the surveillance tape."

That damn surveillance tape, I quietly sighed. "I saw your press conference the other day. You mentioned search warrants." I emphasized the *s* in the word. "Plural. So you're searching for other things, in other places. Other leads."

"We have more than one search warrant," he answered minimally.

"And I heard you offer a tip line on the air. So you must have lots of people calling in with leads. Ideas. Maybe even photos." I realized that this last suggestion was bit direct, but I wanted to know if they had received my anonymous snapshot of the real killer.

Officer Washington, who had, by now, joined the kitchen table, couldn't suppress a laugh.

"Given the high-profile nature of this case," Donovan explained, "we get a lot of calls, that's for sure. Most of them are crackpots. People looking for fifteen minutes of fame."

"But you check them out," I asked pointedly.

"We do. To the extent possible. Unless it's just so obviously a runaround or an astrologer or some anonymous nutcase with a goofy theory."

"But according to your press conference, anonymous leads were invited."

"Right, and we check them out to the extent possible."

To the extent possible, I repeated in my head. Jesus, I had a clear hunch what that meant. Unless all the dots were connected for the police, they weren't going to head somewhere that felt like a wild goose chase. Especially when they felt they had a good solid suspect sitting right in front of them.

"Should I get a lawyer?" I asked. In my bones, I already knew the answer to this question.

Detective Donovan, in a doctoral way, shook his head. "It's always a good idea in a situation such as this. Even though we haven't identified you as a suspect, we do advise representation."

"It can't hurt," Washington chimed in. I interpreted it as helpful advice. She then grabbed her satchel and surveyed my apartment, still in disarray. "Sorry about the break-in. Hope the officers back at the station can solve it."

"You think there's a connection somehow? With you guys checking into me and this burglary happening right on the heels of that. Unusual, no? Maybe the real killer tried to find something."

"I doubt it," Donovan volunteered.

The female officer put it in more sympathetic terms. "You know, sometimes things happen by coincidence. Just an accident of timing. Wrong place, wrong time kind of thing. Doesn't mean there's an actual connection. Know what I mean?"

Did I ever! It was tempting to blurt out that this is exactly what was now happening to me but decided to bite my tongue.

Detective Donovan was now looking over his notes to make sure he had covered all the ways to humiliate me. Then he privately nodded and added another shot, "One more thing, Mr. Witt. In view of the circumstances, I think it's best to hold your passport at this time. Did the burglars take that?"

"I don't know," I answered honestly. I held up a finger to wait and checked my desk drawer. It was still there.

"I don't feel good about this," I admitted as I handed over my travel document.

"Sorry, just procedure," Tanya said almost apologetically. As the two officers walked toward my front door, the senior officer had one more blow for me. "We're going to check these items out," he said, referring to the contents of Washington's satchel. "Depending on the outcome of those tests, we might list you as a 'person of interest.'"

"Great," I sarcastically sighed.

"So you shouldn't leave town. And if it leads to that, we will contact you. If you do retain a lawyer, he or she should feel free to contact us."

"Great," I repeated.

The detective extended his hand to me. "Again, thanks for your cooperation," he said, as if it were the conclusion of a transaction at Best Buy.

And then they were gone.

I returned to my kitchen table and buried my head in my hands. It was almost enough to make me forget about my earlier daze involving the late Joey Roach. Almost, but not quite. Everywhere I looked it my ransacked apartment, I saw evidence of the true killer.

Chapter Twenty-Two

"I have a scoop for you," I announced with some fatigue.

"Hey, I figured as much from the picture and message you sent," Alba Gonzales answered into her phone.

"It's more than that."

"Great! Jackson, you know I always love scoops." "Well, this one is a damn doozy."

"Then get your ass over here," Alba said with some brash encouragement.

I had unsuccessfully tried to calm myself over the last hour. Too many bombarding hits were jamming my brain in one day. By far, the worst image was Joey Roach falling from the sky, capped only by the visual of his brutal impalement from my perilous perch on the very edge of the rooftop. However, I had this hunch that this crime would never be discovered. At least, I hoped not. Even so, it haunted me.

By contrast, my greatest fear was this "person of interest" stuff. I knew this was trouble, especially given the pressure to resolve this high-profile case. The fact that I was seen on subway surveillance cameras was downright disastrous. Intuitively, I knew the video comparison of the red muffler and baseball cap would nail me. The knife, of course, was another story. They would find nothing on my steak knife, other than perhaps week-ago residue of sliced Brie.

Given all that transpired, I decided there was clearly no advantage in following my own instinct and going after it alone. Too much had unraveled in the past few days, and I couldn't help but feel that more difficulties were now headed my way. Alba was the one who could steer things right. Of course, she had already given me good, sound advice—turn the damn phone over to the police—and I had ignored it. OK, my misguided mistake, but that ship had sailed and now the cops had Joey Roach's image.

Despite this miscue, Alba knew how to improvise. She knew how the system in New York worked. Most important, I knew she would be in my corner. On my phone call with her, I promised to be at her apartment in twenty minutes.

Lately, I had resisted the subways. Superstitiously, I blamed the constant publicly delivered private conversations as the source of all my problems. Besides, I needed the think time. So I walked to her place at the Gilsey Building on Twenty-ninth and Broadway.

When she opened the door and greeted me with a big hug and kiss on the cheek, I instantly felt better.

"Jackson, Jackson, Jackson . . . what am I going to do with you?" She smiled and shook her head at my foreshadowed hints of a predicament. "C'mon, I've got all evening, and I think you have some interesting new developments. You still drink vodka?"

"Rocks, please," I happily responded.

She poured two glasses, handed me mine, and walked me over to her living room. It was a barely evolved college apartment—bookshelves crammed with upward and horizontally crammed editions, magazines on the cocktail table and the floor, framed posters on the wall of Andy Warhol and James Rosenquist prints, plus a framed poster of *Rosencrantz and Guildenstern Are Dead* at Temple University Theater, where I had performed the role of Guildenstern to rather nice college reviews.

She caught me staring at the poster and acknowledged it.

"Our last weekend together," she said and quickly changed the subject. "So talk to me."

I knew her well enough to lead with a headline. She already had my forwarded picture of Joey Roach. Rather than explain the new details chronologically, I got to the point and delivered the news, "I am fairly certain I will be named a 'person of interest' in the Martin Ziegler murder. Probably tomorrow. Could be the day after."

"Wow," she quietly reacted with a slight head jolt. She took a sip of her vodka and looked at me. "Wow," she again reacted.

"Yeah. They got me in their crosshairs," I admitted. After a pause, I added, "And they're ignoring the real target, a guy I now know as Joey Roach."

Despite my awful situation and pressing problems in every corner of this case, I did admire my theatrical timing in this delivery. Perhaps the *Rosencrantz and Guildenstern* poster reminded me of my buried talent. Or perhaps it was just being in the presence of the one woman who seemed to enjoy my performances.

After a pause, she smiled. "Wow," she repeated the word yet again and let this bombshell sink in. "I got a feeling we're going to need all that vodka." She went back to her kitchen cabinet and put the Absolut bottle on the coffee table.

Over a few more shots, I explained almost everything that happened over the past forty-eight hours—the ransacking of my apartment, my lunch with Melanie, the still-missing incriminating photos of this affair, my snapshot of Joey Roach at Grand Central Station, the search warrant, the surveillance photos at the Barrow Street station, and the impending "person of interest" interrogation.

I say *almost* because I didn't really have the heart to admit the catapult of Joey Roach into the empty elevator shaft. Too painful to disclose. Not really germane to my immediate predicament, I had already reasoned in my walk over to Alba's apartment.

"Egads," Alba grimaced.

"It's a mess," I admitted.

"That's an understatement," she corrected me. "How much have you told the police?"

"Not much."

"Well, that's going to be a problem because they already know stuff about you. Hey, every decent reporter in this town suspects there was some relationship between Melanie Ziegler and someone. I heard it myself on Day One, which is why I called you."

"I thought maybe you just wanted to say hi," I tried to lighten the moment.

"So the police know you're covering up. And listen to me, Jackson. When a cop senses you are covering up, they jump straight to 'must be guilty.'"

"Which is pretty much where they are now."

In a seemingly abrupt change of topic, Alba took a deep sigh, plopped her feet on her rustic coffee table, and then said, "You still like Philly cheese steaks?"

It was our favorite meal when we were an item at Temple University. At least once a week, we would make the trek down to Geno's on South Ninth just to devour this hometown delicacy. Once or twice during the week, we would get lesser versions from food carts right off the campus just to satiate this craving for onions, beef, and gooey cheese.

"Haven't had one since college, but it brings back fond memories."

She got up and walked over to her kitchen phone. "Well, there's a pizza joint down the street that offers it as a topping. Not the real thing. Not as good as Gino's. But hey, they deliver, and I'm hungry."

"I'm game."

While we waited for our thick concoction on a crust, we both let my data download marinate for a while. A few minutes of exhausted silence felt good and not at all uncomfortable. When I looked over to Alba, she was shaking her head as it all registered. Then she grabbed a steno pad, uncapped her pen, and began writing.

"Jackson, I need to make some notes. You mind?"

"Not at all. It's a lot to take in," I answered.

As she continued to scribble, I thought back on my morning with Leandor. Damn, with all that happened today, it seemed like months ago. And yet, it was only about fifteen hours since I was reading the *Advocate* in his apartment.

The cleave in the gay community over Ziegler's death was curiously unreported in the mainstream press. And what about that blurb on Robert Lévesque as the champion of gay-friendly condos?

"Can I Google a few things on your computer while you scribble away?" I asked.

"Help yourself. It's on," she answered without looking up from her notes.

I sat at her desk in the living room and typed in *Robert Lévesque*. I found a ton of articles about his history as a mogul and real estate developer in Manhattan. Blah, blah, blah, blah. Mr. Success. Fine. Not what I was looking for.

I then typed in *Robert Lévesque's gay connections*. There were fewer stories under this Google prompt. Yes, there was a repeat of the *Advocate* article on co-op and condo rankings. There was a link to his Orion House real estate development. There were several subsequent articles on this apartment house. But there was nothing of a personal nature relating Lévesque directly to the gay community "What are you looking for?" Alba asked as she recapped her pen and put it down next to her steno pad.

"The gay connection," I answered. "Judge Ziegler was a raging regularly practicing homosexual, according to Leandor. Remember him?"

"Speaking of homosexuals." She nodded with a smile. "Yeah, of course, I remember him. Great guy."

"Leandor tells me that in the gay community, there are lots of people who have a grudge against the judge, given his brutal judgment against the 'sin' as he once called it."

"I've got that in my notes," Alba agreed with thumbs-up gesture. "But nothing has turned up. At least, not yet."

"And what about this guy, Robert Lévesque?"

"The new friend and alibi for Melanie Ziegler." Alba nodded.

"More than that. He's got some kind of gay connection. An award-winning gay condo. Some business connections in that area. But other than that, there isn't that much on Google."

Alba reached for her notepad and scribbled. "I can check on that with our resources and records and get better results than you'll ever find on my Mac."

"That would be great," I said, gratefully.

Alba closed her steno pad and looked me in the eye. "I want to help you, Jackson, because I always liked you. But I really have to ask you one serious question."

"Shoot."

"Have you told me everything?"

I reacted with a slight startle at the honest directness of her question. "Alba, listen to me. Every single thing there is to tell about my situation, I have told you." It was delivered with Oscar-worthy sincerity. Admittedly, my answer also contained a Bill Clintonesque weasel: the careful phrase, "there is to tell." In my mind, the launched death of Joey Roach was something that was not is told. Never.

Fortunately, as I was struggling to justify these linguistic and moral gymnastics, the buzzer rang. "Pizza delivery," the voice on the intercom said.

We scarfed down our Philly cheese steak concoctions as if we were ravenous scavengers. Even with that thin crust of pizza dough, it was a nostalgic taste treat. OK, not on par with salmon en croute or boeuf bourguignon, but nonetheless yummy. For the first time of the evening, I saw Alba giggle.

"The last time I had this with you, you were dressed as an Elmer Fudd."

I recalled the Halloween Party sponsored by my theater group. It turned out to be a big turnout and there just wasn't enough food, so we headed to Geno's." And you were Little Bo Peep," I reminded her.

"A damn good one, I might add. You, on the other hand, looked ridiculous." "My costumes have gotten a little better," I piped. At least, I hoped so. However, my recent efforts had admittedly been less than stellar. That Toulouse-Lautrec imitation, for example, didn't seem to convince anyone other than the busy subway commuters.

We finished another slice or two and flashed back to easier college times. After wrapping up the pie and putting it in the fridge, Alba looked back at me. "Enough fun for one night. Let's get back to work."

She brought out her notes and told me the areas that she might be able to pursue from a journalistic perspective. She contended they would all be helpful for my defense. One, however, had been underlined three times and circled. It looked like her priority, and I just knew it would be a dead end.

"Joey Roach," I said, pointing to the encircled name.

"Right, it's critical that the police find him for questioning. And I'll check around. Maybe I can find him. Either way, we need to get this guy out of the bushes and into the spotlight."

"I don't think you're going to be able to find Joey Roach," I cautioned her, without going into details.

"Oh, I'll find him."

"I don't know. I don't think so. I've been looking for the guy for the last few days and nothing. Zero. Gone. I think he may have left town."

"I'll find him," she repeated confidently.

After a pause, I had to shrug. "I just don't want you wasting your time. That's all."

Brushing it aside, she launched into a topic not listed on her pad. "Jackson, one more thing. No matter how things go in the next few days, you really should get a lawyer."

"I don't know any other than the real estate hacks."

"I do." She turned the page of her steno pad to a fresh sheet and wrote down a name and phone number. She then handed it to me. "I will call Ian Rockmore tomorrow. He's the best criminal defense attorney in town. I know him, and he'll do it for me."

"Is he expensive?"

Alba did a double take. "Dirt cheap," she said mockingly and let it play for a second until she knew I got her sarcasm. "Jackson Witt, my dear, there are no inexpensive lawyers. None. And at this point, you shouldn't really give a shit about saving two nickels. You should be more concerned about saving your ass. And he's the best."

I took the paper with his name on it. "I'll call him tomorrow," I said.

"Now we both have a big day ahead of us." Alba winked at me and brought out bedding linens and two pillows. She asked me to help her set up the sleeper sofa, and I complied.

"I don't know how comfortable this is," she admitted.

"It'll do," I answered and walked over to her. "Alba, I don't know how to thank you. Other than Leandor, I didn't know who else to turn to."

"I'm glad you called."

Somewhat awkwardly, I gave her a good night kiss and didn't quite get her cheek. Not a full plant on the lips, but it felt good. Quick thoughts of our time together flooded my brain, but I flushed them aside. Not the place. And definitely not the time.

"Thanks," I simply stated.

"If I remember correctly, you like a lot of coffee in the morning. I've set up a full pot. All you have to do is turn it on. And if you get hungry in the middle of the night, don't eat all the cheese steak," she kidded me.

"I won't."

"Good night," she said and walked into her bedroom. I followed her every step, and wished I had visited her earlier.

Chapter Twenty-Three

Breakfast bagels with Alba Gonzales tasted magnificent. Over our second cup of coffee, she shared her fear that Joey Roach would again break into to my apartment. "It could happen," she warned me and demanded that, for my own safety, I must stay at her place again tonight. Unwilling to admit that I had sent the man into a spiky death yesterday, I promised I would.

We left her apartment together. Alba persuaded me to be careful out there and gave a sisterly hug, and we walked our separate ways.

I headed toward West Chelsea to revisit the Open House apartment and view the resumption of construction on the neighboring condo. By the time I hit the site, the hard hats were lined up by the food cart to buy their double-egg or double-bacon sandwiches, coffee with mega sugar, and maybe a side of morning fries. I was tempted to belittle their culinary tastes until I reminded myself that I couldn't get my fill of Philly cheese steak pizza last night.

Over the rumbling noise of the concrete mixing truck, I could hear the foreman encourage his workers to finish up their breakfasts and start their days. A few of them pointed to their breakfast sandwiches and held up their big fingers, indicating, "First things first."

I got a cup of my third coffee of the morning from the food service van and approached the foreman.

"Pouring concrete today?" I volunteered.

The foreman slowly looked back at the mixing truck and then back at me. "That's the idea," he succinctly replied, obviously unwilling to explain the mechanics of his job to a non-hard hat. He looked back at his still-hungry crew and snapped his fingers a few times. "Guys, we're pouring."

A few of them dumped their crumpled napkins in the trash and headed toward the mixing truck. Others headed into the various parts of the construction site.

Coffee in hand, I walked over to 325 W. 18th. The doorman recognized me. "How was your open house yesterday?" he asked. "Everything go OK?"

"Fine, fine, fine," I answered. "But I left some stuff on the roof. Mind if I take a look?"

He gestured for me to take the elevator. Not surprisingly, there was no one on the roof deck at 9:07 in the morning. After climbing the deck guardrail and moving toward the end of the building, I peered over the edge to see yesterday's unfortunate accident. Yesterday's "event." Yesterday's "incident." I continued to call it anything but "yesterday's death at the hands of Jackson Witt."

It was self-defense, I repeated again to myself.

I looked. He was still there. The bright red blood was more auburn now, but the gaze in my general direction was just as visible, at least from this small postage-stamp size of the roof.

It was every bit as graphic as yesterday, but with all that happened in the past twenty-four hours, the whole spectacle did feel a little more surreal. Maybe the initial shock was gone. I did not feel the need to instantly drop to my knees again.

Instead, I watched.

A combination of morbid curiosity and self-preservation drove me to this vantage point. I suppose I partly wanted to witness the reaction of the hard hats when they saw the body. It would help prepare me for what kind of tracks I would need to assume. Discovery of the victim would dictate a defense. If it were linked to me, I would need to implicate the Dolan family, who had personally observed the aggressive behavior of Joey Roach as he smugly sat and smoked his cigarettes at my open houses.

While I wondered about this, I saw the wet concrete rise up in buckets on the conveyer belt. They were headed for the unfinished shaft, which contained the body of Joey Roach.

By now, there were now two hard hats at the scaffolded opening of the elevator shaft. I recognized one of them from the food cart below. He was still picking at his breakfast fries as the wet concrete buckets neared. I presumed they would evidently guide this conveyer of the concrete into the shaft.

From where I stood, I couldn't hear them, but they seemed to be sharing a story or maybe a joke. The noneating hard hat reached for the first rising bucket and tipped it into the elevator shaft without even glancing downward. Same with the next bucket. And the next.

The french fry laborer appeared to have finished his yarn by now and aimed the next bucket into the shaft. The same with the next bucket.

Finally, his partner actually leaned his body over the shaft to make sure that the wet concrete was effectively hitting the bottom. He took one quick look and then began his own story to his friend.

I instinctively mimicked his action and leaned my body over the edge of the building to see what he was seeing. Fresh concrete now covered the once-gory, impaled body of Joey Roach.

I looked back at the twosome as they continued their yada yada. More buckets of concrete were guided into the shaft. The hard hat from the food cart appeared now to be laughing out loud at some outrageous punch line. He lightly shadowboxed his partner in the stomach like guy culture, macho men do. He took one last fry, crumpled the wrapper, and then flicked it into the shaft as one would send a spent cigarette in the street. Another bucket of concrete. And then another.

Clearly, it was not important to these men what was in the shaft. Concrete would freeze it anyway. Years of wet concrete and yukkity-yuk tales had evidently convinced them of that.

I took one more look over the edge of the building into the shaft of that neighboring half-built condo.

Joey Roach no longer existed. He would never threaten anyone again. He would never be found. He would never be heard from.

At first I was relieved by that thought.

On balance, it was better than the inevitable nightmare that would ensue if someone found his dead body. This would obviously raise question about where it came from and who pushed him there.

Now there would be no questions.

But there would also be no answers.

Chapter Twenty-Four

The Meyers in 14B were happy to hear that it was a successful open house. I explained to them that I would be following up with a few interested prospects that had visited the place yesterday.

"One thing, Mr. Witt," Mrs. Meyer told me. "We seem to be missing a vase from our dining room table."

"Really? A valuable one?" I asked her with some dismay.

"Oh no. Just Crate and Barrel stuff. But it seems to be missing."

I looked puzzled. "You know, sometimes when it's a busy open house as yours was, I may be showing two different couples the master bedroom at the same time, and there might be another possible customer in the dining area. Very occasionally, they will take things . . . and that's why we advise you to clear the place of clutter and hide valuable items. And you did a beautiful job of that."

"Well, we tried," Mrs. Meyer said.

"But I'll be glad to reimburse you for the missing vase." I reached in my pocket and placed a twenty on the dining room table.

"There's no need for that. I have already forgotten it." She insisted I take the money back.

"Was everything else perfect?" I asked. I sneaked glances toward the dining room table to see if there were any telltale signs from my battle with Joey Roach.

"Everything else was perfect. The house was as clean as we left it," she said with a gentle smile.

I was relieved to hear it, particularly given the runaround in the place to save my life. Fortunately, the overturned table and chairs showed no distress. I told Mrs. Meyer I'd get back to her with future appointments and left the building.

Next stop: my health club to check the killer's cell phone. Over the night, I had wondered if he was just bullshitting me about blocking all calls. Something told me that Joey Roach was not a bullshit artist.

I opened my gym locker and found the phone where I left it, buried behind an old pair of gym shorts. I quickly powered the device up and tried to make an outgoing call to my home just to see if it was still operational. Immediately, a recorded voice announced that service on this machine had been discontinued. Like a black hole, I assumed that all incoming calls would now be gone forever, just like Joey Roach himself.

On the plus side, the existing voice mails still seemed to be intact, albeit inaccessible without Joey Roach's password code. Too bad I hadn't asked for that when I had a chance, I mused with gallows humor. The missed calls could still be displayed, and the snapshot of the murderer in Grand Central still appeared. I took another look at it and wondered what good it would possibly be now. Unless someone could actually speak to Joey Roach's involvement, my redemption would be equally shafted.

"Fuck me," I uttered aloud. Without a living culprit, I began to wonder if this blocked hunk of circuitry could truly serve as my lifeline. Rather than check the text messages in a smelly locker room, I decided to carry my once-prized possession to the juice bar.

"An OJ," I ordered and took one of the tables.

The man behind the counter saw me take out the phone and called out to me.

"Sir, no cell phone conversations pleases in this section. Just as a courtesy for other members."

I felt like barking back that there were no fucking voice capabilities on this damn cell phone since the real killer had frozen them all, but decided it was too much information to impart. "I'm just checking text messages," I responded, and the clerk motioned that that was OK.

As I scrolled down, I recognized the first three Melanie messages that I had already seen. But now there was a fourth text message that had not come from her home or cell number. It had been received shortly after

I had sent the Roach photos and evidently before the killer had called Verizon and been catapulted to his death.

The new text message was a request to locate the missing murderer. It simply stated, "Good job. Where R U? Are U OK?" Unlike the others that listed Melanie's number as the source, this one came from an unverifiable party the number listed was 212-222-2222. *Odd number,* I thought. Still, it was something, perhaps even a new lead as to who actually orchestrated this whole thing. I wrote the number on a napkin, along with the other unrecognizable number from the missed calls, and promised myself to try to ascertain their source.

I powered down the cell phone, took another sip of my citrus, and pondered my situation. I stared at the dead phone and recollected my last conversation with Joey Roach. He himself admitted that Melanie had not hired him. In his words, "the other guy had." From my Melanie lunch, I learned that that other guy was Robert Lévesque. Somehow, I needed to prove that he had actually ordered a hit even though I had no hard evidence to point that way. I'll admit this: I wanted him to be guilty. I secretly hoped he was the man who phoned Roach on the subway car and provided the locale even though there was no saved record of that call. I wanted him to be the guy who had texted "Nice job" even though it came from an unverifiable caller. I feared that the answers to these hypotheses were now unfortunately buried in concrete.

As I sat in the juice bar, I thought back on Alba Gonzales advice to me: eventually, the truth will come out. With a forever-silent murderer and frozen cell phone, it would now be more difficult. Discouraged, I finished my citrus, put the cell phone back its safe locker, and headed for my office.

Chapter Twenty-Five

The Stribling real estate office was always busy on a Monday morning. Agents had to file their open house reports, compare leads, and always liked to regale their weekend entertainment stories.

On this particular morning, the atmosphere felt chilly. I sat at my desk when Diane Farin, the managing director, approached me. "You seem to have a lot going on in your life right now, Jackson," she said.

"Busy time," I responded and handed her my report. "I had a pretty successful open house on Sunday."

She took the report and did not react to it.

"Are you OK," she asked with some concern, obviously knowing more about my situation than she was willing to disclose.

"Oh yeah," I scoffed. "As a matter of fact, I'm going to meet with one of those prospects in about thirty minutes."

After a pause, she simply replied with a noncommittal OK and walked away. I didn't want to be in this environment today. Too tense. Too many nosy gossipers. I gathered any condo sheets on my desk as if they would be useful for my imaginary sales meeting. "Later," I said to no one in particular and walked out, hearing indecipherable whispers in my wake.

When I arrived at my ransacked apartment, my automatic first activity was to check missed messages. There were two. The first was from Leandor. "Hope you're holding up well, boopie. I'm around if you need a friend." It was nice of him.

The second message was news I hated to hear. "Mr. Witt, this is Detective Donovan. I wanted to inform you that at a 1:00 p.m. press conference, we will be naming you a person of interest. While you are not yet classified as a suspect, you are not to leave town. And if you have retained an attorney, he or she should feel free to call us. You have our number. Have a nice day."

Have a nice day? My god, he must have been gained his police training at Disneyworld, I groused.

With forty minutes to go before the press conference, I started picking up my piles of sloppily tossed garments and folded them mindlessly. It was just a reflex action to provide me some inane activity to keep my mind from completely obsessing on the upcoming circus—featuring me as the evil jackal. After twenty-five minutes of this diversion, I gave up the charade and planted myself in front of my thirty-five-inch plasma screen, which had been untouched by Joey Roach's miserable mitts.

The scroll on the bottom of the screen screamed the tune-in announcement: "Person of interest to be named in NYPD press conference at 1:00 p.m." Just to add insult to injury, there was a time clock that kept ticking on the right-hand side of the screen. It displayed the minutes remaining to the press conference and ticked away. At this precise moment, it read 6: 42. Then 6:41. Then 6:40. It was almost like a Times Square ball drop, except I wouldn't be celebrating this time.

At precisely 1:00 p.m., Chief of Police Bobby "Buster" Byrnes strode to the podium, followed by Detective Donovan. Even for me, it was impossible to ignore the anticipation in the pressroom and the TV audience. Byrnes was a man in his midfifties and imposing figure of about six feet four. He had earned his nickname not from early playground days but rather from the drug busts, mafia busts, and gang busts that had significantly reduced the street crime rate in New York City. Given his accomplishments, he was a widely respected figure and a regular talk show panelist. Byrnes waved his hands to settle his audience and tapped the microphone a few times to make sure it was on.

"We are here to provide a progress report on the slaying of Judge Martin V. Ziegler," he announced stone-faced. "As you all know, this tragic incident has been a subject of a full-court investigation on the part of the NYPD. Extra police officers, forensic resources, and investigative techniques have been deployed, given the gravity of this crime against a public servant."

Why not put a glowing halo on his Ziegler's head? I mused. Nevertheless, the chief's statement did capture the citywide urgency to solve this crime.

"We continue to chase many leads and pursue search warrants. However, we are prepared at this time to identify a person of interest in this case. I will now turn it over to Detective Thomas Donovan to discuss this development."

Even in the electronic distance of TV land, I could feel the buzz of excitement in the pressroom. Acknowledging the excitement, Donovan took the podium and gestured for the crowd to quiet down.

"We have today named Mr. Jackson Witt as a person of interest in this case."

Hearing one's name mentioned like this is definitely an out-of-body experience. Of course, I expected the revelation, but even so, the announcement of my name in this context was jarring. In earlier years, I had dreamed of my name being called as best supporting actor in a Tony presentation. Or for the Emmy's. Or even dare I say, for the Academy Awards. In my fantasies, that would be thrilling. In today's reality, it was far from it.

As the detective spoke, my photo was projected behind him. I recognized it as my real estate portrait and immediately understood that had contributed to the earlier chill in the Stribling office.

"We believe Mr. Witt had motive. And we have evidence that he was at the scene of this heinous murder at the precise moment of the crime. Surveillance videos at the subway stop place him arriving shortly before and departing shortly after the slaying of Judge Ziegler. In addition, certain specific articles of clothing, which we have now seized, help confirm his identity and presence at the scene."

As he was taking a breath, there was an onrush of raised hands from the ravenous press corps. The detective motioned for them to be patient as he finished his statement.

"I would like to stress that Mr. Witt is not at this time classified as a bona fide suspect and is certainly not charged with any specific crime. However, we are interested in his whereabouts at the time and have asked him to remain in the NY area as we conduct our investigation on this and other leads."

Again, more hands in the air.

The detective gestured over to the police chief, who again took the podium. The chief thanked Donovan and turned back the crowd. "Given the ongoing nature of this investigation, there will undoubtedly be some issues we will not be at liberty to fully address at this time. You folks from the press understand the process, we are sure. However, in the interest of transparency, we do open this conference to questions."

Even though they were not milked, I could hear a cacophonous chorus of journalists pleading, "Chief," "Chief Byrnes," "Question, sir," and other outbursts.

The first few questions were lay ups for the chief—basically, congratulations to the force for such quick work and specifics of the evidence against me, which he dodged.

"Have you found a murder weapon?" one journalist called out.

"No, not as of yet. But in a case such as this, that is not unusual. However, we will continue our search."

"Are there other suspects?" a news reporter screamed.

"Technically, Mr. Witt is not yet a suspect," Donovan corrected him, and then the chief edged over into the podium mike. "And I must say this, we will continue to chase every avenue, follow every scent, and investigate every thread of evidence until this matter is resolved."

It was the perfect political answer, and I'm sure he meant it as an applause line. But the hands in the air and the chorus of questions continued.

"One more," the chief stated and pointed into the audience at a person to his right.

I instantly recognized the voice of the questioner. The TV camera panned around and discovered Alba Gonzales of the *New York Times* with her hand in the air.

"Chief, a question about the search. Given the lifestyle of Judge Ziegler and the apparent widespread antagonism in the gay community toward the judge's conservative bench decisions, is there any further speculation on the part of the NYPD that this may be a sexually related slaying?"

The questions seemed to catch the chief off guard since it did not directly link to his emphasis on me, but he recovered quickly. "Well, Alba, that's quite a few topics wrapped in one question," he said, and there was a slight titter from the crowd at his funny. "I will only say this. Our search is not driven by sexual profiling . . . or any other profiling for that matter."

Before he could pat himself on the back for this politically correct response, Alba jumped in with a follow-up. "So what you're saying is that the search continues for other people of interest beyond Mr. Witt?"

There was no way the chief could imply that he was closing the book, not with the citywide spotlight on this case. He took a breath and then responded, "We continue our search. Now we have to get back to work. Thanks for attending."

As he walked off the stage, he conferred with Detective Donavan and shot a stare back in the direction of my favorite reporter.

I could have kissed the screen and hoped my symbolic bissito could somehow be electronically transmitted to Alba Gonzales. At least there was one person in the press corps who was not quite ready to accept this news as a done deal. Maybe she was just being a journalistic purist. Maybe she had found out something. Either way, I was just glad she was there to keep hope alive.

I watched the TV screen a few more seconds and listened to some live anchor in the NYPD hallway summing up what everyone had just watched. "Well, there you have it. A person of interest has been named in the Martin Ziegler murder case, and yet the search still continues for others." Blah, blah, blah, blah. More pictures of me. More repetition. More recap. More rehash. Finally, I just turned it off.

Despite Alba's last minute "not so fast" moment, I just knew there would be ugly days ahead. I took the folded paper out of my pocket and dialed Ian Rockmore.

Chapter Twenty-Six

Rockmore told me he had watched the televised press conference and had been anticipating my call. "Alba says you are worth defending, and that's good enough for me. I've already cleared my schedule for you," he said and advised me to come into his office immediately.

It was a swanky multi attorney outfit on East Fifty-seventh Street. Lots of beige paint, a few landscape oils on the walls, recessed lighting just short of dramatic. The effect was intended to be calming, I imagined. Everyone, including the receptionist, seemed to already know me. Perhaps they had all been watching the TV when my picture was plastered on the screen as a person of interest.

"Mr. Witt," the receptionist told me, "Mr. Rockmore will be right out. Meanwhile, can I get you a cup of coffee?"

I demurred, anxious to get this meeting started. To be honest, I was also anxious to get this meeting over. Fact is, I had never really liked lawyers.

After graduation, I had played Captain Jack Ross in a touring company production of *A Few Good Men.* It was one of my least favorite roles. Kevin Bacon had played it in the movie, and I consciously tried to avoid his mannerisms and speech patterns in my portrayal. However, the cocky cut-a-deal personality was built into the character.

I had several lawyer clients in the real estate world and almost never enjoyed the experience. I always felt they unwittingly tried to convey their superiority, by virtue of their JD from some Ivy school. They tended to drag out every real estate closing by several hours. In all correspondences with me, they signed their name with the suffix, esquire. Really! It's another damn reminder that we should all bow to their rank.

Maybe Ian Rockmore would be different. After all, any friend of Alba couldn't be all bad.

"Mr. Witt, glad you could come in on such short notice," the voice said. The man in the blue gabardine suit extended his hand to me and shook mine firmly and professionally. "I'm Ian Rockmore, and I'd like to help."

"I could use it," I admitted.

"It certainly sounds like it from today's press conference. Come on, follow me." He walked in big strides toward his office, approximately15' × 20' and decorated in that mahogany style made popular by *Law & Order* and other TV shows.

He was younger than I anticipated. Fit as a soccer player. Maybe early thirties. From Alba's "best in the business" description, I halfway expected him to be a silver-haired sage, perhaps like F. Lee Bailey, Robert Shapiro, or maybe even Matlock. Instead, he moved with a great sense of drive and purpose, almost like an MBA.

He reached in his file drawer and pulled out some papers that he placed in front of me. "You already come qualified, thanks to Alba Gonzales," he explained. "But the firm needs some contact and background information, so just fill out these few sheets, and we'll get started."

He placed a pen down and moved to the door. "I need to use the rest room a minute, and I'm going to get myself a cup of coffee. Want one?"

"I'm OK," I told him and started writing. Name, address, phone, and e-mail. Employment history. Bank accounts. Credit card numbers. All this probably makes their billing easier, I assumed.

When I had just about finished, Rockmore reappeared with his coffee. He didn't beat around the bush. "Mr. Witt, first off, everything we talk about is completely protected by law and 100 percent confidential. So you need to be perfectly honest with me if I'm to ably defend you."

"I didn't do it," I blurted out in my own defense, thinking that's what he first needed to know and wanted to hear.

Rockmore just smiled at me in a rather patronizing way. "That's nice to know, but not actionable right now or even germane to a solid defense. It has to do with 'blunting the prosecutors' theories and ultimately creating a credible alternative story line."

This is one of the things I find so maddening about lawyers. It's the game. The thrust. The parry. The three-point play. The face-off. The one-two punch. And every other sports analogy that comes to mind. However, I had to assume the other side played the same game, so at least it was good to have someone on my side that understood the rules and was at least as skilled, if not more so.

"Tell me everything," he said.

I did so, except, of course, that bit about Joey Roach being thrown over the balcony into a concrete elevator shaft.

"A couple of things," Ian said upon hearing the hour-long completion of my account. "At some point, we're going to have to explain why you went down to Barrow and Hudson at crime time."

"Curiosity," I honestly answered.

"Hmm, maybe," Rockmore winced and looked toward the ceiling. As he thought about this, he began twirling his silver cuff links—an affectation that I found particularly annoying. Then he amplified my response with an alternative theory. "Maybe you were curious about a jazz group or a restaurant down there and then happened to see this awful thing. And then got scared like any normal human being would. I don't know. Think about it."

I had been ever since it had happened. But I was also now thinking that the game had begun.

"Oh, and one more thing, Mr. Witt . . ."

"Jackson," I said.

"Jackson, one more thing. From here on out, don't talk to anyone about this.

Not the cops. Not the doorman. Not Ms. Ziegler. Not the press."

"I already told Alba everything," I replied.

"She's OK. She's on your side. But if the police start questioning you, tell them you've got an attorney now, and he must be present. Here's my card." He reached in his drawer, took out a pen and added his home number, and slid it across the desk to me.

I put his card in my wallet and extracted another one from the NYPD. "Detective Donovan also told me that you should feel free to call him."

"I know his number." Rockmore waved me off. "You forget this is what I do for a living. Oh, and tell Alba to send me that picture of Joey Roach. That's important. We find that guy, and all the focus on you goes away. Pronto. Voila. The police get their guy, and you go back to selling million-dollar condos."

"Right," I answered. Everyone now wanted to find Joey Roach. If only they had been looking for him several days ago, when he was still alive.

Rockmore took the notes from our meeting and packed them in his briefcase. "Well, I got more than enough here to get me started, and I don't want to hold you any longer. As they say in the canyons of commerce, time is money."

"Speaking of which, what is your fee?"

"Eight hundred an hour," Rockmore answered as he fastened his briefcase without even looking up. "It's a pretty standard fee for this kind of thing, but I have a rather remarkable success rate on criminal cases, as Alba knows." He then smiled at me. "I think, in the end, you'll believe I was worth it."

I didn't quite know to respond to this self-belief. Finally, I just said, "Thanks," and headed down the elevator. When I hit the streets, I felt relieved that this first legal meeting was over. Not comforted, but relieved.

Chapter Twenty-Seven

Alba told me to meet her in her apartment around 9:00 p.m. We had swapped a few text messages over the past two hours, and she explained that she was busy chasing some news threads and couldn't break free till then.

I looked forward to a respite from the whirlwind of the past few days. Perhaps my apartment could provide that oasis—some ritualistic folding of ransacked clothes and other strayed belongings might just take my mind off things.

As I unlocked the key and headed into my space, the phone was ringing. It is not my habit to screen calls, but on this particular day, I didn't feel like speaking to a telemarketer, so I let it play. "Hi, this is Bridget Wainright from the *Daily News,* wanting to hear your side of the story. I promise you a fair hearing. Call me at 718-555-8297."

I looked at my phone and saw the blinking light, along with the electronic readout that said, "Message box full." Obviously, I had become a celebrity. There were calls from the *NY Post,* the *Village Voice,* NBC, CBS, ABC, Fox, CNN, the *New York Observer, Newsday,* the *Gotham Gazette,* the *Onion,* the *Advocate,* and six other publications I had never heard of. There were also calls from Leandor and Diane Farin from Stribling Real Estate.

I opened Diane's call first since I already had a premonition of what that that message would be. "Jackson, in view of your circumstances, I think it's best that you take a leave of absence from Stribling effective immediately. When and if all this passes, we can talk. Until then, good luck. Diane." I expected it. No surprise. If I were running the office, I probably would have done the same thing.

Leandor's message was a direct counterpoint to that downer. "Hey, boopie. Tough day. Are you OK? I'm here for you. Remember, you didn't do anything wrong. Call me. Leandor."

I did and invited him over. He promised to arrive in ten minutes.

All the other media telephone messages were similar to the one from Bridget Wainright of the *Daily News*—chirpy invitations to speak off the record and subsequently incriminate myself. I decided to follow my lawyer's advice and return no media calls.

In anticipation of Leandor's visit, I cleaned up the few remaining piles of scattered belonging in my living room. It wasn't pristine. Like a college regimen, I simply gathered the remnants of the ransacked junk and dumped it in the closet. Eventually, I would want to take all these articles of clothing to the local cleaner to eradicate any touches of the intruder's mitts. I then headed back in the kitchen and opened up the cupboard. I could immediately see that the glasses had been carelessly strewn, undoubtedly by my late nemesis. This ubiquitous violation of my personal space was unnerving. I triple-cleaned a glass, filled it with ice, and unscrewed the top of a half-filled liter of Diet Coke. I couldn't help but question if the killer had taken a refreshing swig as he sloppily scoured my apartment. Everything felt soiled. Everything would have to be pitched. Instead of drinking the potentially contaminated cola, I just filled my glass with water and waited for Leandor. Within five minutes, my friend entered my apartment with flamboyant fanfare.

"Tadaa! Hello, Mr. All-over-the-news. Hey, you always wanted fame," he kidded me and gave me his trademark bear hug.

"Yeah, not this way," I replied.

"Well, it's happening, my friend. There are were already a few reporters staked outside when I came in."

I squinted through my miniblinds and could see remote broadcasts just setting up. Ay, yi, yi. I should have expected it. It doesn't take long for the media circus to set up camp. I recalled all those live broadcasts I had seen in front of Scott Peterson's home, Bernie Madoff's apartment, and O.J.'s place. At the time, I figured they deserved the scrutiny because I automatically assumed they were guilty. Perhaps that's how viewers felt about me now. *Ouch!*

"I'd offer you a drink, but I'm afraid the reporters might think it's a party up here," I advised. "Let's slip out of here before this turns into a goddamn feeding frenzy."

I knew an escape route through the laundry room in the basement. I grabbed a baseball cap, a pair of Ray-Bans and showed Leandor the way. After snaking a path through the dark storage bins, I opened up the service door on the side of my building. We walked toward the sidewalk and silently melded with the growing ring of spectators and then headed north. It probably took two blocks of walking before we had reached an area where it was safe to speak.

"How can I help?" Leandor offered.

His friendship and support in this crisis was invaluable, and I told him so. I also asked him to keep his ear to the ground for any scuttlebutt or rumors about Ziegler's enemies in the gay community. I reminded him of the article in the *Advocate* in his apartment about the anger at Ziegler's closeted lifestyle. Given Leandor's particular lifestyle and vantage point, perhaps he could unearth more. Were there any specific ruling or action on the part of Ziegler that particularly enraged his fellow gays? Was there a Martin Zeigler "enemy list"? Admittedly, I was grasping at straws, but maybe there was some connection or at least a diversion from the "gotcha" momentum that was escalating outside my building a few blocks away.

"How about a place to hide from madding crowd? You can stay at my place," he volunteered.

My cell phone rang, and I held up a finger to take it.

"Great. I'll be right there," I said and flipped the phone shut. "I'm covered for tonight, but I may need to take you up on that offer in the next few days. Keep your ears open, my friend. But right now, I've got to go uptown a few blocks," I said and gave him a hug.

"Take care," Leandor called out to me.

"Thanks for being such a great friend," I yelled back to him as I skipped toward Fifth Avenue.

*　*　*

Alba was still in her business blues when I walked into her apartment. With her thin-rimmed glasses (a new addition since college days), it gave her a studious, bankerly appearance. Even so, her contours filled the outfit beautifully, creating a pleasing ying-yang effect.

"We're going to take a break from the Philly cheese steaks tonight," she announced. "I already ordered Chinese, and it'll be here in twenty."

"Mo Shu Pork," I asked, hoping for my favorite.

"Already in the works," she answered and moved to the kitchen, chucked two glasses with ice, and filled them with Absolut vodka.

I took my glass and clinked hers. "Alba, you were magnificent today. I swear, you were the only one in the press room that wasn't completely drinking the NYPD Kool-Aid."

She took a sip and shrugged. "I'm not sure the chief loved my question, but it had to be asked."

"To protect my ass," I guessed.

"Yeah, partly. But also to try to get this investigation focused in more fertile areas. Jackson, there's some crazy shit about this murder that is . . . unsettling." She paused for second after carefully choosing that word and sat down on the couch. She undid her bun, letting her hair flow with a headshake. Nice. After a sip of vodka, she continued, "The whole thing raises questions. And so far, I haven't been able to get to the bottom of all the answers."

"You were busy today," I complimented her.

"I spent most of the morning on Joey Roach."

It was not the pursuit I was dying to hear. However, maybe her research had unearthed something, anything new. I didn't encourage her to head down this blind alley, but clearly this angle intrigued her.

"For starters, he's not a photographer," she started. "I could see that."

"The guy has a violent background. Assault. Battery. Robbery. Five years in the pen. He's lived in tenant hotels and sublets since getting out of jail. And nobody knows where the guy is right now. It's as if he vanished off the face of the earth."

I shook my head in agreement. "I told you. He's gone."

"But I'm still checking."

"I really don't think you're going to find him," I said for what felt like the umpteenth time, in hopes that it might steer her in a more productive direction.

With a shrug, Alba signaled that she was unconvinced. She then took off her high heels and massaged one of her feet. She removed her glasses and rubbed the inside of the bridge of her nose. Then almost as an afterthought, she dropped a bombshell.

"You know he's gay," she said.

I was stopped dead in my tracks. Joey Roach? The man in the peacoat who gutted a judge? The smoking intruder who lunged at me with a switchblade? The guy I threw over the ledge? I looked at Alba and responded with more shock than question.

"No! That's hard to believe," I rebutted.

"Oh yeah. But not always. Like a lot of habits, he picked it up in prison. Or maybe he was always that way and never showed it before. Who knows? But once he turned, he never looked at a woman."

I tried to visualize the killer on Barrows Street, Grand Central Station, and the Dolan's open house. In every aspect, he exuded the persona of a macho stud. It just didn't fit into the stereotype. "Joey Roach?" I repeated incredulously.

The buzzer rang, and the doorman announced that a food delivery was on its way.

"Hey, babe, you can't tell from someone's appearance," she said. "Look at Rock Hudson, Richard Chamberlain, J. Edgar Hoover, Joey Roach."

I had to laugh at her uncommonly linked litany. And I had to smile at her use of the word *babe*. Hadn't heard it since Elmer Fudd days, but it sounded nice. She moved toward the door in her stockinged feet to get the delivery. I arose with my wallet in hand and demanded to pay.

"It's the least I can do," I gallantly said. "Think of it as Dutch. You bought last night. I'll cover tonight."

Over shared dishes on the coffee table, we swapped bites of our stir-fries and tidbits of this maddening day. I must admit, it felt good sitting across from a beautiful ally who implicitly believed in my innocence. Despite the hurricane of events and allegations against me, I felt safe here. She knew my history. She knew my inclinations. Clearly, she knew what I was capable of doing and not doing.

On top of that, she was just as intent as I was in unraveling the roots of mystery. After pinching a piece of my pork with her chopsticks, she asked, "How much do you know about this guy Lévesque?"

"Not enough. He keeps a low profile. But I would bet my last dollar that he's very implicated," I answered. Frankly, I was delighted in this new line of inquiry. It would be far more productive than chasing the dead Roach. I reached in my pocket and pulled out the napkin with the handwritten numbers. "I wonder if he himself had contact with the killer. I got these numbers off Roach's cell phone. They're the only ones I don't recognize. I wonder if one of them belongs to Lévesque or maybe all of them."

"I'll check them during business hours when I can find a live person to answer," Alba said and took the napkin. "Tomorrow's project."

She then went back to her Chinese meal and reached for the remote. After flipping through several channels, some of which featured live remotes in front of my apartment, Alba settled on a *Seinfeld* rerun. It was the one about waiting for a table at a Chinese restaurant and constantly being bumped. I'd seen this episode several times, but it always cracked me up. As a matter of fact, it was the first time I had actually laughed in several days. Wonderful! In the midst of this maelstrom, I had almost forgotten how good it felt to just relax.

"Fortune cookie time," Alba said after finishing her last bite of tangerine beef. She handed me a cookie and took one for herself. "Let's see if it says that you'll be completely cleared in the next twenty-four hours."

"Not likely," I predicted. Like a horoscope, my fortunes are usually rather vague. Sometimes, even indecipherable—like that last one I opened with Leandor that had read, "After the fall, you will feel spring." Of course, a few hours later, Joey Roach did fall to his death. And despite all the ugliness in the aftermath, I actually was feeling a little bounce right now in this apartment.

"OK, you first," I suggested with renewed enthusiasm.

She cracked open her cookie, read the contents, and laughed. "Wow. 'You deserve to be happy.' Sort of the blanket fortune of all blanket statements."

"Short. To the point. Can't argue with it," I agreed and then opened mine. Another cryptic one. "Picture yourself in a new light." I shrugged at its prescient message.

"Maybe they slipped in that fortune after watching the press conference," Alba quipped.

"Speaking of pictures, Ian Rockmore wanted you to send him that cell phone picture of Joey Roach."

"Already sent!" Alba proudly responded. "But I should make sure Ian received it." She then reached in her bag to pull out her buried cell phone. In doing so, she spilled out a few stowed items in the way—car keys, lipstick, and a bright shiny pair of silver cufflinks in a little plastic baggie. They were exactly the kind of gaudy jewelry that Rockmore liked to arrogantly twirl on the edge of his sleeve. I viewed the links suspiciously and then looked back at Alba, who was absolutely not flummoxed by this revelation. Perhaps she hadn't noticed that they had tumbled from her handbag. She seemed preoccupied with the purse's internal paraphernalia as she rummaged through the contents her cell phone. "Here it is," she announced and scrolled down the list of text messages. "Yep, he got the picture," she said and smiled at me.

I was still fixated on those cufflinks lying on coffee table. To my mind, they signified some kind of special relationship. Was it a regular thing? Was it an occasional fling? Was that why she recommended him? Was my brain now so accustomed to suspicious thought that I imagined nefarious motives, even from dear friends?

Without comment, Alba grabbed this debris and put it all back in her purse. She started clearing plates. She then pulled out my pillows and motioned for me to help her set up the sleeper sofa.

"Glad you met with Rockmore," she said cheerfully. "He'll help. He's a very ingenious, creative defense attorney."

I wondered if she was talking about the same Ian Rockmore I had endured earlier. The guy who wanted me to fill out a financial statement before meeting? The guy who looked like he spent more time on a treadmill than in a courtroom? "Creative?" I asked skeptically. "Hey, the guy looks like he spends too much time buying Ralph Lauren suits."

"That's just the legal look," she answered and continued to set up my bed linen.

"Well, he obviously has a high regard for you."

"That's good."

I couldn't resist. I did not want to sound like a jilted teenager, but my curious heart waded in. "Alba, this probably falls in the category of none of my damn business, but how well do you know him? What kind of relationship do you have with this guy?"

Alba puffed up one more pillows and looked me in the eye. "It's strictly a professional relationship."

I had heard these words before, out of my own mouth and also from Melanie Ziegler. On the other hand, Alba Gonzales was incapable of lying. It just wasn't in her nature to even tell a harmless fib.

"Jackson, the courtroom is my beat," she clarified. "I've reported on some of his trials and written positively about some of his courtroom strategies. Given his outsized ego, he would call that fair."

"Fair enough. Just wondering," I responded.

"Jackson Witt, if I didn't know you better, I'd say that sounds like a little jealousy."

"No, no," I scoffed. *No shit,* I thought.

She finished with the sheets, winked good night, and headed for her bedroom.

At the doorway, she turned around and caught me staring at her. "Is the mattress OK?" she asked innocently.

I nodded. Yes, it was OK. Not as comfortable as a big queen bed with a lovely warm body lying next to me, but OK.

"Good night, Alba," I said and threw her a grateful kiss.

Chapter Twenty-Eight

As Alba had predicted last night, I should prepare myself for a trial by media in the days ahead.

The morning newspapers bore that out. My picture was plastered on the front page of virtually every publication. *Newsday* headlined their article, "Person of Interest Named in Ziegler Murder." The *Daily News* screamed, "NYPD Identifies Witt in Ziegler Dlaying." The ever-clever *New York Post* showed a full-page picture of my real estate photo and dubbed it "Witt's End to Ziegler mystery?"

The *New York Times*, thanks to Alba, was the only newspaper that took a more measured approach. Her headline on page 3 read, "Police Report Progress in Ziegler Case." Unlike the other pubs, it contained a small two-inch photo of me, with the following cutline, "Jackson Witt identified as a person of interest as police continue to investigate additional leads." Under the circumstances, it was about as fair and balanced as I could expect.

In my local e-café, I read the other incriminating articles and barely recognized the man called a person of interest. Certain publications reported that I was evidently hiding in his apartment. One article suggested that, given my earlier acting experience, I might be capable of a dissembling denial or, worse yet, a costumed escape.

My cell phone rang. It was from Ian Rockmore.

"I called the police department, and they want to have a conversation with us."

"OK, I guess," I answered. "What's it about?"

"Pictures."

"Ah, Alba sent you the image of Joey Roach?"

"Got it, but this is about other pictures," Rockmore corrected me. "You and Melanie Zeigler together."

So the missing photos had been found. For a fleeting moment, I wondered if Melanie herself had leaked them. Or maybe they came from her new partner in alibi land. I wondered how incriminating they actually were and asked for a sense of how much to brace myself. "Seen them?"

"We'll see them together. Eleven thirty. Fourteenth Street station. And bring Roach's cell phone."

"To give to the police?"

"No no no," he emphatically reacted. "At least not yet. We need to review what's on it."

*   *   *

In the Fourteenth Street precinct conference room, we sat at a table across from the self-satisfied Detective Thomas Donovan, who was holding a manila folder. He explained that he would be handling this meeting himself since his junior partner, Tanya Washington, was busy with an assignment this morning. Selfishly, I wished she were there. She was the only one who could keep his passive-aggressive personality barely in check.

He placed the folder on the table and slid it across to us with one finger, as if he had a perfect blackjack hand. He then smiled smugly and said, "Read 'em and weep."

The pictures were pretty bad. Mind you, nothing naked, as Melanie had earlier feared. But all the same, rather embarrassing. Dozens of pictures of Melanie and me leaving different condos after "canvassing" the properties. A few of them showed more than an afternoon professional kiss on the cheek. One actually had her right leg entwined behind my left calf while we were occupied in a lip-lock.

"Would you like to comment on the so-called businesslike nature of this relationship?" Detective Donovan sarcastically asked.

"We would not," Rockmore answered for both of us. In the lobby, he had advised me to respond to no questions. He would answer if an answer were at all required. "Where did you get the pictures?" my lawyer asked.

"From a search warrant that took us to the judge's chambers," Donovan answered.

At least that, I mused to myself. At least it wasn't Melanie intentionally trying to nail my ass to the wall.

"We have other things to discuss, Mr. Witt," Donovan directed his statement to me as if my lawyer didn't exist and I was free to speak for myself. "From a subpoena of your phone lines, we see that you called Ms. Ziegler shortly after the murder."

Rockmore shot me a glance at this new not-yet-revealed information.

"It was a real estate call. Check the message," I protested.

"What else?" my lawyer signaled to me that he wanted out of this topic.

Donovan continued, "And once your pictures were in the papers, a deli man one block from the scene of the crime has identified you as a customer in his place of business near the time of the murder."

"OK," Rockmore responded like a poker player. "Anything else?"

Donovan looked at both of us and then directed his question to me, "Would you be willing to take a polygraph test?"

"Sure," I quickly answered, thinking it would exonerate me, at least in some eyes of the public.

"We will not," Rockmore jumped in. "No polygraph. Not reliable and not admissible." That assertive answer was partly directed at me. "I have three questions for you, Detective Donovan," my lawyer said with some steam. "First of all, have you had any luck in identifying a murder weapon?"

"Not so far," the detective answered tersely.

"I see," Rockmore smiled. "Two more questions. In view of your new photos and circumstantial information, are you thinking *A*, of holding another press conference? And *B*, are you thinking of changing your designation from person of interest to suspect?"

Donovan reacted to the questions thoughtfully, "Question A? Maybe. And question B? Probably not. As you know, there's no great advantage to us in calling Mr. Witt a suspect. If the situation warrants, we can move directly to charges. But we are not quite to that point yet. We're nearing it, but for the time being, no. As for a press conference, we do owe it to the public to keep them informed of any progress."

"And we have an equal right to access the press and provide an honest defense," Rockmore charged. "That brings me to my next question. And this one, Detective Donovan, is a critical one on my client's behalf. Are you in possession of a photo sent to you with a message that reads, 'This is your killer. I saw him do it'? And if so, why has that picture not been released to the press?"

"In a case like this, we have had all kinds of leads," Donovan finally responded after a few second's pause. "Some of them are wild goose chases. Some are—"

Before he could finish his sentence, Rockmore interrupted him, "I would not call a message that reads 'I saw this man do it' a wild goose chase, especially when connected with an actual photo. In the interest of full disclosure communication and cooperation, I feel the need to inform you that, on behalf of my client, I very well may reference that lead and that photo to the press. Consequently and until that issue is resolved, I would advise you to not escalate this any further than 'person of interest.'"

With this rebuttal, Rockmore impressed me with two things: The first is perhaps silly. I was amazed that someone could actually deliver spontaneous comments with complex sentence structures, as if it were prewritten. More importantly, I was impressed with the serious-as-cancer delivery. Rockmore was capable of imparting his hand with some fire and threat. Amazing! The game was on. Not so nice when you are the ball in the game, but at least my team had a real player who clearly knew how to swing the bat.

The two men had a cordial face-off. As was his custom, Rockmore was twirling one of his damn cufflinks while staring directly at his adversary. After a beat, Donovan responded, as he must, "That's certainly your prerogative in a free society, as the person of interest's legal counsel."

"Good day, Detective Donovan," Rockmore said and gestured for us both to leave. I actually began to think that perhaps that $800 per hour may be money well spent.

Chapter Twenty-Nine

"They have a case," Rockmore told me in the privacy of his office. He took off his suit coat and placed it on the back of his leather chair, revealing a pair of thin leather suspenders over his blue oxford dress shirt. "Let's see the mysterious cell phone," he said.

I reached in my pocket and carefully placed it on his desk. As he checked several phone functions over the next few minutes, I watched him in silence. He then continued hitting several other buttons and frowned. Finally, he placed the phone back on his desk and scratched his head.

"Not as conclusive as I would wish."

"It shows there was communication," I said.

"True, but nothing that couldn't be explained away. For example, when Ms. Ziegler sends messages about introductions, pix, and locales, they could be referring to a real estate transactions. If this language ever came to legal shoot-out, I'm sure her attorney would insinuate that."

Discouraged, I buried my head in the cradle of my hands. "What about the missed calls and the voice mails?"

"Can you open them?"

"Not without his password code," I admitted.

Rockmore shrugged. "Well, maybe we'll get lucky and find the guy, and then it can be unlocked. Short of that, I'd have to turn this over to the NYPD to facilitate that, and I'm not ready to surrender this evidence. Not yet. When they apprehend Joey Roach, the timing of these calls can work in your favor."

"What if no one ever finds Joey Roach?" I was beginning to get apprehensive that so much was riding on his miraculous ascension from a concrete grave.

"Doesn't make this cell phone useless," Rockmore gave me hope. "It suggests some natural curiosity on your part. If I end up serving it up correctly, it might even help explain why you went to Barrows Street that night. But we need to figure out when and where this gets introduced."

My lawyer then strummed his fingers on his desk and starting nodding his head yes from some internal dialogue he was conducting with himself. "It's time to communicate the alternative story line. We need to preempt the department with their press conference and maybe even prevent it." He then called out to his executive assistant, "Miriam, I want a 4:30 p.m. press conference. Let the press know. And can you get Alba Gonzales on the line?"

I was anxious to hear this. When Rockmore knew he had the connection, he picked up. "Alba, at 4:30, I plan to go on the offensive for our friend, Jackson Witt. At the police station. On the outside steps. It'll make for nice optics. I plan to reference the Joey Roach angle. Have you found him?"

I knew the answer to that question but couldn't provide it. After listening to her inevitable dead end, Rockmore jumped back on the line. "Doesn't matter. On behalf of your friend I need to float it out there and slow down the police just a bit. And you're the only one I know who has a photo to run in tomorrow's paper. So you got yourself an exclusive scoop!"

He then twirled his chair around with his back from me and continued his conversation with Alba. "Right," he said and then paused. "Right," he said again and listened further. "Wow, you're too good," he responded with some enthusiasm and encouragement. "Later," he concluded and swirled his chair around again to face me.

"She pretty amazing, huh?" he said.

"I think so."

"Evidently, Joey Roach is gay."

"She already told me," I responded as if I had bragging rights.

"I'm not going to reveal that in the press conference. I'll let her break that story. But that's definitely an interesting wrinkle."

"I guess so."

"Jackson, listen. In my press conference, I am going to have to admit that you and Ms. Ziegler had a relationship. But that's not a crime. I just need to diffuse those pictures. And while I'm at it, I need to hint at a credible other explanation. I need to plant some red flags and create some diversions—something that can get the press thinking that the police have other real suspects." After a beat, he confidently winked at me. "This is when it gets fun."

* * *

Miriam, the executive assistant, invited me to watch Rockmore's press conference from the privacy of his office. That's how I learned I would not be invited to my own defense attorney's press conference. It was probably just as well. I would have undoubtedly been the target of press attention, and Rockmore's objective was to send the attention in a very different direction.

In front of the Fourteenth Street precinct building, my lawyer began by thanking the members of the press for showing up. "My name is Ian Rockmore and am representing Jackson Witt, whom we believe has been unjustifiably classified as a person of interest in the Martin Ziegler case. My client is completely innocent of any wrongdoing, and we intend to fight this injustice."

It was a boilerplate opening that the press had certainly heard from many defense attorneys for many clients. However, it did feel good to hear a legal figure stand up and actually claim I was innocent.

Rockmore stood before the crowd, poised at the metaphorical mound, ready for battle.

"The very loose connection that has led to police to even name my client a person of interest is completely circumstantial and coincidental. There is no weapon. There is no DNA. There are no fingerprints. And most importantly, there is no witness."

I liked his Johnny Cochrane drumroll. However, Rockmore was only in the stretch. He was reading signals and ready to deliver. He looked around, checking the bases. "But there is a witness who has identified the real killer."

From a theatrical standpoint, I appreciated his dramatic pause at this point. Let the big news register. Give the news reporters time to open their notebooks, grab their pens, and make sure their microphones were working properly.

"I have it on good authority that the NYPD, thanks to their hotline, have been sent a clear photograph of this person, along with the message, 'This is the man who killed Martin Ziegler. I saw him do it.'"

There was a stunned silence from the press corps. If I were there, I could probably hear pens furiously writing on paper.

Rockmore delivered his fastball, "I have no idea why the NYPD have not initiated a complete dragnet for this prime suspect. Instead, they have erroneously implicated my innocent client. What I would suggest to the press, as responsible transmitters of truth, is that we get to the bottom of this mystery by finding the identity of the man in this photo and bringing him to justice so my innocent client can return to his law-abiding life."

It was a damn good pitch, but the press corps is not one to applaud.

Instead, they raised their hands and shouted out questions.

"I will take a few question," Rockmore said.

The initial onslaught was on a consistent theme. "Who is it?" "Can you identify the name of the man in the photo?" "What's his name?"

Rockmore, now the impresario for cameras, repeated the gist of the questions with mock respect for the difficult job of the NYPD. "Obviously, many people here would like me to name the real killer. I do not wish to usurp the job of the NYPD. It's their job, not mine. And I respectfully defer to their timing in this matter."

I liked this approach. It would force the NYPD to acknowledge and provide progress on this new search. I imagined it would also shift the press emphasis from me, at least for a few days.

One reporter shouted out a question, "Are you sure they have the photo?"

"I am convinced they have the photo."

"Have you yourself seen the picture of the man?"

Rockmore paused for a second. To the untrained eye, it looked as if he was struggling for how much to reveal. To the trained professional, it was a very good act. After a thoughtful moment, he came clean. "Yes, I myself have seen the photo of the man."

Whoah. Those pens and pencils were racing, and the microphones were definitely whirring. Nice timing, I had to admit.

One hungry reporter asked the inevitable question, "Can you provide us with a copy of the photo?"

My attorney acted torn by this request. As the self-appointed white knight of fairness, he appeared to be grappling with jurisdictional boundary lines. "I honestly believe the release of the photo is truly within the timing and purvey of the NYPD," he carefully answered. "I'd suggest you ask that of the chief investigators on this case."

Instinctively, I knew his response would have the right effect. It would force the press to hound the NYPD for more details on this mysterious image. Rockmore definitely understood his audience. Clearly, he knew that news reporters hated to be kept in the dark about key facts. It was automatic that this new lead would be their focus for the next few days.

There were a few more questions, including one about me.

"There seems to be some new evidence that your client had an ongoing relationship with the widow, Ms. Ziegler. Can you comment?"

Rockmore effectively brushed it aside, "We do not deny that. In their past history, there was a consensual relationship between Ms. Ziegler and my client. However, that is not a crime. And as far as we know, it may not be the only relationship that he or she had in past eight months since moving on their separate paths." Rockmore immediately surveyed the room and called out, "Next?"

It was another question about the mysterious photo. "Can you tell us when the photo of this supposed killer was taken?"

Relieved that the conference was back on topic, Rockmore gratefully acknowledged the question. "The question was, when was this photo of the supposed killer taken? Can I share with you the exact time and place? I cannot. Perhaps the NYPD can also provide that answer, when and if they release this photo and choose to fully investigate this heinous crime."

It was hardball.

"Thank you for attending and your dedication to finding the truth," Rockmore concluded and exited the scene.

Not too shabby. A bravura performance, I admitted to myself and began to better understand why attorneys like Rockmore got the big bucks. But I still didn't like him.

Chapter Thirty

"Late night," Alba said. "I've got a ton of things to check out and I've got to file an article by midnight."

"No problem. You go, girl," I responded into my cell phone, sounding atypically like a cheerleading rap star.

"Hey, I checked those phone numbers you gave me," she reported.

"And?"

"Nada. One missed call was from a pizza delivery place. One was from Blockbuster. Sounds like Joey Roach has a late fee. I'm still checking on that text number."

"Great," I said with some disappointment. OK, more fruitless cul-de-sacs, just as I knew the piqued interest in Joey Roach would ultimately pan out to be. However, it was definitely a plus that the New York media world would now be focused on this fresh lead. My smooth-talking sartorial attorney had effectively tantalized and teased the news-hungry reporters. It would at least serve as a pause in their obsession with me.

"The press conference was good, though," I added.

"Nothing like a new angle to get the press corps breathing."

"Can't imagine the NYPD is too happy."

"Livid."

"Rockmore handled himself well," I conceded.

"I'm sharing a cab with him uptown right now. Why don't you tell him yourself?"

Omigod, I couldn't help but imagine the two of them crammed together in the backseat of a taxi, basking in his latest moment of glory.

I could hear the cell phone being passed and jostled. In the background, Alba's voice could be heard, "It's Jackson Witt." After a beat, the lawyer spoke, "Right."

"Good job," I admitted.

"It's a start. But we still got a lot of work to do." I wasn't sure what he meant by *we*. He and his staff? He and I? He and Alba?

"Well, good job," I repeated. "Can I speak with Alba?"

Again, I could hear the ambient sounds of a cell phone being transferred. I hate to confess this, but I could feel a real rising resentment toward my lawyer's *bravissimo* performance. *All wrong,* I told myself. Both he and Alba were working on my behalf, just hopefully not side by side.

"Jackson, I can call my doorman, and he will gladly let you in. Because of this deadline, I'm going to be late," she said.

"Alba, I don't feel right about that. I don't want to get in the way."

"You're not in the way."

I struggled to communicate my discomfort. "I just . . . I don't know . . . I don't want to overstay my welcome."

"You're not," she protested. "And where would you stay anyway?"

"I promised to see Leandor tonight." Not exactly true, but I did intend to touch base with him.

After a few seconds, Alba responded, "Well, I don't want to twist your arm, but, Jackson, you are more than welcomed. My sleeper sofa will be lonely."

"Not tonight," I told her and wished her luck in completing her article by deadline.

*   *   *   .

I didn't stay with Leandor. He was out and about at some club, and I didn't wish to cramp his style, especially if it could somehow lead to intelligence on Ziegler.

The press had, at least temporarily, abandoned their stakeout of my apartment. I walked freely through the lobby, waved at my sheepish doorman, Javier, and headed up the elevator by myself. It struck me a metaphor for my life these days. Yes, I had some people in my corner, but I confess to feeling very alone, without many answers. When I opened the door, I stood there for a few minutes and wistfully viewed my once-loved apartment. I no longer felt comfortable there. With Joey Roach out of the picture, there was no fear of a midnight surprise. But his violating touches were everywhere.

Just as unsettling, the possible liaison between Alba and Rockmore surprisingly affected my mood. I say surprising because I was not really accustomed to this gnawing feeling of jealousy. Despite my multiyear flings with Melanie, I never really envied Martin V. Ziegler. True, he had some surreptitious flashes of passion, but he struck me a boring stiff and, now literally, more so than ever. Ironically, I didn't even covet the life of Robert Lévesque.

But Alba Gonzales and Mr. Cufflinks? It just didn't seem right. I tried to remind myself that I had no rights to her. After all, the woman was a grown-up, and so was he. However, other than his subdued giggles on the phone with her, he just didn't fit easily together with her in my book. Besides, Alba had struck me as so damn generous and helpful to me lately. It even felt like she enjoyed being around me. The whole thing didn't make sense.

To take my mind of this dilemma, I put on a Bob Marley CD and tried to transport myself to another place and time. I listened to the late reggae star sing, "Let's get together and feel all right." It normally put a smile on my face. But tonight, it didn't really work. Too many troubling triggers all around me. Just to sanitize my environment, I stripped the sheets and outfitted my bed with fresh linens. I still tossed and turned. Finally, fatigue took its toll. After about forty minutes, I did conk out.

The morning newspapers buoyed me. Most publications covered Rockmore's press conference and were vaguely critical of NYPD's inability to come up with the photo by press time.

The *New York Times* was the notable exception, given Alba's head start on the information. Her article, headlined, "New Mystery Man Revealed in Ziegler Case," showed my Grand Central image of the killer. It was a similar-sized photo as the one of me a day earlier. The blurb underneath said, "Joey Roach, the possible missing link in the Ziegler murder case."

Her story, undoubtedly filed right before deadline, contained a few threads of new revelations. "Roach, who had been convicted of assault and battery, was paroled from the state penitentiary earlier this summer after serving eight years. His exact whereabouts remain a mystery." Her article also contained the following tease: "According to reliable sources, Roach has associations with the gay community in Lower Manhattan, and speculation continues that this connection may prove useful in ultimately solving this case."

"Good work, Alba," I whispered to myself.

The only publication that gave scant coverage to the Joey Roach story was the right-wing slanted *New York Observer*. While it did briefly reference Rockmore's press conference, the thrust of the piece was on the new evidence that Jackson Witt had a simmering romantic relationship with the judge's widow. According to the account, "This supports the NYPD contention that Mr. Witt had ample motive and explains why Witt remains the only identified person of interest in this case."

The next passage stopped me in my tracks, "According to Mrs. Ziegler, Jackson Witt continued to harbor fantasies of a romantic liaison, which had ended long ago. This fascination with Mrs. Ziegler included frequent harassing phone calls up to and including the night of the judge's murder."

I couldn't believe my eyes and reread the quote several times. There was very little ambiguity about it. Obviously, the police had leaked their version of the case to a friendly source, the one law-and-order conservative newspaper in Manhattan. Even more disturbing, Melanie had just thrown me under the bus. Clearly, the new focus on Joey Roach had unsettled her team.

She had decided to fight back and attempt to throw the negative spotlight back on me.

I fumed over this damned lie. Finally, after a half hour of pacing in my kitchen, I decided to confront the issue head-on.

"Hello," Melanie answered her phone in a cheerful tone.

"Melanie, this is Jackson. Tell me you were misquoted," I barked. In the background, I could hear her whisper, "It's Jackson Witt." After a few indecipherable back-and-forth murmurs, she spoke again into the receiver, "Yes, Jackson. What can I do for you?"

"This morning, I read your quote in the *Observer*. Melanie, it's patently untrue."

Her answer was cold. "Jackson, I know where I was on the night of the murder. So do the police. So do many eyewitnesses. But as for you? Well, it seems as if you were down on Barrow and Hudson streets."

"I don't understand what you're trying to do," I answered. Inside my gut, I knew the answer. She now wanted to add fuel to the ring of fire around me. Her answer, however, was a little more tangible.

"What am I trying to do? I'm trying to get the phone back, Jackson. We want it. We can't reach Joey Roach. Nobody seems to be able to find him, but his damn phone with our conversations on it? We know you have it. We want it back. If so, everyone can go on and live happily ever after, including you. If you return the cell phone, I might be able to 'better recollect' that you had no contact with me over these past months. Let me translate that. For you, that means no motive, no suspicion."

"I don't believe this," I uttered.

"Until then, you have got to quit these 'harassing' phone calls." *Click.*

Chapter Thirty-One

"Did you read Melanie Ziegler's quote in the *Observer*?" I asked my attorney.

"Not surprising," Rockmore claimed. "At this point, it's every man for himself. And every woman for herself."

"It's bullshit!" I explained, with some exasperation.

"Of course it is," Rockmore calmly explained. "But the game is on. Come into my office. I was thinking about things last night, and we need to talk."

"You were working last night," I asked suspiciously.

"Quite late. But don't worry. I'm not going to charge you for every minute. I get turned on by this stuff." It was not exactly the phrasing I was anxious to hear. But I agreed to meet him in forty-five minutes.

The subway ride up to Fifty-seventh Street was my first venture into public transportation in several days. I buried my head in my collection of morning papers, hoping to become invisible to the late-morning commuters. I fully anticipated that the buzz would be all about the Ziegler-Roach-Witt case, but I forgot one thing: New York is a relentless city of personal self-interest.

"You know my boss, Carl Meecham? I think he's hooked on cocaine," one woman claimed.

"My wife confessed to having an affair last night," a middle-aged male voice to my right said.

To my left, I could overhear a young woman tell her friend, "Laurie is having an abortion today."

Under normal circumstances, I might be lured into these tantalizing tidbits of conversation. Instead, I fought the instinct. *Hey, I've got my own issues,* I told myself. I just didn't feel like broadcasting them to a subway car of total strangers. Of course, I didn't have to. Lately, the morning newspapers and news shows took care of that on a daily basis. Finally, I heard the voices of two businessmen commuters at two o'clock on my directional compass.

"You been following that Ziegler case?" one man asked.

"A little. I guess they got two suspects now, but I'd say that real estate guy is in a heap of trouble," the other voice with a southern twang responded.

OK, my ears did perk up. Hard to resist hearing some free speculation about my situation. I wondered what they had to say about the missing person of interest.

"Speaking of real estate, Marty just bought a new co-op on the Upper West Side.

Nine hundred and fifty grand. Can you believe it?"

"Where the hell does he get that kind of money?" the southern guy wondered.

"Kickbacks," the first guy suggested with a sly chuckle.

Again, I buried my head in my own stories and tried to ignore the personal gossip. Within a few minutes, I arrived at my Fifty-seventh street stop. Soon enough, the conversation would be all about my case.

After a few minutes of chitchat about the weather with the receptionist, she walked me down the hall to Rockmore's office. It looked as if he had been at work for hours, with notepads spread all over his desk. As soon as I entered, he raised his athletic body from behind the desk, gave a hearty handshake, and invited me to sit down with him at his round conference table.

"Nobody knows where Joey Roach is," Rockmore got right to point.

"It would make your life a whole lot simpler if we could find the asshole and have him squirm under police interrogation. Got any idea where he might be?"

I sighed, trying not to reveal my frustration with this dead end. I then shook my head and delivered my answer as flatly as possible, "As I told Alba, I think he's gone."

"So she told me," he said. I chose not to ask where or when. Rockmore, jacket off, twirled one of those cufflinks. This time it was an enameled jewel that suggested a mini golf ball. He then proposed what he surely imagined would be a positive ray. "The press conference yesterday may help flush him out of hiding."

"Nice job," I told him.

"Right, but there's still no sign of the guy. And as for Ms. Ziegler's comments in the *Observer*? Yeah, I read them. That's a good sign."

"Why? How?" I couldn't quite see the positive in throwing me to the wolves.

"It shows that she and her friend don't want the attention on Joey Roach. Obviously, that's trouble for them." He reached in his shirt pocket, took out a Chicklet, and popped one into his mouth. *So that's how he kept those teeth so white,* I told myself.

"I don't really think she's an intentional killer," I said. "But she sure wants me to look like one, at this point." Unfortunately, I couldn't quite reveal that the missing Joey Roach told me as much, right before he was impaled. However, I was still stung by her public attempts to discredit me.

"I know you don't, but it doesn't matter. One way or another, she's involved. And I'd say so is her new boyfriend. I hate to break it to you, kid, but Melanie Ziegler's relationship with Lévesque is a real one. And here's my theory: Maybe Lévesque hires the guy. Maybe your friend Melanie doesn't quite know the 'nature' of the hire. That's possible. Maybe they both have Roach's phone number. Maybe she gets anxious and tries to reach Roach. Maybe she's supposed to pay. Maybe Roach even goes beyond his actual assignment, to take it upon himself to kill the guy. Maybe. Maybe not. Depends on what Lévesque instructed him to do."

I let this plot sink in. I liked it and told him so.

"Yeah, but it's a lot of improvable maybes," Rockmore added.

"So if you can come up with this in a few days, why can't the police?" It seemed like an easy, logical question to me.

"Maybe they have," Rockmore said. "As a matter of fact, they probably have. They're not stupid. But the dots don't connect as neatly as they do with you. And with pressure to show progress on the case, you're still their guy."

"Yeah, but with the cell phone—"

"Not enough," Rockmore interrupted me. It doesn't speak to any motive for Lévesque. And let's face it, the guy has tons of millions, so he really doesn't have a financial motive." Rockmore then pointed to Roach's phone in the center of the round table. "Hell, he was careful enough to not leave any texts on Roach's phone. We don't even have any inkling that he knew Joey Roach. Lévesque is a careful guy. Slippery."

Understanding the truth of these missing links, I involuntarily released a frustrated sigh.

"But we're not done yet. Evidently, your gal Alba was working on the Lévesque connection last night."

"Evidently?" I asked and was rather pleased to hear the term *your gal.* Last time I had spoken with her, she was sharing a conversation with the very man across the table.

"She mentioned that she was going to investigate that after she got out of the cab. I think she may have had a lead somewhere in Hell's Kitchen."

"Good," I said for multiple reasons.

Rockmore left the table and started to collect the scattered papers on his desk, not so subtly indicating that it was time for him to move on to his next assignment.

"So what do we do now?" I asked

"We wait for Joey Roach to show up."

Instinctively again, I expelled a huge sigh of exasperation.

Chapter Thirty-Two

Leandor had left a text message on my cell phone. It read, "I have some answers to your questions."

I offered to meet him at his apartment, and by the time I arrived, he had a full spread of canapés on his dining room table, along with an opened bottle of Montrachet. He filled my glass, then his. By the stem, he raised his glass and invited me to join him in a clink.

"I get the feeling this is going to be good," I said.

"Could be. But first, it's just nice to see you and read about someone else's name in the papers for a change. Eat first." Leandor was consistent, if nothing else. He always liked some of the finer things in life and like the French, hated to mix business with pleasure.

"Taste that walnut Roquefort cheese on one of those crackers," he encouraged me. "It's to die for."

I chowed one down quickly and had to chuckle to myself. "Leandor, you think maybe we could discuss the subject of your text message while we enjoy this beautiful and delicious array of food you so graciously put together?"

"Oh, OK," he assented. "But try one of those crab-stuffed cherry tomatoes first."

I did. "It's great," I said. "Now talk to me."

"All right, first off, I talked with a bunch of my friends downtown and even talked with a few friends of those friends. Judge Ziegler had a lot of enemies in the gay community. A lot of frustration and anger toward this guy. Most of it had to do with the duplicity of his secret hetero lifestyle."

I impatiently winced. This was not news. As I told Leandor, I had already read about that in the *Advocate.*

"I know," Leandor nodded. "But there's more. Leandor took a sip of his wine and paused for a symbolic drumroll. "Brace yourself for this little tidbit. Joey Roach himself—and I have this on very good authority—Joey Roach himself was gay!"

This was his big revelation. Quite proud of his discovery, Leandor opened up both hands, searching for applause. He then performed a very theatrical bow.

I leaned back in my chair and sagged a little. "Actually, Leandor, I had already heard that."

"Oh, really," my friend quietly responded, clearly deflated that he had been beaten to the scoop.

"But I do appreciate the exploration," I quickly added and reached for another one of his specially prepared canapés as a courtesy. After savoring it, I said, "Anything else? Any other grumblings? Anything else that contributed to the distaste for Ziegler?"

"Other than his ridiculous gay-bashing court rulings? What an asshole," Leandor fired.

"Other than that."

Leandor popped a cherry tomato in his mouth and thought for a second. "Well, there was this one thing, and I don't know if it's relevant. But a friend of a friend told me it. Great-looking guy, I must say," he added as an aside.

"Fine," I smiled and gestured for him to continue.

"This one guy told me that he was pissed at Ziegler for the death of a Chelsea gay."

"He killed a gay guy?" I asked incredulously.

"No, not directly. Evidently, this guy was knifed to death about six weeks ago. Police never found the killer."

"What else is new?" I scoffed.

"This new friend tells me he didn't like the timing. He says the damn judge has one of those fund-raising, give-'em-hell speeches to his right-wing constituency. These guys are crazy idiots. You know that."

"I assume they can be."

"Two days later, this gay guy is killed. And this friend of a friend says that if Ziegler hadn't roiled these people into froth, maybe it wouldn't have happened."

I took a deep breath and rubbed my temples at this loose connection.

"Not exactly direct," Leandor admitted.

"No, what's this friend of a friend's name?"

Leandor just shrugged. "George. Or Gerry. Or Gary. Not sure."

"Who was the judge's speech directed to?"

"Don't know, but you can probably look it up. He didn't say."

I gave it one more try for something more than threads. "What was the gay guy's name?"

"I think he said Morgenstern. Adam or Alan. At the place where I heard this, the music was really loud."

"Did you know this guy Morgenstern?" I asked hopefully.

Leandor just laughed. "It's a big city, Jackson. And just because I'm gay doesn't mean I know them all. Hey, until yesterday, I didn't know that Joey Roach was gay. And now I find out that you already did. Sorry I don't have more."

There was no need to apologize. My big black friend was simply doing his best to help in any way. "Maybe there's something there. Maybe," I said gratefully. As Rockmore had told me earlier, all we had was maybes. I secretly prayed that this particular maybe could be some missing link.

"Have another one of those little tomato crab bites. They are really amazing. Not fattening either." Leandor proudly extended the plate to me.

I finished a sip of my wine and took one. "Delicious. Thanks, pal," I said and grabbed my coat.

Leandor gave me a big bear hug, waved good-bye, and said, "Toodles. Be careful out there."

*   *   *

There was an e-café down the block from Leandor's place. At this time in the middle of the afternoon, it wasn't particularly crowded, so I ordered a latte and paid for a booth.

I Googled Allen Morgenstern first. Not much there. An architect in Dallas. A sales executive in Asheville, North Carolina. A profile of an ad guy in Los Angeles. Maybe I spelled his name wrong. Alan Morgenstern yielded nothing better.

OK, how about Adam Morgenstern? I endured the same biographical runaround under this heading. Nothing about a gay guy murdered in Chelsea.

Perhaps Judge Ziegler's file would be more fruitful. Duh! Of course, it was. Given the nonstop news coverage of the slaying over the past few days, it was dizzying and clearly overwhelming. Trying to narrow the search, I Googled in, "Political contributions to Judge Martin Zeigler." After a few hits, I was able to find a public record list of larger contributors. There were about forty significant contributors. None of the names were familiar to me, but I printed out the sheet anyway.

Under a separate heading, "Speeches by Judge Martin Ziegler in June 2010." Several answers were revealed. There was one he had given to his Columbia University alma mater on Appellate Judicial Process. Not much meat there. There was one he had delivered to the East Side YMCA on Citizen Law. It amounted to a primer on the jury process and the boilerplate rights of the accused.

And then there was an address he had given to the Citizens of the American Way on June 16. It was a blurb from the *Advocate* that dubbed the group a "gun-toting and right-wing extremist group that had long supported law-and-order justices like Ziegler."

According to the account, Ziegler had excoriated the penal system for the early release of several gay pornographer dealers that he had years ago put behind bars.

"This lax attitude puts our entire community at risk, especially our young impressionable children," Ziegler was reported to have said. "It is this type of rhetoric, in this type of conservative setting, that inflames tensions between the nongay public and the largely law-abiding gay community," the blurb concluded.

There were no names mentioned of the released criminals. There was no cross-reference to any subsequent slayings. When the print out of this page was completed, I compared it to the judge's list of political donors. Yes, indeed the Citizens of the American Way were a contributor to the reelect Martin V. Ziegler's campaign chest.

Could this be a one of those "maybes" Rockmore had hoped to uncover? Probably not, I concluded. Especially since the events don't overtly connect to anything. It's difficult to criticize a man for addressing the very people who provided money to him. I then Googled "Citizen for the American Way murders." Nothing. Then "Gay Murders in Chelsea." Just statistics of violent crimes in every neighborhood of New York.

Egads, it's tough being a sleuth. I had new respect for reporters like Alba Gonzales who searched below the surface of government-prepared propaganda. No wonder so many other reporters simply published exactly what the NYPD suggested and accepted those talking points as gospel. It was too difficult to unearth any other angle.

Chapter Thirty-Three

The mayor of New York was on the six o'clock news.

After a ribbon cutting of a new Battery Park Bike Path, he was questioned about the Ziegler case and the Joey Roach dilemma. As the mayor walked to his car, he tried to reassure his citizens, "I really don't have a comment on the phantom anonymous photo of this new mystery man. But having spoken with the chief this morning, I just want to reiterate to the New York citizens that I have great confidence in the investigative work of the NYPD and believe this case is progressing nicely. That's all for now," he concluded and started to enter his dark-city limo.

"One more question, Mr. Mayor. Are you planning to ride a bike yourself on this new path?" another reporter asked.

It was exactly the kind of question a vote-seeking politician loves. He stood up again outside the car and surveyed the pathway. "I definitely will. It's a great outlet for recreation in Lower Manhattan and a way that we can keep this city ecologically green. And as many of you know, I'm a big supporter of a better New York City environment."

Well, that was that, I reflected, as I watched the TV broadcast switch to happy smiling families gliding their bicycles down the freshly paved asphalt. Obviously, the city did not want to amplify the Joey Roach detour, especially with no apparent clue of the man's whereabouts. I flipped the channels, saw a few more happy cyclists, and heard a few more reports that the missing man in the photo remained a mystery. And then Alba Gonzales called.

"Did you get a good night's sleep?" she asked.

"It was OK," I answered. "And you?"

"I was up late. Got the story in on time. My editor liked the scoop. Kudos, kudos. I chased loose ends all day—unsuccessfully, I might add—and I'm at my wit's end. I am not working late tonight. So when are you coming over?"

I loved her unabashed directness. Unless she was a far better actress than I ever imagined, it suggested no guilt or secrets. Maybe she just had a gift for compartmentalizing her romantic interests. Or maybe there was not as much between her and Rockmore as I had thought. I couldn't tell. Given my current unsuccessful record at "reading" people, I decided not to try. I just knew she really wanted some time with me. And hearing her voice, I felt the same way.

"Seven thirty," I immediately answered. It would give me time to shower, shave, and actually put on a fresh paint of clothes.

"See ya," she responded promptly and hung up.

I came to her place fifteen minutes late, just to allow her time to handle a last-minute work crisis or get delayed in the perpetual New York traffic jams. As it turned out, it wasn't necessary.

When I entered her apartment, she had already changed into blue jeans and a white oxford shirt—one of my absolute favorite outfits. Just to make matters more enticing, she was chopping garlic on a wood block, rubbed her fingers together, and pinched them under my nose. "Like my new perfume?" she kidded me.

"I'm not sure I would bottle it," I answered but did enjoy the fragrance of the tuber.

She opened the refrigerator and uncorked a bottle of Pinot Grigio and then poured two glasses. "I was thinking of your fortune cookie the other day," she said as she handed me a glass.

Oh yes, the little wisp of a message that read, "Picture yourself in a new light." I flashed on the picture of Joey Roach that might change my life and the pictures of Melanie and me that could do exactly the same thing in a completely different direction. Rather than reference either, I simply said, "And?"

"So here we are in a new light." She then reached over and gave me a sweet kiss on the lips. It wasn't necessarily a seductive come-on. But it was good, and it was as unexpected as Grace Kelly's smooch of Cary Grant in *To Catch a Thief.* I'm sure I looked as pleasantly startled as Mr. Grant.

"I forgot how much I liked being with you, Jackson Witt," she said and went back to her garlic.

I was so damn tempted to put me arms around her, embrace this new moment, and forget all my nagging questions. But it was an opening I couldn't resist. "We were in a good light once," I verbally tiptoed in.

"It was great." Alba cheerfully nodded while she chopped away.

"So why did you choose to break it off?"

I could tell it immediately struck Alba as a question with a very easy answer. She put the chef's knife down and smiled at me. "Because it was the absolute wrong time for both of us. C'mon, Jackson Witt, we were kids . . . with so much grunt work to do, so many long hours to work, so many hills to climb. And besides, you agreed . . . without a whimper."

"I was younger and stupider then," I said.

"Younger, yeah," she laughed. "But as far as stupid goes, your situation with the police these days pretty much still qualifies."

"Tell me about it," I sighed with a chuckle.

"I'm not going to. Not tonight. But I can assure you I had my whimpers back then." She then went back to her chopping board. I considered quizzing her again about Mr. Cufflinks but thought better of it. After all, she had already answered my queries about that once and seemed happy to be with me right now. Why break the mood?

Alba looked up again from her garlic. "Anyway, that was then. And here we are in a whole new light. And as part of that, I'm picturing you as my sous-chef tonight." She handed me a wooden spoon. "I don't want to eat out tonight. I don't want to order in. I don't want to talk shop really. You OK with that?"

More than OK. It would be a nirvana to get away from the 24/7 fixation on my predicament. I nodded at her suggestion and asked, "What are we making tonight?"

"Fettuccini alfredo," she answered as she poured the Ronzoni into a large pot of boiling water. Then she gave me a stick of butter in a large frying pan. "Low heat. Stir," she commanded like a language-challenged immigrant. I added the perfume of the chopped garlic, then the heavy cream. When it was reduced, I added the fresh-shredded Parmesan and whisked it all together.

Alba added the drained fettuccini and mixed it all together. With the addition of some freshly chopped parsley, it was a beautiful thing. Smooth and sharp. *Al dente* and creamy. Comforting and sophisticated. All the contradictions I could think of, including "I shouldn't be fantasizing right now," and "How can I resist?"

This looser, freer Alba Gonzales was not a total figment of my imagination. I recalled the same phenomenon from our college days, when she would pull all-nighters for an assignment or exams and then want to walk away from the pressure or, better yet, sleep away the pressures together.

"I'll wash, you dry," she ordered me after we had practically licked our plates clean. She rolled up the sleeves of her white dress shirt and rinsed the few pans and dishes. She threw me a towel, and I willingly obeyed her command.

In some ways, Alba had indeed changed. Put more accurately, she had evolved from a damn good core that was always there. Now she was a bit more professionally aggressive, but that drive was always there, even on the staff of a more relaxed college newspaper. She was more womanly for sure, but the jeans were definitely a throwback to the Temple University daily costume. They fit her well. For all I could guess, she was still the same size 4. Maybe they were the same jeans.

Once back in the living room, I took a sip of the Pinot and eased into work territory. "What time you have to go in the morning?"

"I don't. It's Friday, stupid. And tomorrow's Saturday."

Without my Stribling schedule and with all the recent twists and turns in my life, I had totally lost track of the days. They just seemed to blur together.

For the most part, it felt like a breakneck, nonstop journey of bumps in the road with no exit.

"No work tomorrow?" I asked.

"Slow news day. Rehash heaven. I will have to check some things out in the afternoon and file a story for the big Sunday edition, but hey, no shop talk tonight. Remember? You promised."

"I am definitely game," I concurred, without trying to overtly sound too suggestive.

"I'm in the mood for a movie," she announced and hit the remote button for her TV. It automatically opened to MSNBC. "Enough news for one week," she announced and then started surfing her cable options—CNBC, CNN, Fox. "Movies," she barked to the set and then finally arrived at HBO pay-per-view. She scrolled down the options.

I was definitely not in the mood for a crime story or police drama. An indie flick felt too heady for now. She clicked on the selections for comedy and musicals. Oh yeah, some déjà vu thoughts began to flood my mind. I remembered how she always wanted to watch reruns of *Evita* just for the music. At this point, I would probably watch anything, but I wasn't really up for long-gone *Evita*.

"*Mama Mia!*" she bellowed. "Ever seen it?"

I shook my head no, and she immediately hit the Play button. "Jackson Witt, it may be a little 'new man' for you . . ."

"Hey, I'm up for anything," I responded, again aware that it could sound like a come-on.

I would later hate to admit this to any man but Leandor, but I really liked this movie. I knew all the tunes. A mental escape to an island in Greece. Meryl Streep was awesome. It has a happy, happy ending. Along with it, the Orville Redenbacher microwave popcorn was outstanding. And so was the warm body of Alba Gonzales, who was curled next to me.

Over the credits, she nudged me in the ribs. "I love this ending where Meryl says 'You wanna hear more?' and then sings another Abba biggie." I watched Meryl and her friends. Then Pierce Brosnan and his friends, all in ridiculous multicolored feathered bell-bottoms, belt it out. It's hard to not like that.

"It always makes me happy," Alba giggled.

"And as the fortune cookie says, 'You deserve to be happy.'"

She nodded and looked at me.

This time, I did not miss her lips nor she mine. It was delicious and wet and wonderful and all-inside-tingly.

She turned off the TV set. I escaped the sleeper sofa. And that night, we were very, very happy. Together.

Chapter Thirty-Four

By the time I woke up at 10:00 a.m., the warm lovely and newly familiar body next to me was missing. From the slight opening of the bedroom door, I could hear the click of computer keys and see the streaming light of the living room area. I slipped on my T-shirt and boxers and followed the attraction.

There was Alba Gonzales in her terry bathrobe peering into her desktop screen.

"Hi," I sleepily said and announced my entry. "That movie was good."

"Yeah," she agreed. "Especially that ending. A very, very happy special ending."

"I'll say."

Alba got up from her computer and gave me another sweet kiss. It was a nice signal that last night was maybe not just an accident of mutual escape. "I didn't want to wake you. Figured you needed your beauty sleep," she said. She then gave me a love tap on the cheek and headed for the kitchen. "I got some coffee brewing."

"Scram eggs?" I asked and opened the fridge as if it were my home away from home.

"That would be great." She smiled. She poured two cups of java and filled mine with a little half-and-half, just the way I always liked it. As she sipped hers on the breakfast island, I kept the egg mixture moving over low heat to result in a creamy smooth texture, just the way she always liked it. I plated two portions and took a stool next to her. "What are you working on?" I asked, gesturing my head toward her computer.

"Guess."

"Me?"

"These are good," she nodded, referring to the eggs. Then she sighed. "I'm at a little bit of an impasse. No one has seen Joey Roach anywhere. He's disappeared."

"I know."

"And I spent all yesterday afternoon checking on Robert Lévesque. Not much there," she said and took a sip of her coffee. "That text message that you think he might have sent? It came from a bogus number in an e-café two blocks from his headquarters."

"Unlike the subways, I don't suppose they have surveillance cameras?"

"No such luck. He's a very private guy. Self-made man. No real brother or sisters. Dad died young. Put him through college. And then made zillions in New York developing high-rise real estate condos and apartments. Never married. Very eligible. No apparent dirt. A real success story."

"Not so glad to hear it," I quipped. I was getting tired of hearing his litany of attractive achievements from everyone. "Is his mom still alive?" I innocently asked.

"I think so." Alba carried her coffee over to her computer table and then brought a pile of her notes back to the island. She paged through her tablet and then paused on a page. "Yeah, his mother now lives in the Hamptons with her second husband. I think she remarried after his dad died. Yeah, she now calls herself Mrs. Walter Morganstern."

"Excuse me?" I put my coffee down and leaned in to Alba.

"The mom remarried and now lives in the Hamptons."

"Her new name?"

Alba looked down again at her notes. "Morgenstern," she said.

I held up my finger for patience and walked back into Alba's bedroom. In my pants pocket, I found my scribbled notes from yesterday's Leandor meeting and my printouts from the nearby e-café. As I scanned down the words, I stopped at one name and rushed back to the kitchen island.

"This is a little freaky and maybe nothing. But maybe not," I said. I then laid out the printouts to Alba. I explained my meeting with Leandor and that some friend of a friend felt that a gay was murdered because of Ziegler's inflammatory speeches. As I went through this Rube Goldberg maze of a story, I could see Alba eyes begin to glaze over. "But here's the interesting thing," I told her. "The gay guy's name was Morgenstern. Is the step dad still alive? Is he gay?"

Alba looked down at her notes. "Evidently, still alive and kicking in the Hamptons with Mrs. Morganstern nee Lévesque. So I assume he's not gay."

Damn. Almost a connected dot. I sagged and took another sip of the coffee. "Does Mr. Morganstern have any kids? Put another way, does Robert Lévesque have any stepbrothers or sisters?"

"That I don't know," Alba answered. "But I'll check." She put her dish in the sink. Soon, it would be time to get back to work and get some words down on paper for the Sunday behemoth called the *New York Times*. I could sense her frustration with a lack of concrete answers. I lived it myself every waking hour. But thanks to her, I almost forgot about my lingering mystery all of last night.

Alba walked behind my stool and then stopped. She put her arms around my waist and kissed below my right ear, which always drove me nuts.

"You know, until last night, I don't think I ever slept with a person of interest."

"Maybe you just forgot," I suggested, alluding to the fact that we had a history.

As she walked toward her bedroom, she turned and smiled. "No, I'd remember. Last night was new."

*　*　*

While Alba toiled away finding something fresh to write, I walked the streets of Manhattan, wearing my Ray-Bans and stocking cap for added anonymity.

Saturday was my normal shopping day at the Union Square green market. It is always a seasonal cornucopia of fresh fruits and vegetables for the restaurants of Chelsea and the Village. Farmers from as far away as Ulster County truck in their fresh produce to provide a taste of the country. On weekends, it tends to be a haven for all the foodies of the Lower Manhattan. It was a usually warm day in late October, and the sweater weather brought out a throng. After squeezing my way into one stall, I eyed the butternut and acorn squash. From the abundance of the selection, they appeared to be at the peak of their season. As I reached for one, I heard a familiar voice behind me.

"Mr. Witt," she said.

I turned around in my incognito outfit and saw Officer Tanya Washington. She was not in her NYPD blues. Instead, she looked like every other shopper in the blocks-long marketplace: slacks, sweater, even a recycle sack for freshly picked produce.

I walked out of line and found a small clearing before speaking to her.

"Trailing me?" I suspiciously asked.

"Not at this moment. We figure now that we've got your passport and you've got a lawyer, you're not going anywhere."

"Just here." I looked down at her recycle bag. "Shopping?"

"Every weekend. I live near here."

It's weird what happens when you see someone out of his or her authority uniform. They appear less threatening—almost like a real human being. After a pause, I made conversation, "I haven't seen you for a while."

"I've been busy trying to find Joey Roach. Thanks to your lawyer, they got me on that detail."

"Roach is a hard man to find."

"Impossible," she answered.

Given the initial reaction of the NYPD, it surprised and pleased me that, at the very least, they were chasing this lead. I suppose they had to, if only for appearance sake. It was indeed an impossible hunt, and I felt some guilty sympathy for anyone who was put on that trail.

"Well, good luck," I told her and began to walk away.

"Mr. Witt, have you ever met Joey Roach?"

The question stopped me in my tracks. I slowly turned around and looked at her incredulously. "Me?" I responded noncommittally.

Could she have seen me throw the body off the balcony? No, of course not. No one had seen anything. But why the question out of left field?

"I was talking to your friend, Mrs. Ziegler, yesterday and she suggested that maybe you somehow knew him. Or should I call her your 'former' friend?"

Wow. Not only was Melanie willing to cover up, she and her new boyfriend were also now willing to link the man directly to me.

"Did you know him?" Ms. Washington repeated.

It was served up in a sincere manner. Unlike Donovan, Tanya did not ask questions with a judgmental, accusatory tone. It sounded like she really wanted to know. However, my defense mechanism kicked in, as well as the ringing advice from Ian Rockmore. "Ms. Washington, I have an attorney now. And I really think it's best to have him with me for questions of this nature." Washington nodded, then looked around toward the playground. Then she turned back to me. "I understand. I know your attorney. Very clever guy. Smart too, and he usually has his own theory how things unfolded. At least with us, he keeps those theories close to the vest."

"Maybe that's his job," I answered, again defensively

"At trial time, yeah. But I'm just trying to get to the truth."

I looked at her cautiously, in view of dragnet around me. Given my previous contact with the NYPD, I couldn't help but think this was perhaps some kind of trap. On the other hand, maybe the Joey Roach lead actually got her thinking; I hoped she was having some last-minute second thoughts. But if so, why was I still in the hot seat?

"The way I see it, your bossy partner, the chief, the mayor, and everyone else at city hall is trying to nail my ass to the wall," I told her. Then I looked her straight in the eye. "And I didn't do it."

To my surprise, she did not scoff at my protestation of innocence. I am sure she had heard the same plea from every circled person of interest. But instead of laughing it off, she simply sighed and motioned for me to move closer for privacy.

"I'll admit this. The dots pretty much connect to you. And they may be enough for a trial. But then it becomes a jump ball. And between you, me, and the fence post, all those dots don't completely point in the same precise direction, at least not yet." As she said this, she again looked around for eavesdroppers. It felt like a Deep Throat conversation.

"Nice to hear, but it doesn't sound that way from the NYPD press conferences."

"I'm just telling you this, Mr. Witt. If your team has a theory or a lead, I would share it with us. Soon."

"Why?" I asked. In my mind, it was not my mission in life to make their job easier, especially since they were obviously trying to hang it all on me.

"Because we are under extreme pressure to resolve this damn thing quickly," she admitted. Then she exhaled a huge sigh. "You gotta understand. I love the police department. There are a lot of us trying to do the right thing. I just don't want us to look embarrassed if we end up charging the wrong guy."

I looked up into the air and thought about her advice. Of course, there were things we could bring forward, including the cell phone. But right now, our own theoretical scenario was still too fuzzy. Still too unsubstantiated. Still too many maybes.

"Think about it, Mr. Witt. It might help us. And it might help you."

Just then, a young voice called out from the direction of the playground. "Mommy," the young black girl screamed. "I'm tired of being on the swings." The little girl raced toward Tanya Washington and threw her arms around my interrogator-turned-advisor. "Can we go?" the young girl pleaded.

They started to walk away and then Ms. Washington asked her daughter to wait for a minute. The out-of-uniform officer turned back to me. "By the way, this conversation never happened."

"Of course not," I replied, as if I were being filmed in a spy movie. I watched Tanya and her young daughter walk over to the fresh corn kiosk and pick out a few ears. I had to admit that the woman's counsel surprised me. I always believed she was more open-minded than her arrogant partner. However, when they were together, they tended to present a unified, albeit disparately, dialed front. As I watched Tanya laugh with her daughter, I began to better understand the "good cop/bad cop" roles they must have to play in public, the NYPD need for a cohesive stance and the contradiction this can create in private.

I also understood that there were some internal bubbles of doubts about my guilt and a rushing desire to charge some real suspect. Without any further evidence, that would soon be me.

Eventually, I turned back to the acorn squash stand. I weighed a few choice pieces, along with Ms. Washington's advice.

Chapter Thirty-Five

Sunday was a ritual for Alba Gonzales. She liked to watch *Meet the Press*, *Face the Nation*, and *This Week* in remote control, channel-surfing fashion. It was not her particular beat, but as a news junkie, she truly enjoyed the opinionated, heated, round table arguments. The literate and intelligent jousts sometimes led to a raised fist, "yes" reaction—not so dissimilar from me watching a NY Jets touchdown.

While she flipped around on her remote, I offered to bring in bacon and egg sandwiches from the nearby deli and pick up the multipound editions of every New York Sunday newspaper. It would be a dishless "no wash/no dry" Sunday brunch for Alba and me.

Every news rag featured my story somewhere in the first section. Most carried the untraceable cell photo of Joey Roach and hinted at the fact that this mystery man was evidently unlocatable. Other than that, most stories reported that Mr. Jackson Witt was still the only identified person of interest.

As Alba hoorayed the George Stephanopoulos interview of Valerie Jarrett, the soft-spoken Chicago-based advisor to President Obama, I served her the egg sandwich.

"Fantastic," Alba said. But I wasn't quite sure whether she was responding to the egg sandwich or Ms. Jarrett's on-air comments.

After Wolf Blitzer's noonish recap of all the Sunday news shows, Alba killed the sequential TV talk fests. "What now?" she asked.

The Kandinsky exhibit on every floor of the Guggenheim seemed like the best option, so we went. Neither one of us were disappointed although any museum visit beyond sixty minutes tends to make me want to take a nap.

Rather than succumb to this temptation, we hit a Starbucks close to her apartment and carried two grande lattes to her place. "So how are you feeling about things?" Alba asked with some subtext.

"About what things?"

"About us," she answered with her usual directness.

I was in the midst of a Starbucks sip but immediately put the Styrofoam cup down so as to not look as if I was stalling for a dodge.

"I think you and me are fantastic and probably meant to be."

She put her coffee cup down on the kitchen island and looked back at me.

Without waiting for a response, I continued, "And I can't remember a time in recent memory when I have been as happy over a weekend as I have been with you."

It truly was not a rehearsed line. It just came out completely unvarnished, sort of like the Pierce Brosnan delivery in *Mama Mia*.

I waited for the stereo chorus of "Dancing Queen." But it didn't materialize. After a full minute of uncomfortable silence, my lovely Latina advocate and *amorosa* filled the empty pause, "Then we better figure out this damn thing."

She went back to her computer station to recapture her notes of the day. It was the move of a determined woman on a no-nonsense mission to identify the dots and determine how they might connect. As soon as he could read her notes, she recapped her summary of the situation to me.

"OK, we know Melanie is fucking Robert Lévesque."

"Check," I responded, without any old emotion.

"This new guy is a first-class prick, but slippery."

"Check."

"Somehow we think he must have set this thing up, maybe with her help."

"Check."

"But with a ton of money in the bank and no incriminating pictures, he doesn't really have a motive."

I paused and shook my head in frustration. "Unfortunate check. Alba, I gotta tell you, I like the more positive checks better."

"So we must find some plausible motive for Mr. Robert Lévesque."

"Check."

We sat across each other, stared into space, and waited for the other person to deliver a brilliant hypothesis. Neither one of us could. The black humor of the situation actually brought out a laugh on both of our parts.

"OK, let's go over my Lévesque notes," Alba said, finally breaking the logjam. It all looked clean.

"What about that gay condo?"

"I checked it out. It just seems like a new millennium business decision. Smart one too."

"And no brother or sisters?"

"I found something out about that," Alba said, turning the pages of her tablet.

"Right, no brothers or sisters. But evidently, the stepdad did have two kids."

"What are their names?"

Alba looked at her fresh scribbles in the margin. "Here it is! Anna and Aaron."

I let the name sink in and pounded the surface with my fist at this possible discovery. "Maybe it's not Allen Morgenstern or Adam Morgenstern. Maybe it's Aaron Morgenstern. Let's look him up!"

We both huddled around her computer, and I Googled the name. After wading through the Aaron Morgenstern bankers, artists, and auto dealers, there it was! "Aaron Morgenstern slain in West Village." It was just a short blurb from the *Village Voice* dated June 28. I compared the printouts from my Leandor meeting to check the date of Judge Ziegler's gay-bashing speech to the Citizens of the American Way, June 18."

I started doing a high-five victory dance all the way to the kitchen. "It's perfect. Lévesque's dear gay stepbrother is cut down as a result of Ziegler's mad speeches. So Lévesque gets even."

Alba had her hands in the air with a "whoah" expression. "It doesn't say that Aaron Morgenstern is gay."

"Would it?" I asked.

"Probably not," she answered. "But I can find out tomorrow morning."

"Great!"

Alba still had her hands up, signaling, "Not so fast." Ever the analytic journalist, she could clearly see a missing link. "Oh, and one more thing," she broke it to me gently. "It doesn't really explain Joey Roach. Why would Lévesque hire him specifically? How would he know him?"

I winced. True enough. But it still didn't dampen my enthusiasm. "OK, I'll give you that. But you've got to admit this, it does provide Lévesque with a motive."

"Check," Alba answered.

I reached into my wallet to find a business card. "I think we should call Rockmore. He said that if there's any new wrinkle—"

Alba interrupted me. "He's not going to be there, Jackson. It's Sunday. He'll be in Bucks Country with his girlfriend."

"He's got a girlfriend in Bucks County?" I beamed at the news.

'I don't know if she's from there, but that's where they go most weekends."

"I'm beginning to like this guy more each day," I said and put Rockmore's business card away.

Chapter Thirty-Six

Ian Rockmore had agreed to meet at 1:00 p.m. to hear what I described as an exciting new breakthrough. Alba had promised to join the meeting and told me over the phone that she had unearthed some news that corroborated our theory.

I could barely contain my enthusiasm when the lawyer invited us all to sit at his round conference table. His secretary had fresh coffee for all the participants. He had brought over a fresh blank tablet, and he himself seemed to psychologically sit on the edge of his chair. "I'm all ears," he said in an encouraging tone.

The story knitted together quite well, in my opinion. There was this bubbling anger in the gay community toward the judge. Ziegler inflamed it with a speech he gave to the Citizens of the American Way. At that moment, Alba opened her briefcase and placed some printouts on the table. She had found some of the more explosive quotes from the address and shared them with all of us.

"Go on," an intrigued Rockmore urged.

I explained that ten days later, a gay man was brutally slain. "But not just any gay man. A man named Aaron Morgenstern."

The name meant nothing to Ian Rockmore.

Alba clarified. "Indeed he was gay. And more importantly, the stepbrother of Robert Lévesque. They were raised together." Alba turned to me after cementing this connection. "I found that out this morning, Jackson." Then she turned to Rockmore to deliver more. "The two stepbrothers took different paths but were close when they were growing up. And he was family—family that, at least in the eyes of the gay community, was mowed down in the aftermath of Ziegler's reckless statements."

"So there! Big motive!" I crowed.

Rockmore nodded, smiled, and glided his chair out from the table. He walked over to the office window and let all this information sink in. When he turned back, he said, "It's good," and then walked over to Alba. "How much of this can you get in the paper?"

After a second, Alba shook her head and responded, "Not much. Right now, it's just a circumstantial path."

"But it's a credible one," I chirped in. "And with Joey Roach's cell phone, hey, it's perfect!"

"It's good," Rockmore repeated. "It's more than good. It can provide a plausible alternative story line for the trial."

The last word sent shudders through every bone of my body. "Trial?" I said, almost choking on the word.

"It could play very well for a jury, especially if there is a gay or two in the group," Rockmore confidently stated and twirled away at his new cufflinks.

"Trial? I don't want to go to trial," I objected.

"I'm sure you don't. Not too many people do. That's why God invented lawyers."

"Hell, I don't even want to get charged." I could hear my voice rising in frustration. My damn lawyer had already calculated that that's where this was going and was already envisioning a plot line he could dramatize to the jury in his summation.

"Well, I hate to break it to you, buddy, but that's where this is headed unless someone can find Joey Roach."

"No one is going to find Joey Roach!" I blurted and slammed my open hand on the table. The certitude of my statement created a reaction on the part of both Alba and Ian Rockmore. Almost like a Marx brothers cartoon, I could see their heads swoon toward me in what seemed like slow motion. They were both clearly startled that I was so sure. Seeing their response, I took a breath and kicked back into character. In a calmer tone, I attempted to cover my outburst.

"No one has heard a peep from Joey Roach. At least not yet. Everybody's looking for the guy. Every newspaper. Every TV station.

Even the NYPD . . . but I get discouraged. I hope he turns up. I really do. It would make my life a lot simpler."

Rockmore seemed mollified by my sincerely expressed wish that Roach could be somehow found. I guess he had heard similarly suspects wish for a miracle. He turned to Alba. "Does your staff have any leads on the guy?"

"Nothing so far," she confessed.

"Nothing anywhere," my lawyer quietly added.

It was my turn to push my chair from the table and make my argument standing on my own two feet. "That's the problem. If the NYPD can't find Roach, they'll want to identify another guy and call him the killer. Right now, their target is me. I get that. But with this information, it could be Lévesque. And that's why I think we should share everything we know with the cops."

From the expression on Rockmore's face, you would think I had just presented an unchanged box of kitty litter front of his nose. "I am really not in favor of that," he said.

"Well, I am really not in favor of being charged with a crime I didn't commit."

Alba jumped in, "What's the risk in sharing what we have? What's the downside in sharing our thoughts with the NYPD?" she asked.

Rockmore heaved a sigh, frustrated that he would have to explain his sophisticated strategy to such amateurs. He then tried to elucidate the intricacies of his advanced legal approach. "It destroys any competitive advantage we may have. It completely takes away the element of surprise."

"Don't we have a responsibility to lay it all out on the table?" she persisted.

Rockmore just shook his head at our Pollyanna approach.

"I think the police would like to know what we know. They're looking for leads too," I encouraged. It was not about to reveal my tip from Tanya Washington, but her advice was resonating, especially that part about doing it soon.

Rockmore again sighed at our naiveté. "Listen, kids, I hate to be the one to break the facts of life to you, but that's not the way this game is played."

"The game!" I exploded. "My life is not a game."

My attorney immediately backed off, apparently sensing that this type of description would upset any client in my shoes. "I realize that, Jackson. Poor choice of words on my part. I meant it metaphorically only.

But the fact is, we have no obligation to share our theories on this case with the police. And I am not prone to do so."

As he said this, he got up from the circular table and started to gather his papers as a signal that this discussion was over.

To use Rockmore's sports analogy, it was time for hardball. I decided to deliver it right down the middle. "What if I were to call the NYPD and tell them we have Roach's cell phone with calls on it, but my lawyer doesn't want to turn it in to the government?"

Rockmore quit putting papers in his satchel. He slowly walked back to our round table. "That's not a good idea," he solemnly admitted.

"Because they would most likely subpoena the damn phone?" I added. Rockmore did not answer my question, but I assumed it could happen. And it wouldn't look so good for an attorney to withhold evidence, even if it were a partially blocked electronic box of limited value.

"Let me think about this," my lawyer finally answered.

There was a standoff pause in the room. Alba filled the gap, "Ian, what's the worst that could happen? The police totally ignore our take on all this?" Rockmore nodded at this possibility, Alba continued, "If that happens, you can always hold another press conference—at which time, you explain our theory and imply that the police are ignoring these very promising leads. Wouldn't look good for them."

Rockmore mulled over possible next steps. "Let me think about it. Maybe there's a creative way to connect the dots." I wasn't quite sure what he had in mind but was at least encouraged that he had opened his mind to a police rendezvous.

"Let's see if anything turns up on Roach this afternoon," my attorney suggested, apparently praying for a Hail Mary.

"That would be nice," I said, again hoping to portray some openness to this nonpossibility.

When Alba and I headed down the elevator, I chided her on Rockmore's safe defense strategy, "I thought you told me this guy could be very creative."

"He can be," she answered. "And my guess? He will be." When we got to the lobby, she told me she had to get in an honest day's work, gave me a kiss, and headed off to the *New York Times* office.

Later that day, the NYPD would report no current sightings of the mystery man on the cell phone photo. "We do believe his name is Joey

Roach," the chief conceded. "But for all we know, he may be out of the country. And for that matter, for all we know, Mr. Roach may be a foreign tourist caught in a happy snap by some crackpot, who wanted fifteen minutes of police confusion." Obviously, the chief was now interested in diffusing this blind alley. "However, the department continues to pursue promising leads in directions we have already discussed and hopes to resolve this mystery swiftly."

An hour later, I received a call from Ian Rockmore on my cell phone. "It's time to share with the police what we think about the Ziegler case," he said,

"At 10:00 a.m. tomorrow. It'll be you, me, Donovan, and a woman named Tanya Washington."

I was glad to hear her name included. Maybe it was her eco-green shopping bag and impatient eight-year-old daughter. Maybe it was the fact that she was assigned to the mission impossible of finding Joey Roach. Maybe it was the honestly confessed concern that her beloved department could end up with egg on their face if they nabbed the wrong guy. Whatever. I had seen another side of this woman and thought that maybe she might be open to our case.

"One more thing," Rockmore added. "I've been trying to figure out the missing links. Would you be willing to talk again with Melanie Ziegler and, if possible, her new boyfriend Robert Lévesque?"

"Absolutely," I said. "Especially if it meant a better path for me."

"It just might," Rockmore said. "Jackson, here's how I read our situation. Some dots are there. But unfortunately, there is no link from Lévesque to Roach."

"So we still need to connect that dot?"

"Right," the lawyer answered. I could tell from his tone that he really hated having a situation like this one, which was not completely buttoned up. Missing links were frustrating for a perfectionist like Rockmore, who loved to have all his ducks in a row. After a beat, the lawyer admitted his insecurity about moving forward. "It would help to know if Lévesque hired Roach. Or even if he ever talked with him. It would help to have a message from Lévesque—any message from him on the phone. But as we both know, that's all been erased."

I did my best to reassure Rockmore of our secret advantage. "He doesn't know that. And neither does she."

Chapter Thirty-Seven

It would be an extreme understatement to call the meeting at the Fourteenth Street precinct statement interesting. Rockmore had warned me in the taxi that he would be unfolding our point of view in the sequence that he thought most advantageous to my defense. He advised me to not interrupt his flow. "Eventually, it will all come out," he reassured me.

In the police interrogation room, Detective Donovan asked if we would mind if this conversation were recorded. My lawyer shook his head. "Yes, we do. This is not a confession. It is a meeting of the minds to try to get to the bottom of this case."

Donovan waved a "chopped head" gesture to a small window at the back of the room. My lawyer asked for reassurance that this conversation was secure, and Donovan confirmed that status.

Somewhat to my surprise, Rockmore reached in his pocket, plunked the cell phone down on the table. He then revealed the train of events sequentially—the subway ride, the overhear, the temptation to explore, the witness of the murder, the cover-up, the snapshot at Grand Central, the subsequent ransacking of my apartment.

"My client admits to having a consensual relationship with Ms. Melanie Ziegler," he offered. "Right, Mr. Witt?" Since this was all too well documented in the press, I nodded affirmatively. Barely waiting for my nod, Rockmore continued, "However, this is a matter of past history. It was an eight-month-ago affair that has no record of any ongoing phone or physical contact other than the panicked night of witnessing a murder . . .

despite Ms. Ziegler's contention that there was no ongoing harassment, but we suspect that you already know that from your own investigations.

"Now here's where this whole thing gets a little trickier," my lawyer acknowledged. He then heaved a huge sigh and took a big psychological step forward. "Rather atypically of me, I am willing to share our theory on this case in the hopes you might be able to fill in some of the missing blanks."

This suggestion, so at odds with the usual adversarial relationship of defense attorneys, caught the attention of both police officers.

"Go on," Donavan said.

Rockmore outlined the intricate theory. He presented printouts of Ziegler's protect-our-community-from-the-depraved-gays speech to his right-wing support group, the subsequent murder of Aaron Morgenstern, the documented fact that Morgenstern was a close stepbrother of Robert Lévesque, the suggestion that among militant gays this might cause anger and outrage, and the revenge motive that Lévesque might have in participating in this crime.

While Detective Donavan digested this download, I stole a look over to Tanya Washington. Unobtrusively, she appeared to steal a glance at me. I couldn't quite tell whether it was intentional or not.

Donavan broke the silence. "First of all, Mr. Rockmore, we thank you for coming forward with your hypothesis. And you too, Mr. Witt." I assumed he included me in his compliment only as a sop, fully believing that the only matter that counted was that between the NYPD and my defense attorney. "It's interesting," Donovan continued. "It corresponds with some of our own questions and conflicts with some of our own theories. I would like to verify the contents of the cell phone and consider next steps. Can you please wait?"

Rockmore answered, "Of course," and watched our adversaries walk out of the room and caucus in private. Once they left, he turned to me and threw his arms in the air. "Well, we'll see what sticks." After a few seconds, he added, "But I must say, it does string together as a rather interesting scenario."

While I sat waiting in the conference room, my attorney paced. He also resumed that annoying habit of twisting his sleeve jewelry. "You like these cufflinks?" he asked me.

I really was not in the mood for small talk, but with nothing to do but stare at off-white walls, I glanced at his links. They looked familiar. I squinted and could visualize them strewn from Alba's purse on her coffee table some days ago.

"Alba gave them to me," he announced.

Whataprick, Iimmediatelythought. Itwasprettyeasyforanyone, including Rockmore, to see that I had some feelings for the woman, and I assumed he wanted to engage in a little joust of Alba's gift-giving generosity.

"I think she picked them up from a street vendor, with a nice little note saying thanks for taking on your case."

"I'll be damned, I thought. So the gift was just a gesture for my benefit! I immediately felt ashamed of myself for suspecting worse.

"Not really my style, though," Rockmore said with an eye roll. "I like heavier ones, you know?"

"I'll keep that in mind if I ever decide to wear them myself," I said sarcastically.

Fifteen minutes later, I got a text from Alba. I wrote back, "So far, so good," and agreed to meet up with her later. When I closed off the communiqué, I pointed to my cell and said, "Alba Gonzales."

Rockmore smiled and said, "You know, if it weren't for your girlfriend, I don't think I'd be here this morning." It was nice to hear the word *girlfriend.* I liked the sound of it. "How so?" I asked.

"She called me after our meeting yesterday and told me to quit being a prick, get off my ass, and get her main squeeze out of the hot box. Good woman," he said, pointing to my cell phone.

When Donovan and Washington walked back into the police interrogation room, it was difficult to immediately read their mood. Tanya Washington broke the drama and placed the phone back on the table. "The calls check out and correspond with our Verizon record of incoming calls to this number. So that's good. Wish you had brought it in sooner."

Rockmore just shrugged. I'm sure he felt it was already above and beyond the call of duty to surrender this crucial piece of defense to the cops.

Detective Donovan then looked at both of us and took hold of the meeting. "First of all, we appreciate you coming forward with your point of view. I must emphasize that you, Mr. Witt, are still a person of interest to us in connection with this case. However, your cooperation is meaningful to us." He then cleared his throat and more directly addressed our proposed scenario. "Since you have both taken the unusual step of sharing your alternative theory, I would like to discuss that and perhaps, to the extent possible, share with you some issues we have and some of the roadblocks we have hit.

It may surprise you, but we have drilled in some of the same areas."

He then ticked off the points of agreement. Ziegler's secret gay lifestyle. The antipathy toward him in the gay community. Joey Roach's gay status. Joey Roach's mysterious absence. To my surprise, they were also aware of Ziegler's inflammatory speech and the resulting murder of several gays, including Aaron Morgenstern.

"But the connection of Morganstern to Lévesque is new and damn interesting," Donovan admitted. He then looked at Rockmore. "As I'm sure you already calculated before bringing us this fact, it would probably also be damn interesting to a jury."

"I would think so," my lawyer said.

"We do not think Melanie Ziegler orchestrated this thing. She's too sloppy and not calculating enough," Donovan said. "Otherwise, she wouldn't have had her multiyear fling with you, which everyone in the Stribling office knew about." I took his shot like a man.

Tanya Washington added her own spin, "And she wouldn't have entered into another romantic liaison with Lévesque . . . which everyone but you, Jackson, evidently knew about."

"So that leads us to Lévesque," Donovan said. "Thanks to your research, he now has a motive. But what remains are two dots that are not easy to connect. First of all, he has a rock-solid alibi at the time of the murder. And second—even more important—he has no direct link to Joey Roach. With all due respects, Joey Roach's cell phone is of limited value. It can implicate Melanie Ziegler since her text messages still are intact, but none of Lévesque's actual calls to this number."

"Do you know that Lévesque actually called this particular cell phone?" My lawyer asked. It evidently struck him as new important evidence.

Washington brought forward some Verizon printouts. "As part of our investigation, we subpoenaed your phone records, Mr. Witt, and those of

Melanie Ziegler and Robert Lévesque. She texted Roach and called a few times. And Lévesque himself called the number a few times."

"But all his messages are now erased," Donovan said. "Without his voice on the phone, it doesn't really prove anything."

My lawyer had already warned me that the cell phone had marginal value. However, now we knew that the real estate mogul/lover/conspirator had actually called the number.

"I wish we had Joey Roach to confess the content of Lévesque's calls or at least Lévesque's voice on the phone," Washington said, showing some slight frustration at her attempts to locate the missing man.

I couldn't help her on the first point but could address the second.

"They don't know what's on that phone and what is not," I said. "Melanie assumes it has everything. And I would suppose that Lévesque fears the same thing."

I could tell that the tantalizing possibility of this confusion was attractive to all the participants in the room, including Ian Rockmore.

"May I have a private caucus with Mr. Witt?" my lawyer asked. Thirty minutes later, after a private sidebar, creatively exhilarating discussion, Rockmore delivered a proposal to the NYPD.

"My client has agreed to my making an unusual proposal to the NYPD. He will willingly have a conversation with Melanie Ziegler and, if possible, Robert Lévesque to advance our new suspicions, which I believe we all share. In addition, he is willing to have this conversation wired. In consideration for this privilege, we ask that he be declassified as a person of interest and reclassified as a cooperating witness."

Donovan was clearly jolted by the proposal. "You think they would meet with you?" he asked skeptically.

"Yeah, if I told them I would give them the damn cell phone. I think so.

I'm pretty sure Melanie would agree. I'm not so sure Lévesque would."

"And you'd agree to be wired?" Ms. Washington asked.

"As long as they couldn't easily see it," I quipped sarcastically.

I could sense that the proposal made Donovan uncomfortable. Given the pressure of the press, the mayor, and his chief, it would be difficult for him to walk away from me as a convenient person of interest. And yet, his struggling pause suggested that he now had doubts about guilt or at least my ultimate conviction.

"Boss, it's worth a shot," Tanya encouraged him, and I could have kissed her for her courage.

After a few more seconds, Donovan responded, "Here's what I'm willing to agree to. If you can in fact get Lévesque to say something that's useful, I'll accede to your request," he said, referring to Rockmore's proposition. He then looked at my lawyer. "But I won't do so until the conversation takes place. Until then, your client must remain a person of interest."

My lawyer looked at me. "You think you can get Lévesque?"

"I'm for damn sure going to try," I answered.

"It would help to have Joey Roach tell him to do it."

"That would be ideal," I agreed and had, in the back of my mind, an idea to make that happen. After a beat, Ian Rockmore stood up and extended his hand to Detective Donovan. "That's a deal," he said.

Taking that as an example, I stood up and extended my hand to Tanya Washington, who whispered to me, "You did the right thing."

Chapter Thirty-Eight

Alba was pleased to hear the outcome of the police summit. She had ordered some sushi and opened a bottle of Chablis, which tasted particularly crisp after my long hard day of it.

"Thanks for lighting a fire under Rockmore." I toasted her.

"He just needed a nudge." She smiled. "Besides, if it all blew up, the idea of having a jam-packed Ian Rockmore press conference where he blasted the police for incompetence did appeal to the man's ego."

"I imagine so. I could see him impeccably attired in his lawyer duds with a shiny new pair of cufflinks, holding court."

The reporter in her was interested in the complete play-by-play of the day's proceedings. I was glad to comply, including the sidebar conversation where he encouraged me to wear a wire. I explained to her that Rockmore liked the element of surprise in this proposal and figured it could give him some negotiating power with the police to potentially reclassify me as a cooperating witness. "It was a pretty creative proposition," I admitted. "And it seemed to work"

"Provided you can get both of them to sit down with you and say something juicy," she added with a note of caution.

I was fairly confident that it would happen. After all, neither of them would want this damn phone on the loose, and Melanie at least suspected—no, I daresay she knew—that I had the cell in my possession. "She'll meet," I boasted.

"But I'm not so sure Lévesque would agree to such a meeting. He's a very careful guy, and he doesn't know you quite like your dear old friend."

It was a risk, I acknowledged. It was a snap for me to envision the phone call to Melanie—I've got the cell, you want it back, let's meet and make it happen. In my tummy, I did fear that enticing Lévesque to join us might be more challenging.

As an exercise, Alba agreed to dress-rehearse my entreaty to him. It was reminiscent of our times together at Temple University where she would run lines for me for in preparation for college theater productions. In this case, we did it as an improv, with her playing the skeptical, reluctant Robert Lévesque.

It was a ragged rehearsal. Admittedly, I sounded a little desperate for the meeting. We ran the improv exercise a few more times, and it marginally improved until Alba, as Lévesque, posed a question I couldn't easily answer. "Why would you be willing to part with the phone?"

"Why? Why?" I repeated, stalling for time.

Alba as Lévesque then magnified this snag. "Yeah, why? As far as I can tell, that's your only alibi. So why would you offer to give it up?"

Yikes! It was a damn good question. It wouldn't play so well to admit that I wanted to unload the phone so I could get off the hook and place him firmly on it.

For the next half hour, we brainstormed possible motivations for me. All of them sounded self-serving and perhaps even suspicious. Alba was right. Lévesque was a smart, cautious man. Most likely, he would never agree to meet with me if he whiffed that it was some sort of trap.

"You've got to convince the guy that you no longer want the phone. Better yet, let him think it's dangerous for you to hold on to it. And make him believe you don't want to turn it into the police," she summed up the puzzle.

Under the circumstances, the best pretext we could invent was this: according to the yarn, I would now have a rock-solid alibi. My friend, Leandor Montgomery, would vouch for the fact that I was having quick drink with him in his apartment around the corner at the time of the murder. My lawyer believed the excuse would hold. And the damn phone, at this point, just got in the way of that alibi. Its presence would suggest that I had a reason to be right there, smack dab at the scene of the crime. So I wanted to get rid of the phone. And I thought they should have it.

"Think it would play?" I asked.

"Maybe. I don't know," Alba honestly answered. "I sort of hate using Leandor this way."

"I'm not asking him to actually verify all this. I'm just trying to make up a story to get that asshole Lévesque to come to the table."

"What if Lévesque decides to check out this bullshit with the cops?" Alba countered.

"That's a risk," I confessed. "But I would think it's unlikely, especially if he's leaning at all to have this clandestine meeting. Besides, he will want his calls back. I just need him to feel enticed to be there."

"You know what would entice Lévesque the most?" Alba countered. "If he felt Joey Roach was about to come out of hiding. That would scare the shit out of him, and he would definitely want to get his mitts on that phone."

"I know it would," I agreed. "But I don't see Joey Roach coming out of hiding in the next twenty-four hours." Of course, she was right. Any threat of Joey Roach's reappearance would compel both Melanie and Lévesque to come to the table and claim the merchandise. But the chances of that happening were nil. At least, in a true physical way.

Alba and I ran further improv rehearsal of my imaginary Lévesque phone conversations for the next twenty minutes or so. To my ear, it sounded convincing. To Alba's ear, it sounded like a possible, plausible "maybe." She was always a tough critic, and I took that as encouragement.

"'Maybe' may be enough." I sighed.

"I hope so," she responded and raised her glass of Chablis to wish me well on my phone solicitations tomorrow. "I really do hope so," she underscored and started to clean up our sushi dishes.

As she did so, I mentally checked off a litany of things I would need to put into place tomorrow. Already, I could envision it as a daunting day. As I watched her dump our Styrofoam plates into her trash, I couldn't help but thank whoever was up there for Alba's reentry into my life. Rockmore had appraised her correctly: indeed, she was a good woman. If it weren't for her, I would have entered into a Lévesque conversation overly confident and half-assed.

As soon as she rejoined me in the living room, she further reinforced my admiration for her. "You've got a lot to deal with tomorrow. But as for tonight, let's go to bed."

We did. And once again, it was everything I could have ever fantasized about—including and exceeding those long-ago trysts with what's-her-name Zeigler.

Chapter Thirty-Nine

As soon as Alba kissed me good-bye for another morning in the journalistic salt mines, adrenaline snapped me into action. I arranged an 11:00 a.m. meeting with Leandor in his apartment. "No food necessary," I advised him. I could instantly tell that this lack of tapas/appetizer/hors d'oeuvres was a disappointment to my gay theatrical friend. "I can do a little minispread," he pleaded.

"No time," I demurred.

"It would be no trouble. As a matter of fact, it would be my pleasure."

I cut off his gourmet temptations. "Leandor, I really need your help today.

Do you still have your la-di-dah recording equipment in house?"

"Somewhere," Leandor answered. "Are you sure you don't want some caviar? Smoked salmon? Eggplant spread on rice crackers? Rather healthy," he suggested.

"I'm not obsessed with health these days," I engaged back. "Just get your recording and mixing equipment ready to go, and I'll be there at eleven."

After clicking off, I called my attorney. I told him I would be inviting Ziegler and Lévesque to a lunch tomorrow at the Tavern on the Green. Thanks to Alba's caution, I informed him that enticing Lévesque to attend was problematical. He was not pleased with this prediction. "That's part of the deal," he reminded me.

"I realize that," I responded like a man on a mission. "That's why I need the following things from you and the NYPD. First of all, I need the exact time of Lévesque's phone calls to Roach."

"They'll give you that," Rockmore advised me.

"I will need Lévesque's direct cell phone number. I think he needs to hear my voice inviting him."

"Mmm, probably so," my lawyer avowed. "It would probably make contact with him easier, and I'd anticipate the NYPD would agree."

"Fine. I'm counting on you to make it happen," I ordered like a general.

"And now . . . a rather tricky but critical request. I need the NYPD to reactivate Joey Roach's phone so that I can make an outgoing call from that number."

There was a pause. I expected it.

"That's not so simple, Jackson. I hate to remind you, but according to the police, you are still a person of interest."

"I appreciate that, Ian," I responded almost like a lawyer. "But here's the truth.

You are an amazingly creative attorney with a gift for negotiation. I trust that you can make it happen." From enough conversations with Alba, I knew that vanity would appeal to him and was not above employing it in this important instance. "If I can make a call from Roach's cell phone, I am convinced Lévesque will attend the lunch. If I am unable to do so, I think there's a good chance he's a no-show. That's not good for me, for you, or for the NYPD."

After a way-too-long pause, Rockmore answered, "You think I'm that good?"

If there were a camera on the other side of the phone, it would have captured my exasperated roll-my-head-around frustration at this arrogant response. With well-acted enthusiasm, I replied, "Yes, you are that good."

"Well, I'll see what I can do. Will you be on your mobile?"

"Definitely. Call me," I said and clicked off.

I immediately went to my apartment to make the easy phone call. I explained my new Leandor-based rock-solid alibi and my desire to give up the phone. Melanie instantly agreed to meet with me at the Tavern on the Green.

"I am glad you came to your senses on this thing," she said. "And yes, I'll try to make sure Robert is with me."

"Would you please confirm that?" I responded like a concierge.

"I will, but I don't really anticipate a problem," she answered.

Maybe Tanya Washington was wise. Maybe Melanie was too just too dumb or simple or uncalculating to figure out the grand scheme here. However, at this point, I refused to be seduced by this naiveté. "Melanie, dear. You just make sure your friend Robert is there to accept the phone. And if there's any snag, call me on my cell. You remember it, I'm sure." I chose not to twiddle my thumbs or wait for a response I fully expected. Instead, I unplugged my "you have messages" landline telephone and headed for Leandor's place.

The first incoming call rang in my taxicab ride downtown. It was from my lawyer. "The answers to your questions are yes, yes. And thanks to my reassurances that the damn phone would be returned again tomorrow, a reluctant yes."

"You're amazing," I gushed. In the process of all this, I began to understand how the game is played, as my attorney once said. If you didn't have the goods to punish your opponent, it was all about praise and suck-up tactics. In retrospect, this shouldn't have been such a surprise to me. I had learned it in my early acting days in Manhattan when I craved an agent. Without power, I would have probably gushed about any Mr. Big's smarts, looks, and creativity just to get an advantage. Now, clearly, I was willing to do the same to gain that same advantage, albeit with more on the line.

"Here's what I want you to do, Ian," I confidently commanded rather like Jason Bourne in one of his many movies. "Messenger that material up to me at the following address: 558 Hudson Street. Attention, Leandor Montgomery. ASAP." After a second, I asked if he had that address and my sense of urgency. "Yes," Rockmore said, and I clicked off as if it were a filmed cliffhanger.

Ten minutes later, another call registered on my cell. "Yes, Melanie," I answered, reading the printout of her number. "I will meet with you tomorrow. But just me. Robert says I should handle this. So 1'll see you at one o'clock," she asked encouragingly,

"No," I gruffly responded. "Unless your new boyfriend comes, I'm not going to meet with you."

"Jackson, c'mon. Life moves on. It's too late to be stupid about these things," she responded, thinking it was all about jealousy.

"I'm calling your buddy, Lévesque. And if he cares about you one iota, he will be there tomorrow." I then dramatically closed my cell phone, quite pleased with my renewed grasp of dramatic tension.

* * *

Leandor protested that I was so unwilling to partake in the special pot stickers he had ordered from the local gourmet Chinese emporium. "It's just a little bite of heaven," he offered on a tray as I entered his apartment.

"Fine," I conceded, devoured one, but quickly pivoted to my immediately needs at hand. "Leandor, I need your expertise quickly and professionally. You've got all this fancy recording equipment here, and I wonder if you can edit and mix a recording for me."

"Sure. What? A little pre-Thanksgiving message for your friends?"

"Well, not exactly. Joey Roach? Robert Lévesque? I would hardly call him them friends."

"Ohh, juicy, juicy." Leandor winked at me. He was always a man who loved a drama, and this assignment promised to provide one. "What do you have? A CD? A tape?"

"A phone message," I answered.

All that advice from Alba, Rockmore, Donovan, and Washington had registered with me. The key to enticing Lévesque to come to the table was to have Joey Roach reappear. Since the chances of that actually happening were zero, I had a plan to create the next best thing: bring him to life through a carefully edited recording.

I explained to Leandor that if I got lucky, I might not need it. Perhaps I could convince Lévesque to meet with my own persuasive skills. But given Lévesque's first refusal, I doubted it. "If the guy continues to resist, this has to be my trump card—a gruff personal phone call from Joey Roach telling him to meet with me.

"Let's hear what you got," Leandor said.

I plugged in the home phone and message machine I had brought from my apartment. I knew it was message no. 5. As I advanced through the first few messages, I glanced at Leandor. "Don't let me erase it. Wouldn't that be the shits?"

"You're doing fine," Leandor encouraged me.

When I got to the fifth message, I paused the button. I looked over to Leandor to make sure he was ready to digest it and envision edits. He motioned to me to let 'er rip, so I played it.

"Hello. Hey, Jackson Witt, you fucking asswipe. This is Joey Roach.

I don't know how you got it. But one way or another, I'm gonna get . . . that . . . fucking . . . phone. You hear me? You ain't gonna know from where or when, but I'm coming after it. A little birdie let slip who you are. And now I know where you live. If You get in the way, I'm coming after you. So play ball now. Don't be a dumbshit." Leandor listened intently and cringed. "That is one nasty motherfucker."

"He's not a sweetheart," I agreed, consciously referring to him in the present tense. I hadn't heard the message in a few days but was again impressed by just how guttural and menacing he was. Roach was a dangerous stalker, but at least he would no longer be threatening anyone. It's not that I felt I deserved a gold star for tossing him to him death. But the man was, after all, a very bad guy. The other thing that flooded my mind upon rehearing the taped message: Melanie Zeigler's irresponsible revelation in identifying me as Toulouse-Lautrec. It was a turning point. From that moment, I had to admit she was quite complicit in framing me. Mind you, all these emotions raced through my brain in a matter of seconds. I immediately tried to quell them because Leandor and I really did have work to do.

"Let me hear it again," Leandor requested. I rewound and replayed the message. Then I did it again and again.

"The quality is not so good," Leandor warned me.

"I don't know that that matters," I countered. "It's not for goddamn *West Side Story* on Broadway."

"Granted," Leandor nodded.

"Can you get rid of all that shit aimed directly at me and make it sound like an urgent appeal to Lévesque to meet with me?"

"I think so," Leandor said. I raised my fist in the air like a triumphant tennis star who just served an ace. I knew my friend could make magic out of nothing and applauded his answer for encouragement.

"First, let me get a recording of your recording," he said. He started connecting wire after wire, checked sound levels, treble, bass, and timber, and put a new disk in his own gizmo equipment. He then played the Joey Roach message several times while a blinking red Record light flashed.

"Now it's time for surgery," Leandor said. "Why don't you entertain yourself with some pot stickers while I conduct this operation?" I took this hint to get out of his hair and lingered by his island while I overheard the ugly rewinds of Joey Roach's threatening call—snipped here, paused there. Replayed again and again.

"Come take a listen," Leandor eventually invited me back to his operating theater. Like an artist about to unveil his experimental creation, my friend raised a finger for patience and then lowered that same digit to hit the Play button and reveal the revised phone call.

"It sounds great," I said.

"I can hear the splices," Leandor frowned. "I want to add some ambient sounds, like maybe a bus or New York street sounds . . . like it's coming from Forty-second Street."

"You don't have to go overboard," I cautioned.

"I'm not. But it'll mask the edits."

Leandor sampled several sound effect tracks he had in his system. Eventually, I heard him say yes and saw that blinking red Record button again. After hearing it in headphones several times, he proudly turned to me. "Listen to this," he said and hit the Play button. By god, it sounded convincing—a call from an angry man in the streets of New York commanding his benefactor to meet with Jackson Witt.

"It's fantastic," I happily reacted.

"Hey, I'm good," Leandor responded, theatrically declining applause.

After five minutes of pacing and a reminder that, if lucky, I may not need his superbly produced recording, I announced to Leandor that it was showtime. I opened the package from Rockmore that had been sent by messenger. Inside, I found Robert Lévesque's personal cell phone number. I crossed my fingers to Leandor, took my own cell phone out of pocket, and dialed.

"Robert Lévesque? This is Jackson Witt. I will deliver the cell phone that may be useful to you, if you agree to meet with me tomorrow."

"Melanie will handle that," he succinctly replied.

"No, I want to meet with both of you."

"Melanie will handle that," he repeated and clicked off.

As I let this rebuke sink in, Leandor watched me like an unsatisfied audience, waiting for the next line. I shook my head in disappointment and threw my cell phone on his kitchen table.

"It was not a very convincing performance," my friend critiqued "I'm not going for a Tony award here!" I replied. "I'm just trying to get the man to take a meeting."

"Give a different interpretation," Leandor advised, as if we were in the midst of acting class.

I paced in his kitchen a few more minutes trying to get into character and eventually confessed to Leandor, "I may need the 'Hail Mary' pass. If it comes to that, how will your recording be transmitted?"

"I'll have to pipe it live through the phone. Not ideal. But the sound effects will cover it," Leandor reassured me.

I shook my arms repeatedly as a relaxing exercise, took a deep cleansing breath, and dialed Robert Lévesque's personal cell phone number again. After a few rings, he picked up.

"Bob," I opened, hoping that this unfamiliar nickname may catch him off-guard.

Meet with me or your girlfriend goes to jail."

"She can handle the pass-off," he coldly responded. "And, Jackson, listen to me. I will not be accepting any further calls from you."

"Wait! Listen to me," I quickly said. "If I can't convince you to join me, maybe Joey Roach can. He wants the damn phone back. You want it back. And he's going to call you in a few minutes to tell you that. If I were you, I would take Joey Roach's call."

"What?" he replied, but all he heard was the click of an end call.

I took out Joey Roach's reactivated cell phone, dialed Lévesque's number, and cued Leandor to be prepared for the main event. As soon as Lévesque answered, I gestured Leandor to hit Play.

Like a cue in any Broadway production, Leandor's reaction was perfectly timed.

The Play button signaled On, and with the handset next to the speaker, the following message was relayed, "Hello. This is Joey Roach. Get . . . that . . . fucking . . . phone . . . from Jackson Witt. You hear me? Don't be a dumbshit."

As soon as the last word was played, Leandor pointed to me to end the call. I did so without a glitch. In unison, both of us looked at each other, silently grinned, and proudly did a thumbs-up.

"It sounded good," Leandor admitted.

"It sounded great," I corrected him.

I tried to imagine the reaction from Robert Lévesque upon hearing Joey Roach's voice. It had to be disconcerting, especially since the killer had kept such a low profile since tumbling to his death in the elevator shaft. After a moment, an incoming call came in on Joey Roach's cell. It was from Lévesque. After a few drrings, I simply disconnected the call. The same thing occurred again after a few seconds. Once again, I repeated the disconnect.

"And now we wait for the reviews," I announced. True to form, Leandor pushed the plate of pot stickers in my direction and said, "They're really scrumptious." I demurred, anxiously awaiting an answer from Lévesque.

About five minutes later, I got a call from Melanie on my cell. "I just heard from Robert. We're on for 1:00 p.m. tomorrow. We'll both be there."

"Good call," I said and hung up.

Chapter Forty

As promised, I came to the precinct station at 10:00 a.m. to be fitted for the wire and better understand the police procedure of the taping. Through most of the night and even at the breakfast table, Alba had given me a crash course on Lévesque. Over the past few days, she had leaned on every source she could find to get the skinny on the smooth real estate developer. In addition to his high-powered connections, he was evidently a significant contributor to the mayor's campaign.

"Are you suggesting—"

"No," she interrupted me. "There's nothing wrong with that. Most bigwigs in town contributed to the mayor's campaign chest and get no special police treatment. All it means is that it helped grease the skids for his real estate developments, including the Orion House."

Alba had snooped around the inner workings of this gay-friendly co-op. She had checked into the array of services offered and the employment records of the place. According to her sources, his stepbrother Aaron Morganstern was briefly installed as assistant manager of the place until he was murdered. "It was basically a job gift to get his paroled, very gay stepbrother on his own two feet. Of course, it didn't quite work out that way," Alba reported.

"Who killed the kid?" I asked.

My friendly resource simply shook her head. "Unsolved mystery." Unlike my own case, there was no urgency to immediately identity some suspect. After all, Aaron Morgenstern was not some vaunted, venerated judge. He was just a gay dead-end kid with a prison record and a powerful stepbrother. Alba explained that everyone in the gay community downtown was still convinced that Morgenstern's death was spurred by Ziegler's nasty "keep our city safe from gays" speech.

"And Lévesque?" I asked.

Alba nodded. "Some folks at the Orion House claim he was crushed by it all," she said. "But the guy has a way of recovering. The Orion House still became a huge financial success—with or without Morganstern—so it counts as a win on Lévesque's balance sheet."

"Did he go to Aaron's funeral?"

"I hear he did not," Alba reported. "Apparently, he claimed to have immovable business concerns that conflicted with the dates."

"What a self-serving prick," I reacted.

"Business is business." Alba shrugged. "And I guess the guy was determined to keep them separate." She then prepped me again on Lévesque's personality profile. It was consistent with everything I had heard—careful, very cautious, smart, aggressive in any negotiation, and extremely protective of his personal life.

"He's happy to talk about his own self-made achievements and conquests. That sort of vanity appeals to him. And remember this. In any negotiation, he will fight back and try to personally bury you. He's tough as nails, and he can be nasty. But you're going to hit a speed bump when you get into his family. When it comes to his personal life, he's not going to wade into any of these topics willingly. You may have to spring things on him. You might even need to provoke him. Otherwise, he'll deflect."

I thanked her for the advice, the caution, and the support. She gave me a big luscious kiss for good luck and promised she would be there in the truck to "hear your greatest performance and nail the real culprit."

My lawyer accompanied me to the prelunch session with the NYPD. In advance, he told me he was going to do his best to limit expectations of my face-to-face with Lévesque and Melanie.

Before fitting me for the wire, Ms. Washington shared one piece of further police reconnaissance. "We checked criminal records of Joey Roach and Aaron Morganstern. They served at the same time at Ossining," she told me. "Because of the closemouthed attitude of most criminals, we can't get anything further than shared penal incarceration at this time. Maybe you can probe that link," she encouraged.

"What do you hope from this taped conversation?" I asked Donovan.

"A full confession would be nice," Donovan answered.

Ian Rockmore immediately jousted back, "Given the very acknowledged reticence of the target to speak freely, that's frankly unlikely."

Ms. Washington seemed to instantly understand the uphill mission of this fact. "Make him admit something," she advised. "More than something," Detective Donovan corrected her. "We need to hear that Lévesque, by his own admission, had a conversation with Joey Roach. We need to hear that he directed harm on Martin Ziegler. In an ideal world, perhaps even fatal harm. But short of that, we need to hear that he was complicit in the crime against Martin Ziegler."

"Does intent to harm qualify as complicity?" Rockmore asked.

After a second, Donovan responded, "That's probably close enough."

My lawyer pulled me aside and explained this legalese. "What they are asking you to establish in your conversation with Lévesque is the probability that danger could ensue. Do you understand that? All you must establish is that the phone conversation took place and an expectation of risk was assumed by the caller."

"I think so," I answered.

When we came back to the NYPD, Rockmore reminded the police of my "extraordinary effort to resolve this case so as to not compound the injustice of naming the wrong person of interest."

"Yes yes yes," Donovan replied in a perfunctory manner, quite accustomed to this posturing by every defense attorney in town. "Let's see how this turns out," he added. He then explained the game plan for the ultimate meeting. "If we feel you have what we need to prosecute Lévesque and Ziegler, we will make our presence. We will come to your table and immediately read them their rights. If you don't see us, that will mean we need to hear more. In other words, if we don't see us barging through the front desk to cuff them, you need to press on and get him to actually admit something."

They then demonstrated the wiring apparatus and outfitted me with the equipment. Thank God I wore a big loose-fitting crew neck sweater. Officer Washington taped the device on my bare back; I put on my sport shirt and covered that with big loose-fitting crew neck sweater. When I turned around in the mirror, I could still see a slight bulge from my back. "It's not all that unobtrusive," I claimed.

"Sit down quick, don't turn you back on them, and start asking interesting questions," Donovan advised. I accepted the device and waved everyone away.

Obviously, no one in this entourage had ever studied the theater arts.

I requested my attorney to leave me alone, refused to be further rattled by the NYPD, and chose instead to get into character. I rehearsed my imagined performance, envisioned possible rebuttals on the other side of the table, and built up the courage to face the opening curtain. As I walked toward the Tavern on the Green, I saw Alba walk toward the police truck, parked several blocks away. She pointed toward her temple for smarts, raised her fist for strength, and then blew me another good luck kiss. I followed her signals as if she were the most astute third-base coach and will always think it made a difference in my confidence that followed.

Chapter Forty-One

"I have approximately one hour," Robert Lévesque officiously announced to me when I was shown to the reserved table under his name. "Let's not make this longer than it needs to be."

"And how are you?" I asked Melanie as I ignored his hurry-up command and joined the table as if it were a family reunion.

"We are getting through this," she answered. "And I assume from our conversation that you are too. It's generous of your friend Leandor to lie for you. I am pleased that you will not have to take the fall what happened."

I tried to imagine the puzzled expressions of the listeners in the police truck two blocks away. Their raised eyebrows were not important, I reminded myself. The main point was this: I had the two of them in front of me, in need of supposedly incriminating evidence, and I needed to take control of this conversation.

Disenchanted with chitchat pleasantries, the real estate mogul jumped to the meat of the matter. "Do you have the damn phone?" he bluntly asked.

I carefully reached over the crew neck of my sweater and revealed the presence of the valued possession, then buried it again in my front shirt pocket.

The waiter had appeared. "Would you like to order cocktails?" he asked.

Having been prepped by Alba's assessment of Lévesque as a no-alcohol, no-tobacco guy, I answered, "I think my friends and I would prefer tap water. Maybe a pitcher. We've got a lot to discuss." The waitress scurried away, acquiescing to my request.

As soon as she was out of earshot, Lévesque lowered his designer reading glasses and peered over at me. "Mr. Witt, why not just hand over the merchandise so we can call this lunch over?"

"In just a few minutes," I answered. "I am more than willing to deliver these incriminating telephone conversations over to you," I answered with some bravado. "But first, I would like the answers to three questions."

The pushback ultimatum seemed to surprise the couple. She looked at him. He glanced at her with some frustration, and I proceeded.

"First of all, this is a nice place to have lunch, isn't it, Melanie? With two men who have had some romantic entanglement with you? Very civilized and modern of us, isn't it, Mr. Lévesque?" He simply glared at me, and I continued, "But I want to wish the two of you well. Mazel tov! All the best."

"Get to the point," Lévesque pushed impatiently.

"I'm just curious. How long have the two of you been going on? I just want to know how stupid I was."

It actually was a personal self-flagellating question with a purpose. I had listened to Alba's advice that Lévesque only enjoyed talking about his own accomplishments and conquests. I had calculated that this would be a chance for him to boast and embarrass me. It would signal to him that I was just a jilted paramour, a mere boy who was clearly out of his league at this table. I wanted him to feel superior. More importantly, I wanted him to feel free to unload.

"Jackson, I don't really think that is important at this time," Melanie jumped in, hoping to cut off the discussion.

"No, I'll answer that," Lévesque countered and tapped her wrist like a dad would to a daughter. "Ten months," he proudly answered and smiled at me. "If the arithmetic is too difficult for you, I'll help. I came along, and then you became past tense. Put more accurately, because of me, you are past tense. Dem's the breaks, young man."

"Robert, c'mon, you don't need to rub it in," Melanie gently chided him.

"No, the kid asked a question. And I wanted to answer it honestly and fully.

See, when a real woman like Melanie here meets a self-made success"—he touched his chest to emphasize our difference—"a callow young struggling nothing like yourself can't really hold a candle. Once she met me, you were history. These are very easy questions. What's next?"

Without hesitation, I launched into my sneak attack. It was aimed straight at Lévesque. "Did your gay step brother, Aaron Morgenstern, and Joey Roach become friends in prison? And is that where you first met Roach?"

It was a direct hit that jarred Lévesque, especially since it seemed to come out of nowhere. The man's expression quickly moved from smugness to sadness. But as long as he was in a lecturing mode, he shot back at me, "My brother was a good man. And whatever friends he made and whatever inclinations he may have had, that's between him and God. But I'll tell you this, he didn't deserve to die for it."

"I happen to agree with you," I said. "But I'm not sure Judge Ziegler did."

"Do we need to get into this?" Melanie tried to interrupt.

"So that's why you turned to Joey Roach," I said as if it were fact.

"I didn't turn to Joey Roach. Joey Roach came to me because he lost his best friend in the world. You and I may not understand that because we happen to prefer women, but—" And then he caught himself midsentence. He took a deep breath and appeared to regain his composure. "Look, enough of this. Give me the damn phone."

"I'm not quite ready to do that," I answered as dramatically as possible.

"You're not ready to do that?" Lévesque repeated slowly, angrily, and in absolute disbelief. "What the fuck do you want? I don't owe you anything. I just want the goddamn phone. You don't need it. You don't want it. Hand it over, and get on with your little, miserable, loveless, dickless life."

Just as I was worried that the temperature was rising a little too fast, Melanie evidently felt the same thing. "Robert, please," she shushed him and gestured toward another table that had reacted to his outburst. The man pushed his chair back a few inches to take a breather. Melanie leaned over to me and filled the void. "I got one question for you, Jackson. How'd you get the damn phone anyway?"

"I was on the subway where he left it in a rush to catch his exit. But I was also there—sitting right next to him—when your call came into Joey Roach. It was 4:28." I calmly explained to Lévesque. From his phone logs, I knew that he had made a call to the cell at that exact time. "I heard your call, giving Roach directions. How did you know where and when?"

"That's easy," the businessman answered. "We found the address in Mr., Zeigler's appointment book. He called them his important personal meetings." *Ahh, progress,* I thought. Didn't the man just admit he made the call? I was imagining some triumphant fists in police trailer but reminded myself to not get derailed. All I needed to do now was help entice Lévesque clarify his intentions.

"And when I replayed some of the voice message, it's you, ordering the hit." For emphasis, I took the cell out of my pocket and pointed to it. "It's all right here in the playback."

Here, I had taken a calculated guess. In this moment of crisis, I hoped he would not question how I could hear the playback without the access code. I also realized I was perhaps putting words in his mouth, but if he would only say one more yes, I figured the police cavalry would come in and cuff the two of them.

"That message is not on that phone," Lévesque said, staring at me.

Fuck me. Did he actually know that Roach had erased his calls? Could he really count on the killer to be that conscientious?

"If you play it back, you will never hear the word *hit*," Lévesque smugly said. "I'm too smart to ever use that word, especially on a cell phone."

OK, I reassured myself. At least Lévesque still thought something was on the cell. Just not that exact word. "But it's what you intended," I suggested, again trying to lead the witness.

"If you listen to that call carefully, you'll hear that I was only giving the guy directions and what happened after that . . . I guess happened."

Wow, Lévesque was a careful guy. I had to try harder. "But knowing Roach's history of violence and his friendship with Aaron, you had to figure that some harm could come."

"Maybe."

There! I told myself that the dot was at least loosely connected and hoped it would be enough for the NYPD. I looked around to see the rushing officers, but so far, there were none.

"Maybe not," Lévesque slyly added. With this hedge, I now imagined the NYPD stopping in their tracks and colliding into each other, like a *Keystone cops* comedy. In view of his weasel-like out, I had to press on. "But there was a good chance, a very good chance, that it could lead to trouble. Otherwise, why even pay the guy?" I directed this at both of them, at this point hoping that either one would crack.

Lévesque exhaled a big sigh and didn't answer the question directly. "Mr. Witt, The judge was a bad guy. You know that. Melanie knows that. Joey Roach knows that. I know that. And whatever was going to happen to him that night . . . happened."

Again, I told myself that should be enough. *My god, what does the NYPD need?* The man just confessed that something was going to happen. I looked around for the incoming cavalry, but again, there was no imminent arrest from the police.

"Now I think we've had enough small talk for one lunch," the business exec said. "And now, we would like to get on with our life . . . *together*," he emphasized that last word for what he obviously assumed would be hurtful effect. Then he added, "And you can get on with your own pitiful life. Hand over the phone."

Aware that, at least according to the police, I had not gotten enough, I reflexively gripped the phone on the table.

"I don't think so," I said. I then poured myself a glass of water and stalled for time. I somehow rationalized that I should definitely hold on to this bargaining chip. If it wasn't yet enough for the NYPD, maybe I could have another meeting with them. Maybe I could up the stakes and play my cards better. Maybe some improv inspiration would strike. Maybe anything. In any case, I instinctively wanted to hold on to the evidence.

"Hand it over," Lévesque commanded me.

"I don't think so," I repeated.

"You give me that fucking phone or I will sic Joey Roach on you—again."

Melanie chose, at that point, to rejoin the conversation. "Robert, Joey Roach seems to be out of the picture. No sight. No sound. No trouble."

"No, honey, that's not true," Lévesque said and took control of the dialogue. "I heard from him. I got a call from him yesterday. He's around. And listen to me, Mr. Witt, if you don't hand over the damn phone, I'll have Joey get it from you—with maybe the same consequences that happened before. Hand it over. This conversation is now over."

It was a mad stare off at that point that was fortunately interrupted by Detective Donovan and four other uniformed officers.

As they rushed into the restaurant, Lévesque instinctively reached for the cell phone and jarred it loose. Immediately, Melanie grabbed the dislodged cell and tossed it into the pitcher of ice water.

As I watched my lifeline sink to the bottom of the pitcher, I turned around to the ruckus in the otherwise sedate restaurant and saw Melanie Ziegler and an angry Robert Lévesque escorted by the police through the aghast and disturbed tables of the Tavern on the Green.

As soon as I exited the restaurant, I walked a hundred yards or so to look for the police trailer that was recording every word of my conversation. It was parked close to Central Park West, and outside the vehicle, Alba Gonzales stood waving both arms to welcome me.

I walked toward her, and she closed the gap, racing into my arms. "Not easy," she said. "But you were magnificent! I think that was the best performance I have ever seen from you."

"He did not want to talk," I admitted.

"As I predicted," she completed my sentence. "But it will make a very good story."

When we entered the police van, I first saw Tanya Washington, giving me thumbs-up and then extending her arms, Leandor-like, to congratulate me.

"Thanks," I acknowledged. "But I have just two questions for you. Where the fuck were you? I'm telling you, I was dying in there, trying to extract anything from Mr. Closed Mouth. And you and your police brass are sitting here comfortably, waiting for the grand 'I admit everything' confession. Jeezus, what the hell were you waiting for?"

"Well, Lévesque never actually admitted anything."

"But you felt you had enough to nab him?" I countered, in view of the perp walk both Robert Lévesque and Melanie Ziegler were now undergoing. "Not enough to nail his ass to wall on a murder 1 charge. But enough on other counts."

Rockmore came out of the shadows and shook my hand on a job well done. "Not an easy mission, but I always had supreme confidence you could do it. Otherwise, I would have never recommended it," he added, presumably trying to claim some small credit for the suggestion to put me in the hot seat. As he twirled his monogrammed cufflink, he tried to be funny. "Just out of curiosity, Jackson, you said you had two key questions and you only asked two. The first one, if I recall the wording was 'Where the fuck were you?' Care to share your next bombshell?"

Recalling the essence of theatrical timing, I took a short beat, then answered, "My second question—assuming I could get an 'I did it' response from Lévesque—was directed at the NYPD. It amounts to this: am I off the hook?"

Upon hearing this request, Rockmore sprung into legal posture and demanded that under "the extreme and trying circumstances under which my client sought information on behalf of the NYPD, he should be immediately be declassified on this case as a cooperating witness."

Tanya Washington digested the legalese and threw a knowing wink in my direction. Within two hours, I was an exonerated man.

Chapter Forty-Two

In the next morning's *New York Times*, an article titled, "Ziegler Mystery Unravels" reported the turn of events and the immediate aftermath. The story was a detailed exclusive by Alba Gonzales, who was the only reporter to eyewitness and hear the table conversation firsthand. According to Alba, "As a result of a carefully orchestrated sting operation, the NYPD made dramatic progress in resolving the murder of Judge Martin V. Ziegler."

The story chronicled the Tavern of the Green drama and the subsequent ruckus in the aisles of the restaurant. As one restaurant customer related, "Oh, you could tell something big was happening. The guy in the suit was turning over pitchers of water on the tables, screaming expletives at the cops and yelling, 'You got nothing!' For a lot of us who were hoping for a special lunch in Manhattan, the event certainly made for a memorable day."

The story extolled the "heroic efforts of Jackson Witt, who will presumably be released and cleared of suspicion in connection with the crime." According to Officer Tanya Washington, "We could not have reached this point in our investigation without his help, and we truly appreciate his cooperation."

Alba also saluted the defense attorney, Ian Rockmore, who "creatively brokered the sting operation on behalf of his client." As Rockmore was quoted, "I always believed my client was completely innocent and was willing to bend over backward with the NYPD to vindicate him. It's just what a good defense attorney is supposed to do." I could easily imagine his self-serving, false humility in making the last statement.

True to her constituency, she credited the NYPD for their dogged persistence in the pursuit of the real perpetrators.

Of course, the thrust of her article was on these new targets. Joey Roach was now officially classified as a suspect. According to her account, the dragnet on his whereabouts was expected to intensify, especially in view of some undenied speculation that he had apparently made a phone call only two days earlier. And then the best: "The victim's widow, Melanie Ziegler was identified as a person of interest, as was Robert Lévesque, the high-powered real estate magnate, who are jointly connected in conjunction with this case."

Such a quaint way to describe an ugly affair and the participants who orchestrated a cold-blooded murder! But I accepted the fact that the *Times* had its editorial standards and resisted salacious dirt. I looked forward to the *Post* and the other tabloids, which would have a field day with the Lévesque-Ziegler sex angle.

The NYPD press conference brought few new details to Alba's account.

Not surprisingly, Police Chief Byrne emphasized and underscored the superb investigation of his staff to "leave no stone unturned."

The Joey Roach manhunt was the main topic of the presentation. The police had new pictures of the culprit. In addition to my cell phone snapshot, several other images of the man, including conviction mug shots and prison photos were revealed. He invited New Yorkers to call the hotline with any leads as to Roach's location and then also tried to reassure everyone that Roach did not "present a random threat to the citizens of New York."

The chief identified Ms. Ziegler and Robert Lévesque as potential coconspirators this case but chose not to elaborate further on their status, contingent upon ongoing investigations. He gave scant mention of me, other than to say that I was no longer a target in this search, and appreciated the fine manner in which my attorney and I had assisted this investigation.

That was OK with me. I was happy to be out of the headlines and instead see the afternoon papers focus on the Melanie-Lévesque love motive.

The *Daily News* announced it as "Real Estate Tryst Goes Haywire."

The *Globe* had this lead: "Duo Does the Nasty with Deadly Consequences."

The *Post* screamed, "Lévesque Bang Leads to Ex-Hubby's Bye-Bye."

The *Advocate* was atypically reserved. It announced their article with the headline, "Justice Served."

None of the afternoon rags led with the NYPD focus of Joey Roach. Perhaps they already had sensed that this was a hopeless blind alley. More likely, the newer, sexier angle sold papers. From firsthand experience, I understood this fascination with illicitly behaving persons of interest. However, in this particular instance, I had no sympathy for either party.

I chose not to bring these competing newspapers back to the Gilsey House, where I promised to have a celebration dinner with my dear heart and greatest advocate. On the way, I trashed the tabloids with their more sensationalized accounts and carried in the *New York Times*.

"I've been reading that the police may have cracked that Ziegler case." I greeted Alba with a warm hug.

"Wow, that's good news," she kidded back.

I pointed to her article. "This reporter seems to all the facts straight and is a hell of a good writer. I'll bet she's beautiful too."

Alba placed the newspaper down on her kitchen island and gave me one of her more amazing kisses. "How does it feel to be a free man?"

"I'm not used to it. I may miss the excitement."

"We can fix that this evening," she answered with a twinkle.

We thought of having Philly cheese steaks for old time's sake but opted to postpone that for the real deal someday. Instead, we ordered Chinese and a movie on Cinemax. I actually argued for a replay of *Mama Mia*, but Alba was in the mood for *Hairspray*. I hadn't seen it before and rather enjoyed Travolta's cross-dressing portrayal. I couldn't help but flash on Martin Ziegler playing the same role in real life but chose not to mention it. That was the past, and it was time to put that behind me.

When the credits rolled, we opened up our fortune cookies. Alba first. Hers read, "Not everything must be told." She looked at it curiously and said, "I don't think my editors at the *Times* would quite agree with that."

I opened mine and smiled. I happily delivered its message to Alba. "Enjoy the minutes and the hours will follow."

"I like yours better," she decided.

Within minutes, we were in bed. The hours ahead were indeed more enjoyable than those I had endured over the past few weeks.

Chapter Forty-Three

Four months later, Alba and I were on a subway car toward Port Authority. We had promised ourselves to return to our alma mater in Philadelphia. In the mailings we had received from Temple University, it had been dubbed Alumni Welcome Weekend. The cocktail party reception for all Temple alums would be fun, but actually all we wanted was to have a true Philly cheese steak from Gino's. The college invitation provided sufficient excuse to escape the day-to-day grind of Manhattan, and a taste of the greasy, cheesy sandwich—and all the sweet associations that we had with it.

Leandor had pushed us to attend. He had been invited by the Temple University drama department to join a panel discussion on "Life beyond Acting." His success behind the curtains on Broadway made him a natural. But true to his initial onstage ambitions, Leandor told the two us, "You've got be there. I need an audience."

Leandor, in fact, had just enjoyed a flurry of theatrical activity in the past four months. He was named the sound director of a new *Cirque du Soliel* production that would play on Randall's Island. In addition, he was nominated for a Tony for his special audio expertise in the short unsuccessful production of *Sunday in the Park with George.*

He was not the only one who had a four-month run at notoriety and subsequent rebirth. I had sold my apartment at a tidy profit, the proceeds helped defray the exorbitant costs of a thirty-eight-thousand-dollar legal tab to Ian Rockmore for "services rendered." As he had predicted, I ended up believing he was worth it.

On the heels of this, I had enrolled in the Pace University Law School with the intention to defend unjustifiably accused clients, without ever wearing gaudy cufflinks. The real plus side of this transition? It meant giving up my pad and moving in full-time with Alba—a willing, winning trade-off.

Despite recurrent allegations in the tabloids about Robert Lévesque and Melanie Ziegler's passionate complicity in the judge's death, they had effectively lawyered up.

Ultimately, it would not result in convictions for accessory to murder. Without a talkative Joey Roach to corroborate the exact deal, it would be difficult to pin a hit order directly on them. As predicted, the few remaining text messages on Roach's phone would not be sufficient to indict them.

Instead, he was charged with extortion on the basis of his recorded threatening ultimatum "that unless I handed over the phone, bad things would happen to me." She was charged with tampering with state's evidence since she had chosen to submerge the Roach's cell phone in a pitcher of ice water.

For Melanie, it would mean four months in the same cushy penal institution that once housed Martha Stewart. Lévesque would eventually have to serve two years in Ossining for extortion.

The degree and length of the sentence was not important to me. As I was later told by Diane Farin at Stribling, Melanie would visit him once a week to console her new "lover boy" while he awaited parole. It no longer matters to me. They were both discredited and destroyed by the media. I couldn't help but contrast that with my own clinched, loving grasp of Alba Gonzales's hand as we headed up the number 6 subway line toward Port Authority.

She leaned into me and whispered the truth, "Can you believe what these passengers are saying to each other within full earshot of the entire subway car? Oh my god, she's having an affair with her neighbor, he's screwing his boss's wife, and this couple is busy plotting a ménage à trois." As she reported her eavesdrop, she pointed to the left, the center, and the right.

"Guess what?" I answered. "I didn't hear a damn thing they said."

We walked toward the Acella high-speed line for our Philly cheese steak dinner. Along the way, Alba bought every newspaper at the kiosk and pored through them as we waited for our carriage. The headlines had moved onto new salacious topics.

"Superstar Steroids Scandal," one headline announced.

"Miss America Nude Pix," the *Post* teased.

"Senator's Love Child, "the *Globe* beckoned.

"I wonder whatever happened to Joey Roach," Alba mused with a more intelligent appreciation of things that mattered.

"Who knows?" I answered her with a question and silently reflected on that fortune cookie prediction we had opened on the night of my freedom. *Not everything must be told,* it read, and it somehow stuck with me.

"Let's catch the express to Philly and make a damn mess of each other with a cheese steak," I invited her. She grabbed my outstretched palm, and we headed toward happy heartburn together.